# BEFORE IT'S TOO LATE

Following an argument with her British boy-friend, Chinese student Min Li is abducted whilst walking the dark streets of picturesque Stratford-upon-Avon alone. Trapped in a dark pit, Min is at the mercy of her captor. Detective Inspector Will Jackman is tasked with solving the case, and in his search for answers discovers that the truth is buried deeper than he ever expected. But as another student vanishes and Min grows ever weaker, time is running out. Can Jackman track down the kidnapper, before it's too late?

*Books by Jane Isaac*
*Published by Ulverscroft:*

**THE TRUTH WILL OUT**

Jane Isaac studied creative writing with the Writers Bureau and the London School of Journalism. She was runner-up 'Writer of the Year 2013' with the Writers Bureau. She lives in rural Northamptonshire with her husband, daughter, and dog Bollo.

You can discover more about the author at www.janeisaac.co.uk

JANE ISAAC

# BEFORE IT'S TOO LATE

*Complete and Unabridged*

# CHARNWOOD
Leicester

First published in Great Britain in 2015 by
Legend Press Ltd
London

First Charnwood Edition
published 2016
by arrangement with
Legend Press Ltd
London

A catalogue record for this book is available
from the British Library.

ISBN 978–1–4448–2814–6

Published by
F. A. Thorpe (Publishing)
Anstey, Leicestershire

Set by Words & Graphics Ltd.
Anstey, Leicestershire
Printed and bound in Great Britain by
T. J. International Ltd., Padstow, Cornwall

This book is printed on acid-free paper

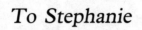

*To Stephanie*

**'And why not death rather than living torment?'**
William Shakespeare
*The Two Gentlemen of Verona*

# 1

A rumble in the background woke me. I could feel something rolling, somewhere nearby. Gently, side to side, like a baby rocking in a crib.

I swallowed, slowly opened my eyes. The images were unclear; bleary dark shadows flickered about in the distance.

The rocking continued, and I suddenly became aware that it was my own body moving. A wave of panic caught me. As much as I tried, I couldn't keep it still. I had no control over my limbs.

Rivulets of sweat trickled down my neck. More blurred images. The sound of an engine.

Darkness, I was travelling in a vehicle with no windows.

I tried to recall earlier: the thump of music, the babble of conversation punctuated by bouts of laughter. Hanging my head over a toilet pan. Pressing my cheek to the cold tiles in the cubicle. Worming my way through sweaty bodies jammed together, moving to the beat, drinks sloshing everywhere. I needed air, and quick. Tom's face contorted in anger, the muscle in his jaw flexing as he spoke through tight teeth. The slam of the pub door behind me. The relief at emerging into the silvery darkness. Alone. The throb of an engine as it revved behind me.

My thoughts fragmented and faded. Little pieces of the jigsaw were missing. I reached for them in the semi-darkness, but they danced about on the periphery.

My head grew heavy, a thick smog began to descend on my brain.

The van stopped abruptly, snapping me back to the present. I was shunted forward. A pain speared through my foot and up into my calf. I couldn't move, yet I still felt the sharp ache.

The engine cut. The grate of a door as it swung open. A soft breeze reached in and tickled my hair.

Footsteps shuffled around me. Hands reached beneath my armpits. Warm breaths on my neck. Dragging.

I mustered every ounce of energy to turn my head and let out a gentle moan.

The breathing instantly halted. The grip released.

A cloth was pressed down on my nose and mouth. A sickly-sweet smell. I desperately wanted to struggle, I tried to, but my limbs felt like they were immersed in a puddle of glue. The world spun around me. Slower and slower. Gradually fading. Until my brain became an empty well of darkness.

# 2

Detective Inspector Will Jackman lowered the window and sucked in a wave of crisp air. Stars peeped down at him through the dark blanket of sky above. A moth flew into the car and fluttered about on the dashboard but he ignored it, relishing the breeze that rushed through his hair as he pressed on.

The sweet scent of grass mingled with wild honeysuckle wafted into the car. The smells were always stronger in the dark hours, especially that gap between 2 and 5 a.m. when the roads were quiet and the people of Stratford rested in their slumber. It reminded Jackman of his early years in the police, working instant response on a rolling shift pattern around the clock. The whole atmosphere changed at night. Jobs were more sporadic but intense. Colleagues rallied around in support. Emotions were heightened. Back at the station things took on a much lighter feel, practical jokes came to the fore in an effort to lighten the load and stave off the fog of fatigue.

Jackman cast the memories aside and pushed on, leaving the town behind him, through a tunnel of trees that cast hazy shadows on the road ahead. By day, Warwick Road Lands was a haven for riverside wildlife, walkers, families sharing their picnics with the ducks in the balmy sunshine. As the sun subsided and the birds roosted it grew peaceful once more, haunted only by the occasional footfall of a passing fisherman, the call of an owl or the swoop of bats, hunting their prey.

He grew closer, turned into the empty car park and stopped the car. Gravel scratched beneath his feet, the sound elevated in the darkness, as he crossed the tarmac and made for the river bank.

He glanced at his watch. It was 2 a.m. Right here. This was where Ellen's body had floated just over a week ago, huddled amongst the bulrushes on the water's edge.

On Saturday 3rd May, Ellen Readman had packed her suitcase into the boot of her black Ford Ka and climbed into the driver's seat. Her face had stretched into a wide grin as she had lifted her hand to wave at her housemate, revved the engine and disappeared down the road. She was off to visit her Aunt in Corfu for a week's break. A missing persons' enquiry later revealed that she'd never even reached the airport.

Media appeals followed, asking for witnesses to come forward, desperately trying to trace Ellen's movements. Her car was last spotted by police cameras leaving Stratford on the A46. But, apart from the usual crank calls and the odd sighting earlier in the week, nothing to reveal what happened next. Until her body surfaced in the River Avon.

If Jackman closed his eyes he could still see her lying there, tossed aside like a rag doll. Her face was concealed beneath a mop of long dark hair, thickly matted with Japanese knotweed. The t-shirt she wore was pulled tight across her bloated body, a short denim skirt clung to her thighs, her feet bare. Jackman let out a ragged sigh. Her parents came across from nearby Nottinghamshire to identify her body. Tissues pressed to tear-stained faces, distraught over the death of their youngest daughter. Twenty-two years old. Barely a couple of years older than his own daughter, Celia.

Jackman sunk his hands into his pockets and glanced across the water. It was calm and still. The pathologist's report indicated her body had been immersed in water for some time. Grazing on the backs of her thighs suggested she may have been lodged somewhere, freed up by the increased flow of the river due to the barrage of heavy rainfall the weekend before.

As soon as the incident room was established, police computers had identified a link with the case of a woman found in the River Nene in rural Northamptonshire, two months earlier. Twenty-two-year-old Katie Sharp's neck bore similar ligature marks, her body no sign of sexual intervention. Just like Ellen. She'd also been immersed in water for some time before a dog walker had stumbled across her.

Jackman massaged his temples. Despite there being separate incident rooms in two counties, less than an hour's drive from each other, neither were close to finding a motive, let alone a suspect. Forensics worked hard on the clothing, the bodies, the surrounding area, and yet any clues were likely flushed away.

The investigation had been code-named Operation Sky and now it felt like the clouds were rolling in, blocking out any gaps of possible light as the lines of enquiry began to dry and shrivel. The irony was not lost on him.

Jackman picked up a stone, skimmed it across the water and watched it plop twice and disappear, before turning on his heels back to the car.

# 3

The bubbling ringtone his daughter had installed as a joke played out as Jackman retrieved his back door key from his tracksuit bottoms the following morning, and fumbled with the lock. Erik, his four-year-old chocolate Lab, jumped around his knees, the lead still attached to his collar slamming against everything in sight. Finally, the key turned. He wrenched the door open and grabbed the phone off the kitchen side.

'Where are you, sir?' The sir followed afterwards, an add-on in an attempt to pacify.

Jackman recognised the gruff tone of Detective Constable Andrew Keane immediately. 'Morning to you, too.' He glanced at the clock. It was 8.30 a.m. 'On my way to Northampton, or I will be in a minute. What's up?'

'The Super's trying to get hold of you. Wants to speak to you urgently.'

Jackman lunged forward and stretched out his stiff calves. The run had failed to release its usual endorphins and his muscles, dogged by sleep deprivation, felt hard and tight. 'What about?'

'A misper.'

'What kind of misper?'

'Missing girl. Twenty-year-old student. The Super wants you in for a briefing, as soon as. Apparently, it's high profile.'

Jackman wiped the sweat off his forehead with the back of his sleeve. 'What do we know?'

'Female, Chinese student at Stratford-upon-Avon College, name of Min Li. Missing person call came in at two o'clock this morning. Argued with her boyfriend and left the Old Thatch Tavern on the corner of Rother Street and Greenhill Street around . . . ' Jackman heard the rustle of a page turn in the detective's notebook, ' . . . 10.35 p.m. Later, her boyfriend couldn't reach her on her mobile, so came back to her apartment at the college to check on her and then alerted her roommates. They called the police at 2 a.m. when they'd phoned all her friends and couldn't locate her. I was the lucky bunny working the CID nightshift, called in to assist.'

Jackman crossed to the sink, filled a glass and took a swig as he listened. 'What do we know about her?'

'Not much. We've checked both her and the boyfriend out. They're not known to us. She's been over here since last September doing an access course in business. Originally from Beijing.'

'And the boyfriend?'

'We've spoken to him. They were celebrating his birthday with a group of friends. Claims he hasn't seen her since she left the pub last night.'

Jackman bent forward and wrestled with the laces on his running shoes. 'Witnesses?'

'We've checked the council CCTV cameras, she was spotted turning the corner from Rother Street into Greenhill Street, probably on her way back to the college. Then nothing. In between Greenhill Street and Alcester Road she disappeared. A few vehicles passed through around the same time, which we're trying to trace. Bloody

8

council footage is hopeless though. We'll have to get it enhanced to read the number plates.'

Jackman thought for a moment. 'Any chance she could have taken herself off somewhere? Gone somewhere to calm down?'

'I don't think so. In the light of current events we've been extra thorough. Luckily, it was quiet last night and most of the uniform shift helped us out. We've made the usual checks — she doesn't own a car, so we tried the trains, buses, taxi firms. No sign of her there. There were no recorded accidents in Stratford last night but we checked the local hospitals anyway and they've no record of treating a Chinese female.'

'What about GPS on her phone?'

'Switched off.'

He had to hand it to Keane. He'd been diligent. Jackman sighed inwardly. With the changes in the recruitment process and the possible introduction of shorter-term contracts, officers like Keane were on the decline.

'There's something else,' Keane continued. 'We talked to her friends at the college. Min Li is a dedicated student. She didn't turn up for an early tutorial at 7 a.m. this morning. We used one of the college's interpreters to speak to her parents in China as it's only her father that can speak reasonable English. They have no idea where she is. Last heard from her at the weekend with a routine catch-up call. Take it from me, sir, this ain't no regular misper.'

Jackman thanked the detective, rang off and drained the rest of his glass. He kicked off his shoes and called Superintendent Alison Janus.

He could picture her right now as the dial tone filled his ear: her duck face protruding beneath a fringed, brown bob, pinched in at the centre at this potential new addition to her crime figures.

She answered on the second ring, as if she were awaiting his call. 'Will. You've heard about the missing girl?'

'I have.'

'Good. I'd like you to lead this one.'

Jackman's frown was tempered with a frisson of excitement. 'I've got my hands full with this murder enquiry at the moment, ma'am. Off to Northampton for a meeting with their homicide team this morning. Is there no one else?'

Janus didn't attempt to hide the frustration in her voice. 'No. Resources are tight enough as it is. DCI Reilly will have to bat on with Operation Sky without you. Liaise with him if you establish any links. But for the moment I want the two enquiries treated separately. The very suggestion of a serial killer running loose in Stratford will cook the press into a fever, let alone the public. Right, I'll meet you at Rother Street station in an hour. Make sure you are up to date. We have a press conference at twelve. And Will?'

'Yes.'

'Put a tie on will you? The new chief constable's taken a personal interest in this one.' The line went dead.

Jackman stared at the phone in his hand. Even with the Readman case pressing on them, why the chief constable would be so interested in a missing person case was beyond his comprehension, although it certainly explained the spur into action. Warwickshire's annual figures for missing persons were far below the national average. Generally, uniform dealt with missing persons; resources were prioritised to the young and the vulnerable. A twenty-year-old college student wouldn't usually fall into this category.

His mobile buzzed again. He viewed the screen. Reilly.

'Will?'

'Yes.'

'I have to attend this meeting with Northants homicide team this morning. I'll need a briefing.'

Jackman closed his eyes and rubbed the bridge of his nose with the thumb and forefinger of his free hand. 'We are looking for any links between the two victims. We know they were killed in a similar manner, but we need to compare the victimology research. If we can establish a personal link between the two — a mutual acquaintance, a similar interest, a place they have both visited — then it strengthens the connection and could point to a single killer.'

'And?'

'It could give us a motive and fresh leads.'

'Can't we do this by email?'

'We've already exchanged emails. This meeting will enable us to talk to the investigating officers, go through witness statements, phone records, credit card statements and bring copies back of anything that might be relevant.' Silence filled the phone line as Jackman continued, 'Look, I'm going to be out of action for most of this morning. You're meeting DCI Stevens at Northants headquarters at 10.30 a.m. Everything's in the

11

policy log in the top drawer of my desk if you need to refresh your memory.'

Jackman felt a thud against the side of his thigh as he rang off. Erik was leaping about like a demented springbok, waiting for his breakfast. Jackman filled a bowl with an unappetising batch of dried brown kibble and left the dog to eat.

As he climbed the stairs and jumped into the shower, his mind turned back to the missing woman. Janus was right, whatever happened, until she was found, speculation would be rife. The press would have a field day. Warwickshire was one of the UK's smallest police forces and Stratford was considered a pretty sleepy town when it came to serious crime, which was one of the reasons he'd moved his family here from North London when his daughter was young.

Even at night, to attack a woman in Stratford town centre was a risk. He pictured the Old Thatch Tavern in his mind. It was located opposite the market square and some way from the theatre and its nearby pubs. Granted, the day-trippers, the shoppers and tourists that flocked in to see the Shakespearean sites, would have gone home and the traffic wouldn't have been particularly prevalent on a Monday evening, but surely there were still some people wandering around? All potential witnesses. Perhaps she went back to the pub to reconcile with her boyfriend, disappeared down one of the numerous alleys that snaked the town centre?

Ten minutes later, Jackman stooped to view himself in the mirror above the fireplace in his sitting room when he heard the letterbox snap and something hit the mat. Erik raised his head and cast a sleepy eye towards the door, then lowered it again. So much for the guard dog.

Jackman moved out into the hallway, fastening his cuffs. He bent down, grabbed a pink envelope and turned it over. It was addressed to 'Mrs Alice Jackman'. He stared at it a moment. Of course. Thursday was her birthday.

As he stood, his shoulder caught the clip-frame on the wall. It wobbled, rattling against the plaster, until he reached up and steadied it. A mosaic of little photographs slipped down inside. His eyes brushed past the jumble of family holiday pics, the photo of him crossing the finishing line at the London marathon a few years earlier, and rested on the small snapshot in the centre: a photograph of him and his wife at their wedding reception. Her white-blonde hair contrasted with his groomed chestnut mop. Their wrists were entwined, poised to drink. The camera had caught them on centre; elated eyes sparkled in the flashlight. Jackman looked back at the card and recognised Alice's mother's spidery handwriting. Why? She knew Alice would never open this. Alice would never open another card again. He pushed it into his pocket, grabbed his keys and left the house.

# 4

I woke to silence. A thick, suffocating silence.

Pain. My shoulders, my back, my legs. I was on my side, curled into a foetal shape. I shifted position and flinched. Every limb smarted. I flicked my eyes open and instantly jammed them shut as a shard of light spiked my pupils. Where was I? In hospital?

No. The floor was hard and rough like sandpaper. There were no covers. I rubbed my forehead and shaded my eyes as I opened them again, gingerly this time. Darkness. A cavern of darkness all around, splintered by the small slice of light from above. I sniffed. A mixture of earthy and sweet, like the trees back home after a rainstorm.

Pain rippled through every tendon as I uncurled my crumpled body. The ground scratched at me. It wasn't soft like mud. More like concrete.

As I sat up, an involuntary shiver made me tremble. Suddenly the dampness penetrated my bones and I felt cold. Excruciatingly cold.

I blinked several times, gradually growing accustomed to the sliver of light from above, and scanned the area. An almost perfect square box about four metres across. A couple of faded crisp packets mingled with a pile of crusted leaves in the far corner. The walls were hard and rough. A covered metal grill blocked the only opening above me. But no window.

14

A mixture of fear and nausea swamped me.

I tugged at my jacket, drew my legs into my chest. Grazed knees peered back at me through the broken threads of material. I reached out, touched one of them and reeled as a bit of skin came off in my hand.

How did I get here? I blinked, tried to recall. A gentle rocking. The hum of a moving vehicle. Limbs paralysed. I wiggled my fingers and toes. The relief at movement was tempered by the reality of my surroundings. My hands and legs weren't bound together, I was free to move around, but only within the confines of this dark pit.

The pain in my head soared. I raised a hand to it and felt my hair, clogged and matted. When I tried to free the congealed strands, I released the unmistakable odour of vomit.

A wave of fatigue reached up and pulled me back down until I lost all sense of recognition and surrendered to the darkness once again.

# 5

'Over three hundred of the students at Stratford College are international. Their parents pay for them to come over here to gain a British education in a sheltered environment.'

Jackman stared at Andrew Keane. The green shirt he wore stretched across his paunch and clashed with a lilac woven tie. He always managed to look like he got dressed in the dark, but the chorus of jokes from his colleagues and peers didn't bother him one bit. Nothing ever seemed to bother Keane.

'So, we are looking at a reassurance exercise,' Janus said. The three of them were seated around an oval table in one of Rother Street station's meeting rooms. The morning sun bounced off the laminated table. A lone filing cabinet stood in the corner, a tower of buff files balanced precariously on top.

'Looks like it,' Keane continued. 'The college principal came in early this morning. His phone is already ringing off the hook from local journos. He's panicking about parents pulling their kids out because they don't feel safe.'

'Hence the chief constable's interest,' Janus said. 'Apparently he had the *Stratford Mail* call him on his personal line first thing this morning. God knows how they got that number.' She snorted. 'Passed it through to me of course.'

Jackman rubbed his forehead. 'How *did* the

press get hold of the story?'

Keane shrugged a single shoulder. 'Most likely someone from the college shared it on social media. Probably one of the students. As soon as they caught a whiff of the police, they saw a chance for some exposure. It seems everyone's after celebrity status these days. I'm amazed somebody hasn't filmed her room on their mobile.'

'Don't speak too quickly,' Janus said. She pushed her glasses up the bridge of her nose and turned to Jackman. 'Make sure uniform's got it locked and contained, will you?'

'Sure.' The room hushed as Jackman inhaled loudly. 'We should probably keep it low key,' he said, speaking through his exhalation. 'Issue a statement to the press to show that we're taking it seriously. There are bound to be comparisons made with the Readman case, particularly as she was missing for several days before her body was discovered. We'll need to refute any links at this stage, try to get them and the public to focus on sightings of Min Li, to track down her last movements.' He stared into space as he spoke. 'Limit the presence at the college. It's early days — we need to find out what we're dealing with first.'

Janus nodded. 'I agree. The last thing we want is international journos on our doorstep. Plain clothes officers only at the college. That'll be more discreet, less alarming.'

The sound of a knock drew their attention towards the entrance. The door opened and DC Kathryn Russell's heart-shaped face appeared.

17

Russell shot a quick smile at Jackman and addressed the Super, 'Phone call for you, ma'am.'

Janus rose. 'Update Judy Pearson in the press office, will you? Get her to draft a statement and tell them we're taking no more than three or four questions. Keep it tight. We don't want any room for speculation.' She checked her watch. 'See you back here at 11.30.'

Jackman nodded and watched as she raced out into the corridor, her heels clicking on the linoleum flooring with every step.

He turned to Keane. 'Right, I think we need to get the boyfriend back in for a formal statement.'

'He's downstairs. I'm just about to interview him.'

Jackman stared at the dark pools that encircled Keane's eyes. 'How long have you been on duty?'

Keane glanced up at the clock. 'Fourteen hours, give or take.'

Jackman raised his brows.

'One last job,' Keane said and winked. 'Can't deny me this one.'

'Okay. I'll come with you. As soon as you're done, you go home.'

They gathered their notes and moved out to the corridor. Just as they were about to turn the corner, Jackman heard a familiar voice behind him. 'Morning, sir. You're looking dashing as ever!'

Jackman turned and smiled at the tall, well-built figure that approached. Most women gave Jackman an uncomfortable wide berth when it came to personal compliments, but DS

18

Annie Davies had always been different which was probably why he liked her so much. Her broad Geordie accent spoke the words with amusing honesty.

He turned to Keane. 'I'll meet you downstairs.'

As Keane nodded, tipped his head at Davies and continued down the corridor, Jackman faced Davies. His eyes caught a white stain on her lapel. 'Thank you, Annie. I've missed you too.'

She followed his eyes, licked her thumb and gave the mark a rub. 'Damn!'

Jackman smiled. 'First day back?'

She looked up at him, raised her eyes to the ceiling, although her face shone like a child's at Christmas. 'Yup! And straight into an incident room.'

Jackman grinned affectionately. Annie and her husband, John, had been the typical childless police couple — indulging in their sports and holidays until she found herself pushing forty and pregnant last year. He suspected their lives had changed more than she'd care to imagine these past twelve months. 'I could use your help. How's the little one?'

She squeezed out a smile. 'Noisy, but cute. What about you? How's Celia?'

'Great. Don't see much of her these days. She's away at Southampton Uni.'

'She managed to get on the course for marine biology.' Annie nodded approvingly. 'Clever girl.'

Jackman suddenly remembered the card in his pocket. He slipped his hand in and ran his finger along the unopened edge. 'She's coming up later in the week, actually.'

'Good to hear.'

A crash in the distance caught their attention. 'Oh, Christ!' Annie rolled her eyes. 'Nothing like a bunch of detectives to rearrange furniture.'

Jackman gave a short laugh. 'Thanks for getting everything set up.' He reached out and tapped her shoulder. 'It's good to have you back.'

# 6

Jackman scratched his temple and stared into the brown eyes of Min Li's boyfriend. 'Let's take this from the top, shall we?'

He'd spent the last twenty minutes sat quietly as Keane questioned Tom on Min's disappearance, although the interview was proving fruitless. Tom had been with friends all yesterday evening and maintained he had no idea where Min would go. It seemed she rarely ventured anywhere but the college.

Jackman leant forward and waited until Tom met his gaze. 'Why don't you tell me about Min?'

Tom dug his fingers into his hair in a comb-like motion. 'What do you want to know?'

'How long have you known her?'

'She started at the college in September. Came over to do the access course.'

'What does she study?' Jackman already knew the answer. But Tom's uncomfortable body language, the way he repeatedly touched his hair, scratched the back of his neck, fidgeted in his chair, fascinated him.

'She's doing a foundation course in business, hoping to go on to study at a British university.'

'When did you meet?'

'During Freshers' week, around the campus. She's very easy to get to know.'

'In what way?'

21

Tom narrowed his eyes. 'She's different to the other Chinese students. Most of them stick together, form their own little clan and rarely mix with the rest of the college. Min loves England: the music, the culture, the clothes, even some of the food. She often says she's not looking forward to going back home.'

'Why?'

'China's not without restrictions. Her parents sent her over here to get a better grounding in business, a solid education. But she wants to stay when she finishes her access course. Maybe even qualify to be an accountant and get residency.'

Jackman leant back in his chair. 'Doesn't she miss her family?'

'I guess so. She talks about her mother. I think they're quite close. She calls her a lot. Her father has a factory that manufactures tooling.'

'Can you tell me anything about her father's business?'

Tom bit his lip and shifted in his chair. 'Not really.'

'Anything you can tell us might lead us closer to finding Min.'

Tom hesitated and then leant forward. 'He started off working for one of the big foreign companies in the nineties and now makes his own range of tools and exports it to the West. But she says the Chinese are very suspicious people. They don't trust the authorities. The government don't actively encourage free enterprise, instead they turn a blind eye to people like him because their business operations boost the economy. But she said his position is always precarious. It seems it's all about who you know, whose palm you grease.' Tom sighed. 'She also said that accountants are low paid in China. Over here she can earn a reasonable living, have more security, maybe even bring her parents over eventually.'

For a moment neither of them spoke. The faint whir of the light bulb in the ceiling filled the room. Jackman surveyed Tom. Earlier he'd watched him struggle to fold his gangly frame into the chair. The photo Jackman had been shown of Min indicated a petite young woman. The contrast between Min's shape and Tom's might have seemed comical in other circumstances.

Jackman rolled his shoulders. 'I understand you had an argument with Min before she went missing. What was it about?'

Tom was quiet for the shortest of seconds. He cleared his throat. 'Her parents. They are coming over in June when we break up. I wanted to meet them, but she doesn't want to introduce me.' Tom grimaced. 'I guess I was being a bit unreasonable. She's an only child and her parents have high expectations for her career.' He cut off awkwardly.

'And those expectations don't include a boyfriend?'

Tom shook his head. 'She's worried that if they find out she's seeing someone they'll take her back home. Put an end to her studies, her life in England.'

'How did you leave it?'

'She got angry, dug her heels in. I'd been

23

drinking. Not too much, but enough to engage mouth before head. I told her if she couldn't be bothered to tell her parents, even to introduce me as a friend, then it was over.'

'Was she upset?'

'A bit. More angry. She got up, screamed something at me in Chinese and stormed out. Actually, it was kind of embarrassing. The whole pub turned to look at me.'

'And you let her go? A young woman? To walk through the streets of Stratford on her own?'

Tom peered up beneath hooded eyes. 'It was my birthday. I thought she was testing me. That she'd gone outside to cool down, to see if I went after her. I really thought she'd come back after a few minutes.'

'And she didn't?'

Tom's face folded. When he spoke, his voice was barely a whisper. 'No.'

'Is there anywhere she might have gone? To calm down, maybe?'

'The other officer asked me that. We've called everyone.'

'How much had she drunk?'

He shrugged. 'She doesn't drink much. She certainly wasn't drunk if that's what you're implying.'

Jackman narrowed his eyes. 'Okay. What about money?'

'She has an account. Her parents give her an allowance, but it's not huge.'

'Is there anyone she might have upset recently?'

'No.' He sat up in his chair. 'She's just a sweet

girl. A little strong-headed, but nice. She's popular at the college.'

Jackman stood. 'I'll need names of all her associates both inside and outside the college, all her close friends, and everybody that was at your party last night. DC Keane will take a note of them.' He moved towards the door. Just as his fingers touched the handle he turned back. 'Tom, as far as we are aware, you are the last person who saw Min last night. Please think very carefully about her recent behaviour and her actions at the pub. If anything comes to mind, however insignificant it might appear, I urge you to give me a call.' He crossed back towards him, dug his hand in his pocket and produced a business card.

'What do you mean?' Tom asked.

'Anything. Perhaps someone she has spoken to recently, an odd phone call, a strange place she has visited, an unusual email or text message, something out of the ordinary. I need to know everything.'

★　★　★

Jackman rubbed his fingers down the shadow of stubble forming at the side of his chin as he wound up his briefing. 'Let's think this one through,' he said. While he'd been busy interviewing the boyfriend and meeting the press, Davies had made a reasonable attempt at turning the only empty office in the building into a makeshift incident room complete with a pin board containing a map of the locality, a white board for briefing and priorities, emergency designated phone lines installed and a team of detectives, albeit crammed into the tight space.

He glanced across at the map of Stratford centre on the board beside him. Coloured pegs marked the location of the college and the Old Thatch Tavern. Red marker indicated Min Li's movements up to where she was last seen. Next to the map was a photo of Min herself, a headshot taken off Tom's phone. She had quite obviously posed for the photo, tilting her head and looking directly into the lens, and it gave the impression that she was now staring back at Jackman. Her mouth was slightly parted to reveal crystal-white teeth. She had a clear complexion, long dark hair. But what really struck Jackman were the eyes. An unusual hazel.

'The cameras track her as she turns the corner of Rother Street, then nothing. We know she was dressed in a long skirt and heels. She couldn't have walked far.' Jackman rubbed his chin. 'We've appealed for witnesses. If she's staying with anyone close by, then surely they would have come forward by now?'

'Unless she's hiding away from someone or something?' Davies' voice shot up from the side of the room.

'I think we need more from the parents,' he said. 'Uniform spoke to them briefly, but . . . ' His eyes scanned the room until they found DC Russell perched on the corner of a desk. Her red hair was pulled back tight from her face and wound into a bun at the back of her head. 'Kathryn, I want you to be a point of contact for

Mr and Mrs Li. Update them on where we are with the investigation, try to establish a relationship and keep the lines of communication open. Does Min have a secret email address, another phone, a confidante? I believe the father speaks reasonable English, not sure about the mother. Get an interpreter on board if you need one.'

Russell looked up from her notes and nodded as Jackman paused. 'Get onto the Chinese consulate as well. See what you can find out about their family background. The officer who spoke to them earlier said they have no other family or close friends in this country, but we'll need to get that verified. Find out as much as you can about her father's business interests. Is there anything unusual there? We can't rule out the possibility of kidnap, although there's been no ransom call yet.'

Silence echoed around the room as Jackman continued, 'According to her boyfriend she is a popular girl, grade A student. No reason for anyone to hold a grudge against her. We haven't located a body. Is that because we haven't found her yet or because she is still alive somewhere?'

'I spoke to the college nurse this morning,' Davies piped up from her makeshift seat on the edge of a desk, which was bowing slightly. 'No record of mental health issues, not being treated for depression.'

Jackman nodded his thanks. That made another line of enquiry less viable. Depressed people sometimes took desperate measures. The possibility of suicide seemed unlikely here, although

27

they couldn't rule out a history of mental illness. They'd have to rely on the Embassy to dig up that information and goodness knows how long that would take.

'Any news on her phone?'

Davies shook her head. 'We can't site it. Been switched off since 10.50 last night. We're just going through billing at the moment but it's not throwing up anything exciting.'

'Okay, let's see what the appeal for witnesses brings in and what we can put together ourselves regarding Min Li's movements yesterday. The local news will put out an appeal on their hourly bulletins and the *Stratford Mail* have agreed to publish the details on their website within the hour. I want a team sent down to the college to interview anybody who had anything to do with her and another team to go through every ounce of CCTV footage from the pub. We need to reach everyone who was in there last night, for whatever reason.

'The town cameras are covered and we're await-ing enhancements on the vehicles that passed through between 10.30 and 12.30 p.m. There's at least two that are of interest, a BMW and a white Volkswagen van. We shared those with the press so hopefully the drivers will come forward.' He turned to Davies. 'Get that fast-tracked, will you?'

She tucked a stray dark curl behind her ear and nodded.

'Right, that's it. Thanks, everyone.' As he made to go, a thought pushed into Jackman's mind and he whipped around. 'I'm sure I don't need to say it, but this is a very sensitive case that will likely attract international press attention. Undoubtedly, there will be links made with Ellen Readman, speculation that we have another murder, maybe even a serial killer. We have no evidence to suggest this, although its early days and we can't rule anything out at the moment. So, everything we discuss, every phone call, every tiny piece of information stays in this room, unless either me or DS Davies says otherwise. Agreed?'

★　★　★

He leant into the screen, pressed rewind and then clicked play. The detective was tall, athletic. Not smooth, but there was a rugged handsomeness about his military stance and chiselled jawline.

He watched the thirty seconds of footage intently, hanging on every word. As the detective said, 'If anybody thinks they have seen Min Li, or have any information about her whereabouts we urge them to ring the incident room immediately,' a smile curled the edge of his lip. No mention of any witnesses. They had no idea where she was. And he'd make sure they didn't find her either. Not until the time was right.

# 7

A damp smell curled my nostrils, pulling me out of my slumber. It wasn't a dream. This isn't a dream.

I folded my body in, bringing every warm fibre together. My skirt felt wet. The stench of ammonia followed quickly as realisation clawed at my insides.

The sound of the wind caught my attention. Distant branches creaked as they shunted about. It reminded me of the bamboo bending and creaking in the wind back home.

A bright street filled my mind. The railway bridge and the college in the distance. I imagined myself heading to class, the strap of my satchel bag rubbing against my shoulder, the traffic on the main road drowned out by the hub of college life; the endless conversations of students roaming the campus. The memory was stark. Lauren checking the timetable, keeping me organised. Steph rummaging through her bag. Tom texting. My friends. Did they miss me?

How long had it been? I considered the time, but no matter how hard I tried to concentrate my thoughts were still foggy. The light that seeped through the tiny gap above me had brightened to daytime. But that didn't mean a great deal.

Tom. I remembered shouting at him. The hurt in his face. I pressed hard on the cogs of my brain, forcing them to turn. We were in the Old

Thatch Tavern. I left him there. Walked out on my own. That must have been when I was brought here.

I hauled myself up, placed my hands on the walls and moved slowly around the square box, my fingertips searching every inch of the concrete walls. There were gaps here and there, areas where the concrete had cracked and worn. But no way out.

I turned my attention to the top. A metal grill sat proud in the centre, covering almost a metre square. It felt cold on my palms, and fiercely rigid. I shook it. Nothing. Not even the slightest movement. Again. This time there was a light shift, and a rattle. I shook harder until tears of anger swelled in my eyes. It juddered slightly and a soft rattle could be heard in the distance, but it remained firmly in place.

Hot tears stung my cheeks as I focused on the grill. It was covered with a flat piece of wood that almost reached the end, leaving a gap for the narrow slice of light to pass through. I tried to reach for the wood through the gaps between the bars, but there was only enough room to hook a couple of fingers inside and they weren't long enough to reach it.

I stuck my forefinger through to explore the edge of the grill and slowly moved it around the cold metal edge, weaving it in and out of the bars. My finger brushed something uneven. A chink of metal rang out. I pushed my middle finger through. Links. Big thick links. Maybe a chain. A spasm of pain shot through my fingers, causing me to retrieve them and rub them into

31

the palm of my left hand. The frustration was unbearable. I needed to do something.

I coughed to clear my throat, took a deep breath and shouted. My voice isn't naturally loud, it softens the consonants of English speech. But today I shouted and screeched like I'd never shouted before, for as long as I could. I paused and listened hard, desperately hoping for the tiniest shred of human presence. Nothing.

Suddenly I remembered something, the words of my father back home: 'When you are projecting your voice, you need to stand tall, open your diaphragm.' I straightened my back, took another breath, deeper this time and shouted louder until my voice disappeared and my throat squeaked.

Crushed, I leant back against the wall and slid to the ground. Where was this black hole? I concentrated hard, desperately listening for something familiar, the sound of life. I heard no traffic, no voices. Just my own breaths and the wind, whistling through branches that felt as though they were planted in the ground above. The thought made me shiver. I am buried alive.

# 8

Jackman checked his phone as he crossed the college car park. A missed call from Reilly. He'd deal with that later. He reached a modern building that curved around the corner, entered and trudged up the stairs to Min Li's apartment. Yesterday Min would have been climbing these steps, possibly on her way back from class.

Their low-key approach meant a distinct absence of police tape. Earlier, he'd despatched a couple of crime scene investigators to comb Min's room for clues to her whereabouts, although he didn't expect the search to yield much. They'd now secured Min's room, but the rest of the building was open access in an attempt to keep everything as normal as possible for the students that lived there.

Jackman entered the main door and scanned the purpose-built apartment that Min Li shared with three other Chinese students. It looked far plusher than any student accommodation he'd even seen. Apart from a pile of used coffee mugs, plates and bowls in the sink of the kitchenette in the corner, the magnolia living area was spacious and surprisingly tidy. A few brightly coloured cushions were squished into the corners of an oversized sofa in the centre of the room, a couple of bean bags strewn on the laminate floor around it; a pile of magazines were scattered beside an armchair in the corner.

The room was empty apart from the plain-clothes officer guarding Min's door. Jackman exchanged pleasantries with him and entered Min's bedroom. It was a small room, less than five metres square he guessed, with a bed in the centre and a desk on the far wall next to a small dressing table and a built-in wardrobe.

He stepped into the ensuite bathroom, which housed a corner shower, sink and toilet. There was no window and just enough tiled flooring to accommodate one person comfortably with the door closed. A single toothbrush and tube of toothpaste filled a cup on the sink, a pink face cloth was folded over the side. A make-up case sat on the shelf above alongside bottles of shampoo and conditioner. All items one would pack if one was planning a trip away. Jackman chewed the side of his mouth and moved back into the bedroom. The bed was wrapped in a lilac and cream silk cover, tucked in neatly at the sides, undisturbed. He opened the wardrobe and ran his fingers along the hanging clothes. Jeans and jumpers were piled on the shelf above. A pink suitcase tucked away at the bottom.

This was a student girl's bedroom, much like Celia's, although he guessed much tidier. He checked his watch. It was 4.35 p.m. Min's bedroom left no indication of what, why or where she'd gone. His eyes fell on the empty desk in the far corner. Officers had seized her computer. Station techies would be examining it now, checking her last movements online. He crossed the room and pulled open the single drawer below. A couple of biros rattled along the bottom as it opened. He lifted out an essay and picked up a photo of a man and woman and another of an older Chinese woman — her mother and father, and grandmother perhaps. He cast the photos aside and sifted through what was left: her passport, a menu for The Thai Boathouse, a hairbrush with a couple of hair bands secured around the handle.

Suddenly, a comment Tom had made tripped into Jackman's mind, 'She was rarely alone.' Rarely alone. Until that night. It suggested an element of planning, a stalker maybe. In Jackman's experience, stranger crime was incredibly uncommon. Most victims were assaulted, abused, or killed by someone they knew. Somebody would have to have been watching her movements for days, weeks even — waiting, planning, ready to snatch her at any moment.

No amount of years in the force made these thoughts any more palatable, although he had to admit that the longer Min remained missing, the more sinister explanations presented themselves. He thought back to the three kidnappings he had dealt with during the course of his career. Two of them had been drugs-related, connected with debts that, once paid, meant the victim was returned. The third was the abduction of a businessman's daughter, a CEO of a major video games company. Ethan Larkin's daughter had been gone less than three hours when the ransom call came through. The advice was always the same: pay the ransom and preserve life. A tacit agreement meant that the press honoured a complete hold on media activity

35

once a demand was received. For this reason, most kidnappings never even got reported to the public. Getting the victim back was top priority.

Although kidnappings were one of the most unpleasant and manipulative of crimes to deal with, they were predominantly a business transaction. But, with Min missing for over twelve hours and no ransom call, it seemed an unlikely prospect.

He considered Ellen Readman, missing for a week before her body was found, and wondered how Reilly was getting on in Northampton. Ellen Readman and Katie Sharp were both dark-haired girls, just like Min. He hoped there wasn't a connection.

The buzz of his phone cut through his thoughts. He glanced down at the text message from Davies. 'Best full shot of the misper, taken from the footage at the Old Thatch Tavern last night.' He clicked to open the photo and came face to face with Min Li.

# 9

Jackman decided to walk back to the police station. He rounded the corner onto Alcester Road, passed the blue-blocked college frontage and made his way over the railway bridge, pausing at the junction with Grove Road and Arden Street. During the daytime this was a busy intersection. Vehicles spilled through it as they headed out of the town centre. He turned around, almost full circle. Directly ahead of him lay Greenhill Street. Alcester Road stretched out of town behind. A turn to the right or left showed lines of Victorian terraces. He thought for a moment. The last sighting of their misper came from the camera on Greenhill Street, almost directly opposite the pub. They knew she'd turned the corner and was heading in the direction of the college. But the camera at the end of Greenhill Street hadn't picked up their girl. So she either didn't get that far, or she turned off somewhere.

He crossed the road, retracing Min's footsteps. The edge of Stratford town still featured many black and white uneven Tudor buildings. Wood Street and those around the theatre had been sympathetically renovated and built up over the years and even the new shop fronts were in keeping with the original style. But further out, many of the ancient dwellings had been interspersed with modern buildings and shop fronts, and Greenhill Street was an eclectic mixture of the ancient and the very new. He made his way to the old red telephone box and halted. A car park sat beside it. There were no side streets during this stretch for Min to take. He glanced to the right and walked into the car park. A camera pointed protectively across its flock of cars, away from the road. He stopped next to a low stone wall and looked over the top. The ground was lower at the other side by a couple of feet, although it was feasible to jump over it, and head through to Grove Road. Well, feasible for him. But for a woman in a long skirt and heels? It seemed unlikely.

He made his way back to the pavement. The Chicago Rock Cafe opposite had long since closed down. He racked his brains. His officers would be working their way down this road checking for witnesses and sightings of the victim. He made a mental note to ensure they requested all available camera footage from the shops and businesses still open and continued on until he reached the pub.

Hanging baskets weighted down with petunias, begonias and strings of variegated ivy decorated the side walls of the Old Thatch Tavern that straddled the corner of Rother Street and Greenhill Street, their blast of colour making the quaint fifteenth-century, white-painted building look almost picturesque in the sparkling sunlight. He stared at the wooden entrance door as he passed and made his way back to the station.

It was another balmy evening. Rush hour was in full swing and the buzz of traffic hummed in his ears, so much so that he was grateful to escape it when he arrived at the station. He strode around the back and walked through the staff entrance.

The first person Jackman saw as he climbed the stairs was DC Russell. She was standing on the landing, texting on her mobile.

'Evening, sir.' She looked up at him. 'Can't get a damn signal inside.'

Jackman smiled at her. 'Any news from the Li family?'

Russell's face clouded over. 'Not much I'm afraid. I've spoken to the father, but as far as I can tell she hasn't been in touch and they have no idea where she is. They're eight hours ahead of us, so I think we're unlikely to hear anything more until the morning.'

'Okay, well done. What about the Embassy? Anything on her father's business interests?'

Russell blew a frustrated sigh out of the corners of her mouth. 'It's all forms and paperwork requests, but no answers. Proper bureaucracy. I don't hold out much hope for anything very soon.'

'Alright, thanks. Keep plugging away at it.'

She looked out of the window and her forehead wrinkled into a frown.

'Is there something else?'

She kept her gaze on the car park as she spoke. 'No, nothing I can put my finger on.'

'What do you mean?'

She shook her head. 'I don't know. The parents didn't sound too upset.' She turned to look at him. 'If it was your daughter, you'd be frantic, choke on your words, angry even. I know it was a phone call to the other side of the world and there are cultural differences to bear in mind, but I found it difficult to get any emotion from him at all. He seemed so controlled.'

Jackman stared at Russell a moment before he spoke. 'People react to things in different ways.'

'Yes, you're right.' Her mouth formed a thin smile. 'Probably just me. We'll see what tomorrow brings.'

He nodded and turned towards the incident room. He'd almost reached the entrance when she called after him, 'Oh, by the way, a package was dropped off for you.'

He turned back. 'Who from?'

She shrugged. 'A brown envelope. It's on your desk.'

Jackman entered the incident room and headed for the box-style office in the corner. As soon as he approached it, he saw the brown envelope that sat in the middle of his desk marked clearly in black biro, DI JACKMAN, ROTHER STREET STATION. There was a short line under his name. A single full stop below.

He lifted it, ripped the end of the envelope and could barely believe his eyes at the contents. It was full of witness statements, phone logs, credit card statements relating to the Readman and Sharp cases. Incensed, he grabbed his phone and immediately dialled.

Reilly picked up on the second ring, as if he was expecting the call. 'Ah, Will. Good to hear from you.'

'I've just found a pile of material on my desk.'

'Oh, you've received your package. Good.'

Jackman bit back his irritation. 'What's it doing here?'

'Thought you might like to have a look through,' Reilly said. 'See if anything jumps out at you.'

'I'm up to my eyeballs with the misper at the moment. I really don't think . . . '

'Don't worry, I've cleared it with Janus. Just an hour or so of your time. Since you've been at the forefront of the investigation the chief constable felt it might be helpful if you cast your eye over it. Kind of 'belt and braces', leaving no stone unturned and all that.'

Jackman ground his teeth together, tossed the envelope aside and ended the call. He could never understand why Reilly had taken a detective role, particularly as a senior investigating officer in charge of major crime where every case decision had to be justified and recorded, every strategic decision outlined in detail. The weight of the press, the family, the public, superiors who all wanted a resolution pressed on your shoulders as each hour passed. Yet Reilly made no attempt to hide his dislike of frontline policing. To him the move was temporary, another notch on his management CV.

But Jackman knew the score here. If something was missed later on, something that they needed, that the evidence relied upon for a conviction, Reilly would be able to say Jackman didn't notice it. Some people would go to any amount of trouble to shirk responsibility.

A knock at the door interrupted his thoughts. Davies' face appeared. 'Sir, I think you need to

41

come and take a look at this.'

He followed her into the incident room. Several officers were crowded around Keane's computer in the corner. They parted to let Jackman through.

Keane turned to face him. 'This is the camera footage from the Old Thatch Tavern last night.' He whisked back to his computer screen and clicked the mouse. There was only one exit/entrance door to the pub for customers and it was in full view. For a couple of seconds, nothing happened. Then a grainy image entered the screen. The figure was tall, wearing a navy shirt and jeans. Suddenly the figure turned back for a split second before exiting the pub. Tom. Jackman checked the time in the corner of the screen. It was 10.45 p.m. Tom must have popped outside to check if Min was still there.

Jackman raised his head, perplexed, and shot Davies a glance.

She lifted a flat hand, said nothing.

Keane clicked fast forward to 10.46 p.m. Tom re-entered the pub.

Jackman shifted position. 'What are we meant to be looking at?'

'Wait,' Keane said. His tongue was visible, pushed against his top lip as he moved the footage on further, stopping at 11.05 p.m. For a moment all was quiet. Then the same figure approached the door and exited the pub. The door swung shut behind him.

Keane swivelled his chair to face them. 'We catch him returning later at exactly 11.33 p.m. He was gone for almost half an hour.'

'What was our devoted boyfriend doing leaving the pub again?' Jackman said.

Davies raised a brow. 'That's the question.'

★ ★ ★

Jackman rested his elbow on the armrest and balanced his chin on his thumb. His forefinger lingered along the line of his lip for several moments as he surveyed Tom Steele.

Tom had been brought back to the police station on the pretence of further assistance. Russell said he'd come along amiably, not an etching of surprise on his handsome face. As he was guided into the same room it seemed any earlier nerves or awkwardness had drained away.

They'd spent the last fifteen minutes going over Tom's movements from the previous night from when he arrived at the pub, to the argument and Min leaving, him wandering out to look for her, then leaving himself with his mates just after 11.45 p.m. He delivered the story with surprising aplomb, as if he'd rehearsed the details several times in his mind over the past twelve hours.

Jackman lifted his forefinger just enough to let himself speak. 'Are you sure there's nothing else you'd like to add?'

Tom's shrug was barely perceptible. He shook his head.

'Only according to our records you were the last person to see Min alive. And that was at 10.35 p.m. when she left the pub?'

Tom nodded.

'And you haven't seen or heard from her since?'

'No, I told you . . . '

'Think.' Jackman paused slightly. 'Think hard. What you tell us now could be very important to Min's welfare. You've had almost twenty-two hours to mull it over. Are you sure there's nowhere else she'd go?'

'Yes, I'm sure.'

'You see I'm having a problem believing you.'

Alarm fluttered across Tom's face. He made to speak, widened his eyes, but Jackman cut in first. 'Tom Steele, would you like to tell me where you went when you left the Old Thatch Tavern at,' he consulted his notes, '11.05 p.m.?'

Tom's face instantly froze.

Jackman threw him a hard stare. 'I'm beginning to think you don't want to help us.'

A muscle flexed in Tom's jawline. He cast a cursory glance at the camera in the corner, then looked down, his eyes darting about from side to side.

Jackman watched him shift inch by inch in his seat so that his feet were pointing towards the door, a movement that made his body appear to be twisted at an angle. This should have been a turning point in the interview, the moment when a dark secret was uncovered. But the creases of sheer desperation in Tom's face gave Jackman the distinct impression that whatever was said next would not be the breakthrough he'd hoped for.

Jackman inhaled deeply. 'Instead of considering your options, why not be honest? We can deal with the consequences afterwards.'

Tom gaped back at him. 'It's complicated.'

★ ★ ★

Back in his office, Jackman swivelled his chair to look out of the window. Dusk was just starting to fall over the car park below, the sky in the distance a mass of yellow, orange and red swirls.

A tap at the door made him spin to face it. Davies cocked her head to one side. 'Thought I might find you here.'

Jackman glanced up at the clock. It was 8.35 p.m. 'Don't you have a baby to go to?'

She plonked herself down on the chair opposite him. 'Already been. He's tucked up in bed fast asleep.'

'Well, I'm sorry to inform you that it's an offence to leave a minor alone,' Jackman said with a slight smile.

Davies' dimple dug into her left cheek. 'Oh, come on, I'm not letting you have all the fun. Anyhow, John's off, delayed his two weeks paternity leave until I returned to work. He can cope.' She leant forward and poked the brown envelope from Reilly. 'What's this?'

Jackman's eyes rested on the package. His anger had refused to allow him to look through it. 'Just some crap from Operation Sky.' He looked up at Davies. 'Anything from the appeals?'

Davies looked back out into the incident room where an array of officers had phones glued to their ears. 'Nothing concrete. The usual cranks and a few possible leads to pursue. Nothing on the white van or the BMW, or any other vehicles that passed through between 10.30 p.m. and 12.30pm. So, what are we going to do about Tom's guilty secret? Do you want her brought here?'

Jackman considered his options. The only benefit to bringing her in here was to interview her formally, scare her. Although she wasn't officially a suspect. This was a missing person case. They didn't even have a crime, so she couldn't be a suspect. Damn protocol.

He looked up and met her gaze. 'Fancy a trip out?'

# 10

Rushbrook Road led into Trinity Mead, a nearly new estate with a variety of different sizes and styles of affordable modern homes. He passed the older, established houses and pulled in halfway down at one of the detached brick-built new homes. As they walked down the short pathway to the entrance he could see the silhouette of a woman, sat in the single armchair beside the window. Just as they reached the door she hauled herself up.

The clunk of a bolt and rattle of a chain reminded Jackman that darkness was closing in. The door eventually opened to reveal a woman with an oval, made-up face and smooth, cropped dark hair in black trousers and a cream silky top. Her feet were clad with gold sandals.

'Jenny Walters?' Davies held up her badge. 'I'm DS Davies and this is DI Jackman.'

'Who is it, honey?' The gravelly voice came from above. Jenny cast her eyes to the ceiling. 'Nothing. Go back to sleep. I'll be up in a bit.'

She turned back to Jackman. 'You'd better come in.'

They wandered a few steps down a dimly-lit hallway and entered the front room. Jenny followed them through and switched on the light.

The sudden illumination revealed a neat room painted pale green and filled with a cream sofa against one wall, a matching single armchair beneath the window and an oak dresser littered with silver-framed photos on the far wall. Jenny gesticulated for them to sit and crossed to the single armchair. The fact that they weren't offered refreshments wasn't lost on Jackman.

'Mrs Walters, can you tell me where you were last night?' he asked.

She took a deep breath. In the soft hallway lighting she could have been mistaken for a woman in her thirties, but under the glaring spotlights the laughter lines around her eyes and deep grooves that edged her cheeks added another ten years at least. 'Here for most of the evening. Had to pop out for a bit, but I think you already know that.'

'Why was that?'

She closed her eyes momentarily before she met his gaze. 'Look I know what this is about,' she said. 'Tom phoned me.'

Back at the station, Keane had married up the grainy CCTV footage of Tom leaving the pub with the private camera footage from Grove House car park on Greenhill Street which showed Tom arrive there a couple of minutes later. Tom had loitered for a bit by the entrance until a green Volvo had pulled in, that they later traced to Jenny Walters. They watched him climb into the car. A few minutes later he emerged with some paperwork which he'd folded and tucked into his pocket before heading back to the pub.

'Why don't you talk us through it?' he asked. Jenny sighed. 'It's awkward.'

48

'I know,' Jackman said, 'Tom's already spoken to us.'

'Then you'll know what it's about. I don't want to get involved.'

Jackman pushed his lips together. He really couldn't deal with dramatics at this time of night. 'We are investigating the case of a missing woman. You were spotted in the vicinity where she was last seen. Why did you drive out to Stratford centre to meet Tom last night?'

A short silence followed. Just as Jackman was going to suggest they continue the conversation at the station, Jenny spoke up. 'I'm an agent for a private abortion clinic. Tom contacted me a couple of weeks ago.'

'How did he find out about you?'

She lifted a manicured nail and scratched the side of her neck. 'He found us on the internet. We're based on the edge of Warwickshire and offer a discreet, confidential service. I deal with all potential new clients. We've chatted a few times over the past two weeks, discussed his options.'

'And why did he contact you?'

'His girlfriend is almost two months pregnant.'

'Have you spoken to her?'

She shook her head.

'Is it normal for you to deal with partners?'

Jenny hesitated for a split second. 'We deal with people in very difficult circumstances. Either partner may make the initial contact. Our success is measured by our commitment to confidentiality. Our clients could be in relationships, married, in executive jobs where they don't wish to be judged.'

'Or international students,' Davies offered.

Jenny gave Davies a dismissive glance. 'This is not folding tables and dirty knives, Sergeant. Nothing that I do or represent is illegal or sordid in any way.'

'What did you talk about with Tom?' Jackman asked.

She switched back to face him. 'The usual. I have all the details in my diary if you need them. I keep a note of every call and every meeting.'

'That would be helpful.'

Jackman caught the faint waft of her perfume as she passed him and disappeared from the room for the shortest of moments, returning with a black leather briefcase. They watched as she foraged through and retrieved a navy A5 diary.

She opened the book and flipped through the pages until she found what she wanted. 'His initial contact was Monday the 28th of April. He wanted to know how it all worked, costs involved, that sort of thing. It was just an expression of interest. I only took his name and telephone number. Then he phoned again last week on Wednesday to ask about availability. I said we could fit them in within a few days, but we had to meet and examine his girlfriend first.'

'How much does it cost for a confidential abortion?' Jackman asked.

'That depends on the duration of the pregnancy and the health of the woman. There are lots of factors to consider, but our prices start from £500 inclusive of consultation.'

Davies raised her brows. 'Steep price for confidentiality.'

50

Jenny ignored her, looked back at her diary and flicked forward a few pages. 'Then I received another call from him last night. He wanted some more information, a brochure. He said it was urgent.'

Jackman leant back. 'Does your job often take you out to meet clients in car parks late at night?'

'As I said, we deal with people in very difficult circumstances. We offer a complete package of assistance and advice before, and counselling and support after, the procedure. My job is the initial contact.'

'A sales person?'

She cleared her throat. 'I like to think I'm more than that. I make myself available to assist with any questions and provide information to enable clients to make an informed decision. Tom sounded upset, so I drove in and gave him some literature. He said he was going to talk to his girlfriend and come back to me in the next couple of days.'

'And that is all?'

She nodded. 'I drove straight home. I was barely gone for half an hour.'

Jackman glanced at the ceiling. 'What does your husband think of you popping out last thing at night to see a client?'

She fluttered her eyelashes. 'Partner,' she corrected. 'He's used to it. All part of the job.'

'Did you see Min, or talk about her last night?'

She shook her head. 'Not at all. In fact very few words were exchanged between Tom and I.' She met his gaze and held it a second. 'This won't become public knowledge will it? I don't

51

want the clinic compromised.'

Jackman stared back at her. 'This is a missing person investigation. I'm not in a position to give any guarantees.'

Jackman closed the interview and wandered over to take a closer look at the photos on the dresser while Jenny gave her contact details to Davies. His eyes brushed several featuring two boys taken at various ages and rested on a row at the bottom in leather frames. These were recent photos taken of Jenny, dressed up for a night out. He picked up the one on the end. The frame was scuffed, as if it had been knocked. Jenny was at the front of a small group of women, her arm hooked around another woman's shoulder, her free hand raising a glass to the camera.

Davies snapped her notebook shut, stood and handed over her card.

The door shook as it shut behind them. Jackman immediately heard the sound of locks being reapplied.

As they climbed into the car and battled with seatbelts, Davies shot Jackman a sideways glance. 'What do you think?'

He wound down his window. The air was cool and fresh, a welcome respite after the stickiness of the day. 'That Min has a major problem which gives her every reason to go off somewhere and mull it over.'

'So we're wasting our time?'

'I'm not sure. What do you make of Jenny Walters?'

Davies was silent for a moment. 'Bit overdressed and made up for her age. Could be her work face.' Her words trailed off.

Jackman ran his tongue across the back of his teeth in thought, said nothing.

'Maybe there was more to it?' Davies continued. 'I imagine Tom's handsome boy band look might catch her eye.'

Jackman thought back to the photos on the dresser. Jenny Walters certainly enjoyed a night out with the girls. And there wasn't a photograph of her with her partner. He considered the CCTV footage from the evening before — their clandestine meeting. They didn't know they were being watched yet there was no intimacy in their body language, no hint of familiarity between them. He paused to massage the pads of his hands into his weary eyes, before he spoke. 'Tom was the last person to see her alive, right?'

'So far.'

'The fact that he was pressing for a private abortion could give him a motive. Where would he get that kind of cash?'

'Background checks showed his dad's a doctor, mother a secondary school teacher. They live in Loxley Road, in one of the big detached houses at the far end. Can't be short of a bob or two.'

'What if they refused to help? Or maybe he couldn't tell them? I imagine they'd be very disappointed at their only son's career ambitions being dashed at this stage in his studies.'

'Maybe she wanted to keep the baby and it became a problem?'

'In any event he chose to keep it from us. Why?' Jackman said. 'I think we should keep a close eye on him. If he's involved he might lead us to her.'

Jackman stared out into the night and percolated his thoughts. Arranging surveillance required authorisation from the assistant chief constable, organising a team of officers, a briefing. This wasn't something they could set up instantly. And he needed something, right now.

'Tom Steele's been dropped back home, right?'

Davies checked her watch. 'Yes. I got uniform to give him a lift. He should have landed about the time we arrived here.'

'Right. Think we'll get a couple of detectives to hang around and watch his house tonight. By the morning we should be able to get a surveillance team in place.'

Davies sat quietly, texting on her phone beside him, whilst Jackman made a few calls. When he finished, she pocketed her phone and inserted the key into the ignition. 'Where to now?'

He narrowed his eyes. 'I'm thinking the pub?'

'Wonderful idea!'

He turned his head to face her. 'You don't change.'

Davies smiled. 'Oh, come on,' she cried, 'give a girl a break. I don't get out much these days.'

He gave a short laugh. 'Okay, only if you promise to behave. We just need to make a quick detour first.'

\* \* \*

He stared at the computer screen, his fingers navigating the keys like water rippling across the stones of a shallow stream. He moved quickly, typing each word like it was his last, although he knew he had all the time in the world. He was calling the shots now. He was making the decisions.

A last read through. A ragged breath, drawn tightly, sent a rush of adrenalin fizzing through his veins. He pressed the save button. The final piece of his plan was in place. Now it was time to execute it.

# 11

Jackman could hear Erik's tail thumping as he pushed open his front door. He followed the sound to the living room.

Celia looked up from the sofa and flashed a wide smile that exposed a row of perfect white teeth. 'Hi, Dad.'

'Hey!' Jackman bent down, encased his daughter in a hug and planted a kiss on her forehead. 'Wasn't expecting you until tomorrow.'

'Thought I'd surprise you,' she said. Her face was clear of make-up and decorated around the edge with messy strands of white-blonde hair that had escaped from the loose tie at the nape of her neck. 'And I rescued this runt from Angela next door.' Erik was curled up beside her, tongue hanging out to the side, tail still beating the cushions.

Jackman rolled his eyes. 'She's meant to walk him, not babysit him.'

'Think she likes the company.' Celia's yellow vest puckered as she stretched her elbows back to reveal a blue stud in her navel, just above the waistline of her denims.

'How was the drive up from Southampton?'

'Fine, apart from the dreaded roadworks on the M40. Took me almost three hours.'

Jackman suddenly remembered Davies who was hovering in the hallway. 'Come on in, Annie,' he called.

Davies' ashen face appeared around the doorway. 'Sorry, didn't want to intrude.'

Jackman waved her in. 'Don't be silly. Celia, you remember Annie Davies?'

Celia looked up and smiled. 'Course. Nice to see you again.'

Jackman turned back to his daughter. 'You eaten?'

'I ordered Chinese. There's some crispy beef and noodles left in the kitchen for you.'

Jackman smiled inwardly at how his daughter had grown accustomed to his unsociable hours. She didn't bat an eye that he wasn't home when she arrived. But still the warm smile greeted him on his return. 'Great, I'm starving. Have to go out again, I'm afraid. Got a case on.'

'Ahhh.' Celia turned her attention back to the television where a girl was playing a keyboard on the rooftop of a high rise.

'What are you watching?' Annie asked, as she squeezed herself into the gap at the end of the sofa.

'*Coyote Ugly*. Love this film.' Celia huddled up with Erik, who licked her forehead in pleasure. 'Mum used to watch it.'

'Oooh, me too,' Annie said.

Jackman watched as both women became engrossed in the film. He was dying to ask Celia about her studies, how things were going in Southampton, but he could see that she was winding down from her journey. Plenty of time for that later.

A rumble in his belly sent him through to the kitchen. He opened a drawer, retrieved his

57

mobile phone charger, the reason he'd called home, and placed it next to his car keys on the side. Although there was a drawer full of them at the station, he hated sorting through to find one that would fit his old phone that Celia affectionately called 'the brick'.

Jackman emptied the remaining cold noodles over the crispy beef and called back into the lounge, 'Want any food, Annie?'

'No thanks,' she said. 'Got to get rid of these love handles.'

Both women chuckled together as he leant against the side and ate the noodles out of the carton. He glanced across at his daughter through the open door. She looked more like her mother every day — the same slender frame, long arms and giraffe neckline, that white-blonde Nordic hair. In fact, the only thing she had inherited from her father were the pale green eyes. 'Striking eyes', Alice had called them. The eyes that had initially attracted her to him.

Striking eyes. His mind switched to Min Li. He reached for his phone and pulled up the photo Davies had sent him earlier.

He was still awaiting details of her father's business from the Chinese authorities. The bureaucracy associated with international liaison irritated him. It would be quicker to take the eleven-hour flight and dig it up himself.

Jackman rolled his shoulders. During his early years in the police he had struggled to settle. He missed the excitement of his old career in the Royal Marines: the travel, the unpredictability, the camaraderie of his colleagues. Dealing with shoplifters, domestic disputes and petty theft just left him numb. But his first murder case had changed everything. Still in uniform, he was tasked with guarding the scene of a stabbing of a young man at a small corner pub in East London. He'd watched the detectives arrive, flash their badges, climb over the tape in their sharp suits. Their very presence demanded respect. And the relief on the uniform sergeant's face at handing over the crime scene to them was palpable. That's the moment when everything changed for him, when he discovered what he really wanted to do.

Officers like Reilly frowned upon Jackman's 'hands-on' approach to investigation. In his view, senior officers were expected to sit behind a desk, bark orders at their team, set strategy for the case. But Jackman wasn't interested in spreadsheets, targets and ticking boxes. Frankly, the bureaucracy and the politics of the senior echelons of the police force, the budgetary constraints and management meetings grated away at him. All he wanted, all he had ever wanted was to piece together the evidence to solve the crime and catch the really bad guys. Jackman took one last look at Min, slipped his phone into his pocket and forked another mouthful of crispy beef into his mouth. There had to be something there — hidden away in the background, something that he was missing.

# 12

A wet sponge touched my nose. I threw my eyes open. It was not a sponge. I shuddered, darted back. A rat. I opened my mouth to scream but only a hoarsely coated grunt gushed out. It was enough to scare the animal. It scrabbled up the walls in the half-light and disappeared from sight.

I recoiled. Thoughts of it, sniffing at me, crawling on me as I slept made me wince. I hugged my arms into myself, my eyes scanning the surrounding walls for more creatures lurking in the shadows.

Yet a part of me yearned for it. Yearned for some company in this black cavern.

I scrunched my body together tighter. Why was I here? Apart from a cut to my head and a few bruises and grazes, I hadn't been attacked. The silver bracelet my parents bought me for my eighteenth birthday still hung around my wrist.

Surely I hadn't been taken? My father was considered wealthy in China, but not by Western standards. Our apartment in Beijing was reasonably sized but not huge, and certainly not opulent — we still had my grandmother's old sofa, the woven mat beside the fire that I played on as a kid.

Kidnapped. The word made me shudder. Had my father upset somebody back home for his family to be punished in this way? It seemed

60

unlikely, he was the most amiable person I knew. Or was it someone from the UK, who had spotted what they considered a rich Chinese girl, attempting to extort money from her family?

I churned it over and over in my mind, but the more I thought about it, the more abduction seemed the only viable explanation. Why else keep me here, alive?

Had they approached my parents yet? If I closed my eyes I could almost see my mother's porcelain face crumble, my father's shoulders sink as the bottom fell out of their world. I was their only child.

And how much money had they demanded? My poor father. All those years he'd spent working long hours, making contacts, networking every waking hour. If the demands were substantial, he would take a loan. Borrowing that kind of money quickly wasn't easy in China. Not legally. If he borrowed it discreetly they would expect a hefty return, and swiftly. Everything he had built up, everything he had worked for could be lost.

It was my decision to study in the UK. I had persuaded, cajoled, plagued my parents for years. Could my decision now mean pain and suffering, not to mention potential financial ruin?

I glanced down at my stomach. But it was worse than that. Even if they paid the ransom, even if I was released and returned to their protective arms, I'd let them down. Because it wasn't just me they'd be saving. They knew nothing about the child growing in my stomach.

A lump caught in my throat. When did it all go so terribly wrong?

I looked up at the grill. If it was kidnap, why hadn't they come back?

My stomach cramped with hunger.

My tongue felt like a sheet of sandpaper. Did that mean that the baby was thirsty too? How long had I been here? How long could a human survive with no food or water, especially in my condition?

Tears stung my eyes as I saw my mother's face again in my mind. Her mouth quivering, her eyes heavy with anxiety. Even after my father gave in to my wishes she had never wanted me to come to England to study, said I was too young to travel the 5,000 miles alone. She had great expectations of me, encouraged me in my studies. But those expectations didn't include me moving to the other side of the world. My stomach clenched. Her face on the day I left spoke a thousand words. It was as if somebody had inserted metal pincers into her chest and pulled out her heart. Her only child. But after much persuasion on my part, my father had insisted and supported my hedonistic obsession to gain a better education in the West. If only I'd listened to her, I would be back home now. Curled up on the sofa whilst she cooked dinner instead of sat here, starving to death.

I rubbed my belly. If only I'd listened to her, I wouldn't be in so much of a mess.

# 13

Jackman took a sip of his mineral water and glanced along the bar. There. Right at the end he recognised it — the stone bust of Shakespeare, the same bust that sat in the background behind Min Li in her photo from the Old Thatch Tavern, now on their wall in the incident room. The front of her long hair was pulled back from her face, her mouth curled into a half-smile.

He thanked the girl behind the bar as she passed over his change. The last thing he felt like was a drink on a night like this, with Celia back home. But although his team had already interviewed the staff working last night, the CCTV footage had been meticulously watched for glimpses of Min, witness statements taken and recorded, he still wanted to visit the pub himself. This was the last place Min was seen alive, by her friends at least, and he wanted to see it around the same time she disappeared.

He turned around and leant his back against the bar. Although an old pub, the Old Thatch Tavern wasn't furnished with the usual jazzy, loud carpet that carried the pungent smell of old spilt beer into the air. An assorted selection of rustic tables, surrounded by wooden chairs, and a couple of cosy leather sofas sat on a polished tiled floor.

Jackman checked his watch, 10.20 p.m. He glanced around. A couple sat at the table beside the entrance, hands entwined. A group of men in suits sat on the only long table in the middle, glasses of lager on the table in front of them. They were laughing loudly, as if they'd just shared a private joke. Another couple filled the sofa at the end, neither speaking, eyes averted. It was a quiet Tuesday evening. He took another sip of his drink. They knew from the statements already taken that there were initially twelve of them in Min's party. They'd come into the pub around eight o'clock and were later joined by others. By the time Min had left, the pub had been heaving with friends and acquaintances. How many bodies had squashed themselves into this small bar area?

The table beside the suits was empty. He approached and sat down. From this position he could see every angle of the pub — the bar, the door, the entrance into the restaurant area and the couple canoodling in the corner. Although last night was a lot busier, it was an excellent vantage point. Perfect for somebody sitting, watching. So far, he was led to believe that Min had no known associates in Stratford, apart from her friends and teachers at the college. Her room on campus left no indication that she planned to go away.

Something puzzled him as he took another sip of his drink. The bar area was very small here, and with the horse brasses that adorned the beams, the old-fashioned bookcase in the corner, the red lamp beside the window, it looked more like a country pub than a town party venue.

The slam of a door in the background

interrupted his thoughts. He looked up as a familiar face appeared around the doorframe that led through the restaurant and out to the toilets at the far end of the building.

Davies beamed as she moved towards him and sat down opposite, blocking his view to the bar. 'What's on your mind?' she said.

'I'm thinking this seems an odd venue for a student party.'

Davies scanned the area. 'Suppose so. But, from what I understand, one of Tom's friends works here. Maybe he arranged a discount on the drinks?'

'Maybe. We need to check the statements of everyone who was in here last night and re-check the CCTV. Who came in? Who left and when? Somebody must have noticed something.'

Davies nodded. 'Sure.'

'And we need to check on the council camera footage of the street outside first thing. Tracing the drivers of that BMW and white van is a definite priority.'

'Okay.'

They sat in comfortable silence for a few minutes.

Davies lifted her hands and tightened the ponytail at the back of her head. As the day progressed it had got messier and soft curls now hung loose around her face. 'How is Alice?'

Jackman stared at his glass. 'No change.'

He fidgeted in his seat. Her words conjured up images of those awkward moments when he'd returned to work after the car accident that had reduced his wife to a permanent comatose state a year ago. Some colleagues shuffled in their shoes, dug their hands in their pockets when they enquired after Alice's health. Others made a beeline for him with their head tilts and soppy eyes. A few avoided him altogether, unsure of what to say. The answer was always the same, 'No change.' Because there never was any change.

The memories made his stomach dip. It wasn't that he was cold-hearted. He knew everyone meant well, but the last thing he wanted to talk about at work, his one area of respite, was his wife's tragic situation.

Some colleagues adapted to this much quicker than others. Accustomed to turning tragedy into humour, a coping mechanism for some of the tragic events they faced during their career, Alice's illness nudged them into unchartered territory — they couldn't make a joke out of it and therefore didn't know how to deal with it, or him for that matter — so they were much happier when Jackman crushed the sympathy and anxiety talk. Others struggled but eventually followed suit. Eventually, Alice wasn't mentioned, apart from by the odd old friend or colleague who popped in, and even then it was only perfunctory. But Annie Davies was a real friend. A friend that had spent many an evening enjoying their joint company over BBQs, dinner parties and birthday celebrations. And Annie never believed in protocol. Not when it meant keeping her mouth shut.

Davies pressed her lips together. 'John and I were only saying the other day we must pop over.

It's been ages. It's amazing how much a little person takes over your life.'

'It's okay, really. It's her birthday this week.'

'Of course.' Silence hung like a threatening raincloud between them. 'That's why Celia's here?'

Jackman nodded.

Davies eyed him a moment. 'And what about you?'

'Oh, you know . . . ' Jackman tailed off. He scratched the back of his ear.

'Still seeing the shrink?'

He gave a single nod. 'Force orders.'

Uncomfortable silence prevailed for the shortest of seconds before she turned her head to the bar and whisked back. She winked. 'Well, you must be doing something right. Lady at the bar's giving you the real once over.'

Jackman leant sideways to look past her and glanced across at the curved end of the bar where an elderly man stood supping from a pint. He turned back to Annie and rolled his eyes. The tension in the air immediately dissolved.

'Got ya!' she chuckled.

'Like I said, you don't change.' He slung the rest of the mineral water down his throat and stood. 'Right, I'm off to see if Celia fancies a nightcap. See you tomorrow.'

★  ★  ★

He pulled into the byway and parked up as soon as the mixture of bramble hedging and established oaks concealed him from the road.

67

He got out of the car, grabbed the bag from the back seat and stopped for a moment to look around.

Satisfied he was alone, he trudged up the path away from the road. The mud beneath him, baked hard from the sun, felt uneven under his feet. His rucksack bounced against his back and by the time he reached the end of the track, it felt heavy. He switched on his head torch to navigate the copse. An arc of light exposed the lush broad-leaf branches above. Thick bracken covered the floor. He had to be careful here. Tree roots protruded and lurked about, ready to trip him. Branches reached out to catch at his jacket. But it didn't bother him. He'd navigated this route several times, always under the cover of darkness. It had become second nature.

Within minutes he was through the copse and out the other side. A rustling in the distance caught his attention. He stopped, moved back towards the trees and switched off his head torch. Several moments passed. His eyes grew accustomed to the darkness and darted about for any sign of movement. Then he saw it; black and white stripes ran down its face, its dark speckled back waddled from side to side as it moved across the path in front of him. The badger stopped and gave him a fleeting glance before continuing on its path.

He exhaled, long and hard, and waited until it disappeared from sight before he felt it was safe to switch the torch back on. Even then he hesitated and cast a slow glance around him, the torch illuminating the area in strips of light. The

68

air was quiet and still. He'd almost reached the old airfield when his feet found the concrete. He pulled the torch off his head, walked across to the shelter and entered. Dropping his bag down, he rummaged for the black hood and slung it over his head, before replacing the torch, then lent forward to unlock the chain.

The grill grated as he pulled it back and looked inside.

She was lying amongst the shadows that danced around the walls. Her legs were tucked to the side, hands lifted to shade her face from the splintering light of his head torch. Her dark hair hung in a tangled mess around her shoulders. He could just about make out the contour of her breast, the curve of her hip. Even in this state her beauty was almost mesmerising.

'Please. Don't hurt me!' she cried.

He said nothing, marvelling at the soft intonation in her voice. Her words couldn't be harsh even if she wanted them to be.

'Please!' She moved her hands back and forth across her face. He could see what she was trying to do — she wanted to catch a glimpse of her captor. But even if her eyes penetrated the bright bulb in his head torch, they couldn't see beneath the hood. The view was for his eyes only. This time.

'Please, let me go. I won't tell anyone.'

He ignored her calls, untied a couple of blankets from the bottom of his pack and threw them down. Then, retrieving the packs of food and water from inside his rucksack, he crouched down and dropped them into the pit. They made loud thuds as they hit the ground. The noise made him jerk back and instinctively grab the grill.

'No! Don't go.' Her words were fractured, urgent. He paused and stared at the figure, now curled up in the corner, her body wrapped around itself like a cat. A film of dirt covered the bare skin that peeped through her torn clothing. And, as he dragged the grill across, he heard her voice fade into a series of muffled sobs.

# 14

Jackman was woken by a wet tongue lashing his ear. He groaned, twisted and pushed the dog away. The movement caused a gentle weight to slip off the sofa beside him, closely followed by a splash below. He looked down and groaned again. The file of case material that had balanced on his chest for the last few hours now littered the floor beneath: photocopies of statements, credit card bills, phone logs all mixed up together.

'Morning!' He looked up to see Celia's bright face. 'Looks like you had a late one.'

'Hi,' was all he could manage. His mouth was dry and his head was pounding.

Celia had already gone to bed when he'd returned last night. He'd popped his head around the door, but her face was lost beneath the duvet, a habit she'd kept since childhood. Erik had lifted his head and thumped his tail a couple of times, but made no attempt to move from his comfortable position next to her.

Jackman had sidled through to his own room in the hope of tempting sleep. After half an hour of staring into the darkness, he remembered the file from Reilly and padded down to the lounge to examine the papers by lamplight. He didn't recall the moment his eyes finally closed. The lamp still shone in the corner, its dull hue merging with the daylight that was now seeping into the room.

Celia moved forward, switched off the lamp and drew back the curtains. Instantly, Jackman jerked forward and shaded his eyes. 'What time is it?'

'Five thirty. Love the air this time in the morning.'

Jackman let out another groan and sunk back into the sofa. Early mornings were another childhood trait that Celia had regained after a few teenage years of respite.

Paper crackled and shifted beneath him as Erik moved over the papers. 'Awww, come on mate,' he said, gently pushing the dog aside.

By the time he'd reached down and pulled them into a shoddy pile, Celia had returned with two steaming mugs. 'Extra strong,' she said. 'Your favourite.'

'Thanks.'

She looked down at the nest of papers beside him. 'You working on that missing girl?'

He blinked and stared at her through bleary eyes.

'I've seen it on the local news,' she said.

He stared at her, willing his brain to life. And as the cogs started to turn, the thought of his own daughter being home while young women were going missing in Stratford made him slightly uneasy. 'Do me a favour?' he said in his softest tone. 'Be extra careful while you're out and about the next couple of days?'

'Yes, Dad.' She spoke the words slowly, an ounce of irritation in her voice.

'I'm serious. Don't go anywhere alone. Especially after dark. Okay?'

She raised her eyes to the ceiling and gave a single, weary nod.

The fresh early morning breeze filtered in from the open French doors at the back of the room. They sipped their drinks in silence and as the caffeine worked its magic, Jackman felt the hazy cloud that filled his head start to disperse.

He turned back to Celia. 'Sleep alright?'

'Not bad. Woke up on the edge of the bed this morning though. Erik clearly needs to be re-educated in the art of sharing.'

They both chuckled as Erik ambled back into the lounge, his tail circling. Celia reached down and rubbed his head.

Jackman rolled his shoulders. Despite being woken at such an early hour, Celia's warmth and energy seemed to spread into every recess, every corner, transforming the house into a home once more. 'What are you up to today?' he asked.

She sipped her coffee and licked her lips before she spoke. 'Thought I'd look up Sam and Mikey. See what they've been up to.'

Jackman nodded. 'How long are you here for?'

'I need to head back tomorrow lunchtime. It's Adrian's birthday too. I promised to take him out for a meal, and don't look so forlorn, I'm back in two weeks and we have our holiday in Newquay, remember? We'll have loads of time then.'

Jackman smiled guiltily. From a young age she always seemed to be able to read his mind. He swallowed his pride. 'This Adrian. Errr . . . Serious, is it?'

'Dad!' She raised a hand. 'I'm not doing this.'

'No, I didn't mean that. Just wondered if you wanted to invite him here for a bit in the holidays?'

'I don't know.' She took another sip of her coffee. 'Maybe. His parents live in Exeter. It's a long way and he doesn't drive.'

Jackman planted his empty mug on the floor beside him and began sorting through the pile of papers on his lap. 'He could join us in Newquay if you want?' he said, without looking up.

'Adrian? I don't think so. He can't even surf! Don't worry, Dad, I'll think of something for the summer. You can meet him then. As long as you promise to be nice.'

Celia rambled on, but Jackman wasn't listening. His eyes were fixed on a single entry on Ellen Readman's credit card statement. He'd seen that somewhere before.

# 15

'Both the victims have a connection to The Thai Boat house,' Jackman said as he eased into his chair.

Janus sat opposite, cradling a mug of milky tea in her hands. Her fringe fluttered as she blew across the top of the drink. She'd caught Jackman by surprise when she'd called in for an impromptu briefing en route to Leamington that morning. Luckily Celia's coffee at daybreak meant he'd been in since before seven, although he had to borrow some milk off the ladies at the front desk for her tea.

'I found a Stratford number on Katie Sharp's phone records, a month before she disappeared, and traced it there. The restaurant also appears on Ellen Readman's credit card statement, a couple of weeks before she was reported missing.'

Janus inhaled deeply, but said nothing. She kept her eyes on Jackman.

'I emailed Reilly with the details this morning, but it does give me cause for concern,' Jackman continued. 'It brings both cases to Stratford. And I found one of their menus in Min Li's room at the college. We might have to brace ourselves for a link. All three women are around the same age, slim and dark-haired. Readman and Sharp disappeared for some time before their bodies were found. None of them have family close by.'

Janus exhaled loudly, pushed her glasses onto her forehead and rubbed her eyes with her thumb and forefinger as she spoke. 'Any more on the missing girl?'

Jackman gave her a summary of their actions from the day before. He finished up with the surveillance crews, which had relieved the weary detectives at Tom's family home that morning.

'What are your thoughts?' she asked.

'The pregnancy casts a new light and gives Tom a possible motive. If she refused to abort, it threatened his future. It seems our best bet at the moment. I'm not convinced about any potential affair with the agent from the abortion clinic, but I've asked the guys to run some background checks, just in case. Of course, it also gives Min a reason to run away.'

'What does that leave us with?'

'The enhanced footage on the two vehicles — the van and BMW car — that were seen in the vicinity close to the time she left the pub should be through this morning. Hopefully then, we'll have number plates and be able to trace the drivers. And we're still tracking down people from the CCTV footage at the pub, and following up from the public appeal.'

'And the parents?'

'Russell is the family liaison officer. She spoke to them yesterday and they claim to have heard nothing. Obviously, we'll be in touch again today. The biggest problem we have is victimology.'

'You've not heard from the Embassy yet?' Janus' forehead creased into a frown.

'A report came through in the early hours — copies of his business accounts and his credit rating which all look in reasonable order. There's very little on her background, and that of the family.'

Janus glanced at the floor a moment and then back at Jackman. When she spoke her words were carefully constructed. 'Okay, Min Li has been missing for almost thirty-six hours. We've checked all the hospitals so we don't think she's been involved in an accident, and her mental state doesn't indicate that she might kill herself. So, we currently have three main lines of enquiry. One, now that we know about the pregnancy, she still may turn up on the college campus after taking herself off somewhere to cool down. Two, her disappearance is linked to the other cases. But I think it's far too much of a stretch to make that decision yet. Three, somebody else has taken her. I'll get Reilly's team to focus on the restaurant this morning,' she continued, 'see what that turns up. You continue with your enquiries.' She placed her hand on the desk in front of him and leant in closer. 'Keep this to yourself for the moment. I don't want anyone chatting in the street where ears are flapping. There's already huge speculation in the media. On Warwick Radio this morning they mentioned Min Li's disappearance in the same breath as Ellen Readman, although they were careful not to link directly. We certainly need to make some decisions and soon.' She paused for a moment. 'Let's see what today brings. Keep me updated on any developments.'

He nodded, expecting her to dash out of the office, off to another meeting, in her usual perfunctory manner. Instead she sat quite still and angled her head back. 'There's something else.' The pithiness in her voice hooked Jackman's attention. 'You've missed your last three sessions.'

Jackman sighed inwardly. Part of the agreement for him returning to work on full duties after the car accident was that he would attend weekly counselling sessions. He'd managed to push them back to fortnightly over the last few months. He was quite aware that he'd cancelled one or two. Was it really as many as the last three? 'I've been busy.'

She pursed her lips. 'That wasn't the agreement.'

Jackman rolled his eyes.

'Quite honestly, Will, I couldn't give a damn whether you attend or not. But I've got welfare on my back and I can do without it right now. They've arranged another session directly with the counsellor for you on Friday at 4.30 p.m. Just make sure you attend your session and keep your nose clean. Then we won't need to waste time having this conversation again.' She jumped up and gathered her briefcase. 'Right, I'm off. We'll speak later.' And with that she disappeared out of the door.

Jackman sunk back into his chair. Bloody sessions, they encroached on his life and hung over him like a permanent raincloud.

That night, almost twelve months previous, would be forever branded on his brain. Travelling down the A46, heading back home after a party,

78

Alice in the driving seat. He remembered it like it was yesterday — a beautiful clear night, stars illuminating the road like little cat's eyes in the sky.

The car came from nowhere, rounded the corner, headlights that were more like strobe lights on full beam. It swerved across the carriageway like a bumper car, there wasn't even time to hit the horn. They felt the full force of the smash, the rumble as the car rolled over and over, lights blinked and juddered. One moment Jackman was spinning in a vortex of coloured lights, being thrust around the car. The next, nothing. He looked over at Alice. Her head was wedged between the crushed roof of the Ford Focus and the steering wheel.

Jackman thought back to those early days and weeks after the accident. Having managed to reach across and feel the pulse in her neck, he knew Alice was alive. But despite all his insistence, they wouldn't let him stay with her. He remembered being whipped away by the paramedics, rushed to hospital amidst loud sirens, his neck in a brace.

It wasn't until much later he discovered that Alice was cut from the car and raced to hospital like himself. But unlike Jackman, whose injuries were mostly superficial, Alice hadn't regained consciousness. A CAT scan discovered a blood clot on her brain. Emergency surgery followed. Brain damage was suspected, although nobody, not even the surgeon who carried out the surgery was able to predict a recovery.

The days and weeks of worry and fatigue that

followed slowly sucked the energy out of him as he travelled back and forth to the hospital, walked up the steps, down the long corridor to the stroke unit, the shiny floor squeaking under his shoes. Celia trotted beside him, the dutiful daughter, having finished her first year of university exactly six days before the accident. The routine became automatic, programmed into his brain. Each time he paused to rub the antibacterial cleaner into his hands and check with the duty nurse for an update. Finally he entered his wife's room where a plethora of machines pumped and bleeped and kept her alive.

For a while the outside world ceased to exist. He was stuck in a time warp, drifting through the days of hospital visits, bedside vigils, consultant appointments.

The diagnosis, when it finally arrived, changed everything. Suddenly, consultants weren't talking test results and treatment, they were talking palliative care as the prognosis wasn't good.

He recalled the specialist's office on that day, four months after the accident. It was barely a box with a filing cabinet and a desk full of brown envelope files and loose paper notes. Dr Simmons had asked Jackman to sit down. The grooves around his eyes had deepened as he'd leaned forward and said, 'As a result of the accident your wife sustained a brain haemorrhage in her basilar artery.' He'd lifted a hand to indicate the lower back part of his skull. 'She is suffering from locked-in syndrome.'

The consultant's fingers wove in and out of each other as he explained the condition that reduced her to the paralysed state she now endured. 'While Alice is aware of what is going on around her, she has no control over her body. Even her eyes are in a state of permanent paralysis.

'I have to be completely honest with you,' Dr Simmons had continued. 'Currently, there is no known cure. Most patients pass within the first few months of onset and those that survive rarely regain functions. There have been incidents recorded of patients regaining some control and communicating via eye movements or even sniffs. There's also been a few notable cases where a full recovery has been made,' he paused, 'but they are extremely rare.'

The consultant's words had tailed off into the room as he spoke about the need for permanent care for the future. Jackman could feel Celia's fingers tighten around his forearm, the desperation that engulfed them both, the indelible reminder of his wife's permanent condition and the fact that their life would never be the same again.

'Aware of what is going on around her.' Those words had clung to Jackman in his darkest hours afterwards. He couldn't imagine anything worse — it was like being a caged animal, sheltered in every respect from the outside world, but with no control over your functions.

The slam of a door in the car park below snapped him back to the present. The police had been very tentative about his return to work in the early days. He'd understood the need for caution, nobody wanted a rogue cop on the loose, especially not on major investigations when clear judgement was imperative. But he'd never given anyone reason to question his judgement. The anger that now rose within him was a manifestation of everything: fate for subjecting his wife to such a condition, the police for forcing him into prolonged counselling, Janus for ordering him to attend. In truth, talking about the incident just served to remind him of the permanent shadow that had followed him around over the past twelve months.

Still, this was the first time he'd been given a case to manage since the accident. He couldn't afford to give Janus any reason to move him.

He wandered out into the main office. It was a hive of activity. He caught Davies' eye and she waved him over enthusiastically to her desk where she was bent over a computer screen.

As he approached she cast him a quick sideways glance. 'Enhanced footage has just come through.' She clicked another key. 'There.' She pointed at the screen.

Jackman drew closer. He could see the white Volkswagen van. The image was still a little blurred, but he could now make out the number plate. There was a rust circle around the diesel cap.

'Belongs to a Guy Taylor in Coventry,' Davies said. 'Not known to us. Keane's gonna head out there.'

Jackman nodded. 'Good. What about the BMW?'

She clicked the mouse and another photo appeared on the screen.

He could see the BMW and number plate clearly marked.

'Belongs to a Mr Galloway of Tiddington Road. Again, no intelligence.'

Jackman thought back to the footage. It showed the car stopping next to Min, before speeding off down the road. 'I'll take that one.'

She turned to face him. 'Are you sure?'

'Absolutely, could do with some fresh air.'

★ ★ ★

Women. All around him. Painted faces surrounded by bubbles of sweet perfume staring into window displays, the clear glass bouncing back a faded reflection in the sunlight. Handbags balanced on open forearms.

Some pushing toddlers in buggies, some in couples chatting as they wandered through the stores. Clinging dresses with scooped backs and plunging necklines. Crescents of curls dangling from tied ponytails.

Royal Priors was busier than he'd anticipated this morning. Shoppers catching the stores early to avoid the heat of the day. A redhead dashed towards him, the trickle of sweat running down her neckline causing a stirring in his groin as she passed.

He stole a deep breath, continued through the mall and glanced around. A department store was what he needed now with ample obliging assistants to tend to his every whim. Assistants that would move quickly from one customer to another. Not like the boutiques and smaller shops in Stratford, where assistants would recognise you, single you out in a crowd.

No, he'd thought this one through. He wandered down the aisles and collected the provisions he needed for stage two. Very soon it would be time to shake things up a bit. And he couldn't help but wonder what the detective would make of that.

# 16

I stared at the two bottles of water that leant against the concrete in the corner of the pit, one almost empty, the part-loaf of bread, wrapped in an orange plastic wrapper, the few chocolate bars and a collection of apples beside. Last night's delivery.

It had been late when he'd come. I knew that because the gap at the top had only emitted a soft grey light and the pit was at its darkest. He. I'm pretty convinced that my captor is male. I've turned it over and over in my head. He needed to be robust, strong enough to carry me down here.

Last night I'd heard footfalls above as he approached. At first I thought it might be a prowling animal, but then I heard the determined chink of metal, a thud as the chain fell to the floor.

Thoughts of what he might have planned had reverberated around my skull. I was trembling even before the dazzling light burnt my pupils, causing me to bury my head in my hands. The next thing I knew packages were being fired into the pit like missiles. Later I discovered they were food parcels and blankets, but at the time I had no idea and I'd never experienced terror like it. Thud after thud made me shriek. A brief silence was followed by the scraping sound of the grill.

Anger tore through me. I had an opportunity

to see something, do something, at the very least pick up on something that might help me later — a slight lilt in his voice, the colour of his eyes, the shape of his frame. But I saw and heard nothing.

I smoothed out the creases in the blankets wedged beneath me, lifted a corner up to my nose. It was fresh and clean, not yet tainted by the musty stench of concrete powder and urine that pervaded everything else in the pit. Clean. Like the scent that fills the bathroom when you step out of the shower. I held it close, not wanting to ever lose it.

My stomach gurgled and swirled around like a washing machine. Sickly bile rose in my throat as a childhood memory wormed its way creepily out of the dark shadows in my mind. I was barely twelve years old when the owner of my father's neighbouring factory disappeared. Ling Chen made metal screens for a Western company. He was a good friend to my father, he and his family lived in our apartment block when I was young. One day, he left home and didn't turn up for work. Days passed and nobody heard any news. Rumours circulated like snakes, sliding their way into the minds of the local community. But no body was ever found, no funeral took place, no explanation came forth. Time passed and his wife and son moved away to the country. Another family moved in. The authorities took over his factory. We all moved on but every time I passed the door to their apartment I could see his face in my mind.

Would that happen to me? One day at college,

the next nothing. But why continue to feed me?

Maybe my parents weren't able to pay the demand yet. Maybe they needed more time. I clung to this tiny thread of hope, closed my eyes and willed a happy memory from home — my mother at the kitchen sink, the pinny tied to her waist, my father sat at the table reading. It was rare we were home on our own. Usually he was entertaining some client or business partner. But when we were, he read voraciously. Constantly soaking up the knowledge of some book or another. Always facts. Never fiction. I could see him now, pointing a forefinger at his temple. 'Books make you clever. Read well, Lan Hua, for they will determine your future.' 'Lan Hua' or orchid was my family nickname. I was rarely called Min outside of school until I came to the UK.

Guilt pained me. When I was much younger I plagued my parents for a sibling. A brother to roll around the floor and wrestle with, a sister to read to and share confidences. My father had a brother. My mother was one of three. I saw the idea of a sibling as a plus, a playmate, someone to play with on long summer days when school friends weren't around. I envied my parents and couldn't understand why I or any of my friends were denied such a privilege.

But my pleading words on this subject were always hushed, my spirits dampened. It didn't stop my yearning though. Even as a teenager I was dogged by a silent fear and loneliness. I read Little Women and, like most readers, I cried when Beth died. But unlike others, I didn't cry because she died, I cried because I wanted to be her, to experience that fun and camaraderie in the circle of those sisters even for just a short time. It made me determined that I would never do that to my own child. I would have a large family, with lots of children running around, playing together, lost in their own little innocent world. Children that would grow up together, support and comfort each other later in life.

I massaged my stomach and wondered if my child could hear my thoughts. I hadn't intended to start my family now. Not here. Not like this. Tom wanted me to abort our baby. In some ways I understood why. It would upset our parents, our studies, present huge problems for our future. He'd talked to me about a clinic on the edge of Stratford where, for a sum, they would discreetly complete a termination procedure. Termination. It sounded so final.

# 17

Fingers of sunshine reached through the gaps in the clouds as Jackman arrived in Tiddington Road. For once, Warwickshire Radio had been right in their predictions that Stratford would be the last area in the region to join the ongoing heat wave that Wednesday, and the light morning breeze that had provided a welcome reprieve now worked hard to wipe the clouds from the sky.

He passed the entrance to Loxley Road, where specially trained officers sat, covertly watching Tom Steele's home, and couldn't help but wonder if the Galloways' close proximity to the Steeles was significant. Their homes would have been less than a ten-minute walk apart.

Jackman glanced at the golf club on his right, continued until he reached a detached sandstone house set back from the road and swept his Honda up the drive to the entrance. He was greeted by an array of large terracotta pots and window boxes, bursting with a range of pansies in a variety of colours.

Gravel crunched beneath his feet as he crossed the drive and pressed the doorbell beside an imposing hardwood entrance door. He couldn't hear the road from back here, just the gentle breeze rustling through the tall hawthorn hedge out front and the distant sound of dogs barking, although it wasn't really surprising. This was the most salubrious area of Stratford. Houses on this stretch fetched almost a million each. Apart from an occasional burglary during his early days, it wasn't an area he'd frequented much in the line of duty.

He pressed the doorbell again. The sound of the dogs grew louder. A sudden bang, metal on metal, made him jerk around. At the side of the house was a wrought-iron gate where two Springer Spaniels were now jumping up and barking in harmony.

'Can I help you?'

He followed the voice that battled with the din of barking and flashed his badge. 'Morning,' he said. 'Would you be Mrs Galloway?'

She squinted to look at his badge. 'Enough! In your beds.' The barking stopped immediately. Two hooded pairs of eyes glanced up at her momentarily before they slunk off around the corner.

She waited for them to retreat, clicked open the gate and stood aside for Jackman to enter. Jackman eyed her navy cotton dress, the smoothness of her grey hair. She wore no make-up but her face held a soft English-rose prettiness.

She clasped her hands together. 'What can I do for you?'

'I'm looking to speak to Mr David Galloway. Is he home?'

She stepped back and narrowed her eyes. 'No, he's away at the moment. Is everything alright?'

'It's nothing to be alarmed about. I just felt he may be able to help with our enquiries.'

The sound of a phone ringing in the distance

broke the conversation. Mrs Galloway looked perturbed. 'You'd better come inside.'

He followed her through the kitchen, across the hall and into a living room that overlooked the drive at the front of the house. 'You'll have to excuse me,' she said as she picked up the phone and wandered out of the room.

Jackman sat on the edge of a brown chair and glanced at the fresh tracks from the vacuum cleaner that looked like broken crop circles on the rug in front of a log burner.

A floorboard in the hall creaked and Mrs Galloway appeared in the doorway. 'Sorry about that. Can I get you a coffee?'

'No, thank you.'

The dull scent of an air freshener sweetened the air around them as she walked into the room and seated herself on the large sofa. 'You asked about my husband?'

Jackman nodded.

'He's not here, I'm afraid. He works in Dubai and won't be back until the end of June. Can I ask why you wanted to speak to him?'

Jackman ignored the question. 'Do you own a black BMW?'

A slight flicker of recognition appeared behind her eyes. 'We do. It's in the garage.'

Jackman vaguely remembered the double garage set back from the house. 'May I ask you where you were on Monday evening?'

Mrs Galloway hesitated a moment and looked at the floor. 'Yes, I was at our book club annual dinner. We do it every May, take it in turns. This year it was held at the pub in Luddington.'

'What time did you leave?'

She glanced down at her hands. 'Around 10.30, I think. I dropped a friend off in the town centre on the way home and stopped for a coffee. I guess I was home around midnight.'

'What vehicle did you use?'

'The Range Rover parked out front.' She shifted in her seat.

'Are you sure you didn't use the BMW?'

'Absolutely! I never use David's car. Can't abide the damn thing. Far too low. Look, what is this all about?'

'Are you sure the BMW is in the garage?'

'Yes. I saw it this morning when I went to fetch some garden twine.'

'Well it was spotted in the centre of Stratford-upon-Avon on Monday night.'

'Impossible.' She shook her head as if to dismiss the thought.

'It was picked up on the cameras. There's no mistake. Is there anybody else with access to the vehicle?'

Mrs Galloway smoothed her skirt uncomfortably. 'No, I don't believe so.'

'Are you sure? Is there anyone else living here with you?'

'Only my son, Andrew. My daughter is away at university. And Andrew is only seventeen. Still having driving lessons.'

Seventeen. Only a year younger than Tom Steele, Jackman thought. They could have been at school together. He fixed a stare on Mrs Galloway. Her son had no licence. No wonder she was feeling uncomfortable.

Jackman softened his tone. 'A girl went missing in the town on Monday night. The car was spotted near to where she was last seen. Whoever drove it may have witnessed something.'

'I'm sure Andrew wasn't involved.' She swallowed.

'I do need to speak to him.'

The roar of an engine filled the room, followed by the sound of a door slamming shut, a chuckle and a chorus of dogs barking.

Mrs Galloway stood, her face twitching with anger. 'Well, it looks like you have your wish. He's here right now.'

A scrawny boy who looked younger than his seventeen years, with blue eyes, shaggy blond hair and oversized clothes appeared in the doorway.

Mrs Galloway stood. 'Andrew. This is Detective Inspector Jackman.'

Jackman wasn't sure if it was the tightness in his mother's voice or the mention of the police that turned the boy's face ashen. He froze, like a toddler caught with his hand in the cookie jar.

'The inspector's got some questions for you.'

Andrew slunk into the room. He cast a furtive glance at Jackman who gestured for him to sit down on the sofa opposite and asked him to run through the events of Monday night. Initially, he denied involvement, until the camera footage was mentioned, then he cast his gaze to the floor.

'Look, I'm here to investigate the case of a missing girl, a Chinese student,' Jackman said. 'She was last seen leaving the Old Thatch Tavern at 10.35 p.m. on Monday. The cameras show your father's car passing through around that time. If you saw or heard anything, it may well help our enquiry.'

A faint glimmer of hope flickered across Andrew's face. This wasn't the admonishment he was expecting.

'Did you see anyone?'

He nodded. 'We'd been cruising around for an hour or so.'

'We?' The interruption came from Mrs Galloway, her voice indignant.

'Jem and I.'

'Might have known.' She didn't attempt to hide the disapproval in her voice.

Jackman ignored her. 'Go on.'

'A girl was walking down Rother Street towards the police station as we drove up in the direction of the market place.'

'Can you describe her?'

'Short, Chinese. She had a long, pale, silk skirt on. We pulled over to talk to her.'

'I don't believe this!' a splintered voice squeaked from behind Jackman.

He whisked around. 'Mrs Galloway, please?' She averted her gaze, but her face was like thunder.

Jackman turned back to the boy. 'What did you say?'

He lifted the corner of his lip. 'Not much. Just asked her if she wanted a ride. It was only meant to be a bit of fun.'

'This is important now, Andrew. Think carefully. You are currently the last person known to have seen her. What did she do then?'

'She looked across at us, but didn't answer.

94

She looked like she'd been crying. So, we just hooted and pulled off. It was only for a laugh.'

'Did you see anybody else nearby, any people or vehicles?'

Andrew looked at the floor and chewed the side of his lip. 'I think there was a van parked on the market place, near the clock tower.'

'Can you describe it?'

'Not really. White. Maybe a Volkswagen.'

'Was there anybody sitting in it, or nearby perhaps?'

Andrew shook his head. 'Didn't see anyone.'

Jackman sat back in his chair and folded his hands into his lap. It was time to change tack. 'Andrew, do you know Tom Steele?'

Tight creases formed along the boy's forehead. For a moment he was lost in thought. 'Yes, he was in the year above me at school. Why?'

Jackman ignored the question. 'When was the last time you saw him?'

★   ★   ★

Jackman took a deep breath to calm his frayed patience. An hour spent with Andrew had yielded little result. He claimed that he hardly knew Tom and hadn't seen him since he left school. Nothing in his body language indicated that he was lying, although the close proximity to Tom's home still bothered Jackman.

He considered the scenario. Andrew had claimed he and his friend had been cruising around for the best part of the evening when they happened upon Min. She was walking in

95

the direction of the police station when Andrew saw her, yet when the cameras caught her she'd turned the corner into Greenhill Street. Had she stomped out of the pub in a temper and taken any direction just to calm down, or was she heading somewhere in particular? And what made her turn back? Did Andrew Galloway, harassing her in his dad's BMW, frighten her? Did he give her a message from Tom, or was there another reason?

He turned Andrew's account over in his mind. 'She looked like she'd been crying.' He wondered if that was due to the argument with Tom, or if something else was bothering her.

Back in the car, Jackman called the station. It was answered on the first ring.

'Sir?' Annie didn't wait for him to respond. 'We've traced the white van, or what we thought was the van.'

'What do you mean?' he said as he pulled out of the Galloways' driveway.

'The owner lives in Coventry. He's been working in Huddersfield. Contract only finished yesterday. He was driving back to Coventry last night, arrived in the early hours of this morning.'

'Are you sure?'

'Completely. We've checked it out. Doesn't look like this is our guy.'

'The number plates match?'

'To the letter.'

Jackman indicated and pulled over. 'Are we thinking cloned plates?'

'Certainly looks that way.'

Jackman felt a surge of adrenalin. But the lead

was marred with a chequered reality. If the van was connected to Min then they could very well be looking for a body. 'Okay, get everyone on it. Try all the garages in and around the region to see if anyone's ordered new plates recently. Also check the police cameras to see when and where this number plate has been clocked over the last three months. Whoever was driving this van has taken careful steps to conceal their existence.'

'Will do,' Davies said. 'How did you get on with the BMW owner?'

'Rich kid snuck out in his father's car. Couldn't tell me much. Claims he saw the victim, but only for a few seconds. Lives around the corner from Tom Steele though which might be significant. Hold on.' He retrieved his notebook from his pocket and relayed the details of the friend that had accompanied Andrew in the car. 'Get someone out to interview him, will you? Let's see if his account checks out.'

Davies didn't answer immediately. The line crackled. Suddenly Jackman became aware of a kerfuffle in the background. Raised voices. Annie spoke quickly, 'Hold on a minute, sir.' She disappeared from the end of the line.

He strained his ears, could hear Annie's high-pitched voice chipping into a distant conversation, but he couldn't make out what she was saying. 'Annie? What's going on?'

It seemed an age before she answered. Frustration itched away at him. When she returned to the call there was a definite edge to her voice. 'Sir, you need to get back here urgently. Looks like there's been a ransom demand.'

# 18

I balled up the bread wrapper, chucked it into the corner. It caught the edge of an empty bottle, causing it to wobble slightly, sending a hollow rattle reverberating around the pit.

Earlier, my dozing had been disturbed by a strange scratching sound. At first I thought I was dreaming, until I opened my eyes to a myriad of shiny eyes glistening in the half-darkness. The rat had come back. And he'd brought friends.

I'd jumped up, screamed, bared my teeth like a vampire until they scurried away. But they would be back. They knew there was food down here, they'd smelt it. I couldn't afford to sleep now. I needed to stay alert.

Two tired-looking apples poked out of the edge of the blanket, one with a few chunks missing. It was all I had left from the delivery. I placed my hands behind my neck, stretched my elbows back. The concoction of anxiety, boredom and loneliness down here was suffocating. I needed something to concentrate my mind, keep me awake. Happy memories.

Tom. It was raining the day I first saw him. He stood out in the wet, water dripping off the edge of his chin, beaming as he held open the main entrance door of the college for me. I remember being struck by how his whole face lit up as he smiled. His eyes lingered for just long enough to make my stomach flutter. 'Welcome to Stratford College,' he'd said with a wink. He made a show of taking me around campus and I played along (even though I'd arrived a couple of weeks earlier and already familiarised myself with it) while he introduced me to his friends.

Almost instantly, I became a part of his friendship group. I thought hard. It was strange, our first meeting was so vivid in my mind yet I couldn't recall the moment our friendship turned into something more. It just seemed to deepen over the following days and weeks. Until one day he kissed me.

The recollection made me smile. We were sitting on the sofa in my apartment listening to Ed Sheeran. I was teasing him, poking his ribs. We chuckled, rubbed shoulders. He smelled so good. I don't even remember how it happened. Suddenly his lips were on mine. Wet and inviting. He felt so deliciously warm and welcoming that there was not an ounce of awkwardness. Not even afterwards. Everything with Tom was like that. He seemed to glide effortlessly through life.

From that moment on, I felt like a warm arm had been placed around me. He didn't seem to notice the longing looks from other girls far prettier than me, and I couldn't fail to be flattered by his interest in finding out all those intricate details about me that you only discover through intimacy. While I forced myself to concentrate on my studies and pored over my laptop, he breezed through his homework and read music magazines beside me. I could still see him making silly faces in my dressing table

99

mirror while I dried my hair.

I took a deep breath, rested my head back on the stone as the memories warmed my insides. I didn't come over here to start a relationship. It had been the last thing on my mind. But during the days and weeks that followed that first kiss, the bond that pulled us together consumed me. Tom was the first man to reach into my heart and he'd laid an anchor deep. Which made it all the more difficult when things started to go wrong.

Tears pricked my eyes. I'd never forget how ghostly white his face turned when I told him I was pregnant. We still wanted to be close to each other, the pull was magnetic, but we were faced with something neither of us had expected.

I reached a hand down to my stomach as a tear escaped and rolled down the side of my nose. We'd argued that night. That's why I left the pub. Alone. Goosebumps stood erect on my arms. Alone in the dark. Stupid. I never did that, I was always surrounded by friends, we looked after each other. But that night I was in a temper. I strode out of the pub. Waited for no one.

I was angry. My feet pounded the pavement with each step.

Tom doesn't understand how different things are back home. My parents expect a great deal of me. I need to excel at my studies, build a firm platform for my eventual career. Right now, it's important to show them that I'm working hard, diligently, being the dutiful daughter. Otherwise they will remove the funding and whip me back

100

home where I will not only be expected to continue my studies, but also mix with all the right people so that I gain a respected position in a progressive company.

Memories of my father hosting endless dinner parties, keeping everybody happy, greasing the right palms to enable his business to stabilise and grow, dogged my childhood. Looking back a part of me understood his motivations. How could I blame him for wanting a better life for his family? But I loathed the falseness of such liaisons, the shallowness. Smiling at people I didn't particularly like, being asked to sing for strangers when I was little, putting on my best table manners.

I tried to explain to Tom that I needed to deal with this, with them, in my own way. Right now they would see him as a barrier, rather than an addition. And that was without the baby.

But I couldn't expect Tom to understand. After all, he was raised in a country where the press freely express their opinions on the state and openly criticise their governors instead of huddling around a neighbour's table and covertly talking in whispers.

I forced my mind back to the other evening, to focus. Monday. I was walking down Rother Street. An image danced into my mind. A black car. It stopped. Young lads. I couldn't catch what they said through their excited smiles. They whistled and drove off, but I was scared. Scared enough to turn back. I reached the pub on the corner, hesitated. But I wasn't going to give Tom the satisfaction. I marched towards the corner, back towards the college.

My thoughts turned misty. As much as I tried to pull and pick I couldn't recall what happened next. It was like somebody had placed a veil over my brain. I'd turned the corner from the pub. I was in Greenhill Street. I knew that much. I remembered a force pulling me back, a cloth that smelt sickly sweet.

The pub. If only I'd gone back inside. If only I hadn't been so headstrong, I'd be back in my apartment right now, Liu watching the television, Lang laid across the sofa reading. Tom beside me.

Instead I was here. In a concrete box with only the rats for company.

I didn't want to cry. Crying only made everything worse — I became thirsty and my head pounded. But I couldn't seem to hold back the tears that dripped from my chin and spotted the blanket beneath.

All alone. All those years of wanting, waiting, planning how I would get to England and this was what happened.

I thought back to my first trip here when I was eleven years old, the trip that sowed the seed that would flourish in my mind. We came over for three weeks in the summer of 2005, stayed at Northampton University, took English classes in the morning and travelled out to Cambridge, Bath, Stratford and London. I loved the way people dressed, spoke, the beauty of the landscape and architecture. I remembered watching a crowd of people marching through the streets in London calling out and carrying banners. I stopped and gawped at them, asked our guide what it meant. 'It's an organised protest about animal rights,' she'd said. Instantly, I was scared. 'Won't the police come?' 'Not unless there is any trouble', she'd replied. I stood for what felt like ages, fascinated by their open display of beliefs, until our guide tugged at my arm and pulled me away.

When I was fourteen I met Karen Hardwick, the English teacher with the blonde hair and eyes that sparkled when she talked of her home on the coast in Dorset. She encouraged me to read Dickens, Austen, the Brontë sisters. My father studied English too and we practised together at home. He was so proud when I came top of the class in our English exam.

The memories dried my tears and installed a sense of steeliness inside me. Why should I be punished for wanting a different life?

As my thoughts cascaded, a rage of anger grew and flourished in my bones. How dare somebody take such liberties with my life, with the lives of my loved ones?

I looked up at the grill. I couldn't break out, I'd tried already. My only hope was to wait until my captor returned and find a way of distracting him.

I sat forward, glanced around. Dead leaves and crisp packets in one corner covered my makeshift toilet. The opposite corner contained the empty bottles. They were too soft. I needed something hard. Something that would hurt him. I searched urgently until I remembered my heels. I was wearing them on Monday evening. Where were my stilettos?

*I moved around the pit, tossing everything aside. But even as I did so, I already knew the answer. He'd taken those too. My only weapon. I was left with nothing.*

# 19

Thoughts raced through Jackman's head as he sat in his office and prepared for the emergency team briefing. A copy of the ransom request, an email in Mandarin, sat before him. He read through the translation:

DO NOT CONTACT THE POLICE OR THE PRESS, IN CHINA OR BRITAIN, IF YOU WANT TO SEE YOUR DAUGHTER ALIVE AGAIN.

*We have Li Min. She is safe and unharmed at the moment.*

*If you want to see her, follow these instructions.*

*We require £25,000 in used bank notes. The notes should be tied together and taken to The Grove Industrial Estate, Birmingham. Enter the lay-by on Brambleside Way and leave the cash in the bin in an orange supermarket carrier bag at precisely 12.30 a.m. on 21st May. Li Min will then be released.*

*At present, Min has food and water and is in good health. If you do not pay we won't kill her. We will fail to meet her basic needs and she will die a slow death of starvation in captivity.*

The words were dramatic enough, yet the email felt lifeless; the Times New Roman font business-like and impersonal. Whoever wrote this chose their words carefully, ensuring that all the information they wished to impart was included, and no more.

There was no sign-off. It wasn't until Jackman scrolled down that the message was brought alive by a photo of Min. She was in what looked like the back of a vehicle. The internal paintwork was white. A couple of tartan blankets were strewn in the corner. Her eyes were closed, her body laid prostrate. She could have been dead, although there was something about the image that breathed life.

Jackman thought back to previous kidnapping cases he'd worked. The emphasis was always placed on building up a relationship with the abductors, not only to open the possibility for negotiation but also to establish the state of the victim. In the Larkin case, he'd actually got to speak to the victim to prove she was still alive. Here, all they had was a rather tenuous-looking photograph.

Jackman rubbed the bridge of his nose. No open lines of communication meant no chance for negotiation. No opportunity to obtain any potential indication as to the location of Min.

He switched back to the email. This single message sent to Mr Li at 11.30 a.m. GMT yesterday had elevated the case to a new level. Min's parents claimed they had followed the instructions, paid the demand. Yet, Min had not been in contact.

Jackman thought hard. Min's father owned his own factory. When Russell had spoken to Mr Li yesterday, he'd claimed that his staff had been loyal to him for many years. No incidents that he was aware of recently, nobody had suddenly left and the majority of his dealings were with European customers whom he had dealt with for many years. But if Mr Li was involved in something illegal, money laundering for instance, it wouldn't show up within his accounts. And they still hadn't received a list of his main competitors. Jackman made a note to get his team to chase this urgently.

A knock at his door broke his train of thought. Davies' face appeared. 'We're ready for you now, sir.'

The sweltering heat immediately consumed him as he crossed the threshold into the incident room. Bodies cluttered the tiny space, thickening the air; some seated, others perched on the edge of desks, a few standing at the back, clogging any possible draught from the open windows. He moved across to the side of the whiteboard to join Janus who had hotfooted across from Leamington to join the assemblage.

DC Russell stood at the front and cleared her throat. The red hair that was usually smoothed back neatly looked ruffled. He could see a couple of amber blotches on her neckline. 'Right.' She paused briefly as the room silenced. 'Mr and Mrs Li received an email at precisely 11.30 a.m. our time, yesterday morning.' She clicked a button on the keyboard and an enlarged copy of the ransom email flashed on the screen in front of them.

The atmosphere of the room grew tense as everyone scanned the message. Jackman could hear the rattle of the venetian blinds tapping the window sill in the gentle breeze that did nothing

107

to alleviate the stifling room.

Davies pulled a face when she read the final line. 'Why didn't they come to us?' she asked.

'They claim they were scared,' Russell answered. 'Thought it would be easier if they complied with the wishes and paid the cash. Anything to get their daughter back.'

'That's exactly what we would have advised them to do, but at least we could have monitored it,' Davies said. 'What about their local police in China?'

Russell shook her head.

Jackman scanned the message on the screen once again. Seeing it there, enlarged, seemed to ramp up the gravity of the situation even more. One word jumped out at him: *we*. Not I, we.

'Li Min,' Davies repeated out loud.

Russell seemed to guess her thoughts. 'It's the Chinese way of writing it. They put the surname first, although many of the students that come over switch to the English habit of writing the surname last to make it easier. It was the same with the Embassy report. The interpreter says the Mandarin is clean, well-versed.'

'So we are looking at a Chinese national, or somebody fluent in Mandarin?' Davies said.

Russell nodded.

'Talk us through what you know,' Jackman said.

Russell turned to face the room. 'Well, as most of you are aware, I've been in contact with the parents since Min disappeared. Yesterday, they gave me every indication they didn't know where she was and hadn't heard from anybody regarding her disappearance.' She paused and glanced down at her notes. 'This morning I tried to call, text and email several times, but couldn't reach them. Finally I took a desperate call from Mr Li at home, just after 10.30 a.m. our time, when he explained about the email and sent me a copy. They paid the ransom but Min hasn't been in contact. They're convinced she wasn't released, as arranged, and are now at their wits' end.'

Russell swallowed. 'I knew something wasn't right,' she said. 'Their reaction. They weren't the typical grieving parents. Their words were exact, serious, almost calculated.'

'You could put that down to cultural differences and interpretation,' Davies said.

'How did he arrange to make payment?' Jackman asked.

'He claims to have been introduced to a contact, a man in a restaurant, a friend of a friend, who gave them the telephone number of a contact in the UK who would help them, arrange the drop and then collect their daughter.'

'What contact?'

Russell shook her head. 'He doesn't know who they are.'

'What about the friend that introduced them?'

'Again. He won't say who it is. He said that he promised not to disclose any of the details. He wouldn't be pressed.'

'What sort of contact did they arrange?'

Russell pursed her lips. 'Mr Li was given a mobile phone number. That's all. No name.'

A heavy weight filled the room. 'This is all we need,' Janus said.

A phone rang in the background. Jackman cast it an annoyed glance, then turned back to Russell. 'Go on.'

'He received a text message at 12.00 a.m. our time yesterday to say that the drop location had been changed. They were directed into the industrial estate at Applewood Way instead of Brambleside and told to leave the bag in a cardboard recycling bin down the side of a building that housed a company called Atom Conveyors.'

Jackman rubbed his forehead and allowed himself a wry smile. Changing the drop location at the last minute showed organisation. Whoever arranged this was not leaving anything to chance.

'They hung around for a bit and watched, and said it was collected by a motorcyclist with a tinted visor,' Russell continued. 'There's a photograph that they texted him.'

Russell leant forward and tapped a button on her laptop. An image of the back of a motorbike filled the screen. The rider was wearing black leathers and a dark crash helmet; the number plate was concealed. On the back of the helmet was the number forty-six, clearly marked in yellow. A deep score line ran through the middle of the six, as if it had been scratched.

Jackman ran his hand down his face. 'Looks like an off-road bike to me. Trawl the nearby units for additional footage and check with local dealers to see if you can trace the make. See if the number forty-six on the helmet means anything too. What do we know about the person who arranged the payment?' he said.

Russell shook her head and sighed. 'Again, very little. Mr Li spoke to a man with a British accent initially to explain what was required. They agreed to lend him the money against his business. Somebody would be in touch when payment was due. Then all he received were text messages from mobile phones to tell him the drop had been made. Every time a different number.'

Jackman sighed. 'Get all the numbers off him and see if you can trace any of them. And get me a meeting with both parents will you, over Skype? I want them to realise the gravity of the situation. There's no room for secrets here.'

The sound of a phone receiver being slammed down immediately hushed the room. Keane jumped up from his position at the far corner. 'That was the techie team at headquarters. They've been looking at the server address for the email. It was sent from a hotmail address, so no luck there, but through the server they were able to trace the IP location to an internet cafe on Hagley Road in Birmingham.'

'Good work,' Jackman said. 'Get yourself across there. Hopefully somebody will remember something. If we're lucky they'll also have CCTV.' He turned back to Davies. 'Anything on the bin?'

Davies shook her head. 'We arranged for Birmingham CID to pick it up. They are examining it as we speak.'

Her words conjured up images of CSIs in white coveralls, hoods and booties picking through the contents of the waste bin, brushing

111

it for fingerprints. But Jackman was pretty certain they wouldn't find anything. It was unlikely that whoever had taken the trouble to plan in such detail would forget to cover their tracks and wear gloves. 'Right. We need to get out to the location of the drop in Birmingham.'

'What about surveillance on the boyfriend?' Davies asked.

Jackman pressed his lips together and switched his gaze to Janus. 'We have authorisation for twenty-four hours, right?'

Janus gave a swift nod.

'Then we leave it there for the moment,' he said. 'The note makes it seem unlikely, but doesn't rule out the possibility that he still may be involved in some way.'

'We need to establish a press strategy,' Janus said.

Jackman was aware of the normal press shutdown in the wake of kidnappings. But this abductor's demand had been met and still the hostage hadn't been released.

He thought hard. 'The ransom note said no police, no press,' Jackman said. 'If there is any chance she might still be alive we need to be very careful how we treat it. Let's step up the press campaign, reiterate that she is missing and get the public to look out for her. It's still possible that she has been dropped somewhere and is wandering around confused. We need to establish a motive,' he continued. 'If this is an attempt by organised criminal gangs, or a rival business interest, then there may well be more to it. Maybe this is somebody's warped way of trying to muscle in on Mr Li's business.'

'There's something else.' Russell's soft tone spoke up. 'There's a brother. Min Li has an uncle in the UK.'

# 20

I stood and rapped my fists on thc wall, screaming as I banged one after the other, harder and harder until they burned with pain and my knuckles, now split and grazed, oozed with blood. I took a deep breath and sucked them into my mouth as Grandmother's voice rung in my ears, 'You are a strong woman, Lan Hua. You can win.'

I suddenly remembered being around five or six years old, sat at the table with my grandmother, practising my writing. Pressing the pen down hard, tearing into the paper; my grandmother gently telling me to press lightly. I'd always been heavy-handed.

An idea formed in my mind. I glanced around the pit. The slice of light from above was at its brightest at this time of day. I grabbed a small stone and scraped it down the wall beside me. It barely made a mark. I tried again, pressed harder this time. A faint mark appeared in the rough concrete. But as soon as I ran my hand over it, it disappeared into a cloud of dust.

I pulled back the blanket and moved the food packets around to search beneath. Desperation itched at me. I got down on my hands and knees, running my hands across the uneven floor. But there were no loose pieces of concrete I could pick out, no sharp edges. It wasn't surprising really. The first morning in here, I'd had to sit and pick so many small stones from the skin on my arms and legs that afterwards I'd spent most of the day moving across the floor, my bare hands sweeping loose stones and rocks into a pile. I sat back on my heels as my eyes landed on the far corner. That pile now lay beneath the crisps packets, the leaves, the rubbish.

A strong smell of fresh ammonia rose to meet me as I approached and crouched down. I grabbed the empty bread packet, pushed my hand into it like a glove, then reached in and sorted through the leaves. The smell of stale faeces floated up into the air. I turned my head back, covered my nose with my free hand and retched. But I couldn't stop now. Eventually I felt the blunt edge of metal and pulled out a rusty nail. I wiped it down the side of the bag before applying it to the wall.

It made a faint mark. I went over it again, and again, then rubbed it with the corner of the blanket. The mark didn't move. This was going to work. I dug the nail in and kept carving.

# 21

Janus followed Jackman into his office, planted her briefcase on his desk and rested a hand on her bony hip. 'I don't like this,' she said as if speaking to herself.

Jackman massaged his temples and turned to face her. He was still digesting the fact that Min had an uncle living in the UK. 'Look, an uncle in Birmingham gives us a lead, especially when the drop was made there,' he said. 'And we're pretty sure that the sender of that email understood Mandarin.'

'Why haven't they told us this before?'

Jackman recalled Russell's feedback. She'd gone on to say that the family claimed he moved to England twelve years ago to work in a restaurant, waiting tables. They lost contact with him around ten years ago. 'Perhaps they didn't think it would be relevant.'

Janus didn't answer.

'It's a new lead,' Jackman continued. 'We have a name, Qiang Li. The family weren't sure whether or not he had a permanent visa. We need to get that checked out. If not, it's unlikely we can make the usual checks, but that doesn't mean we can't trace him. Give it time.'

'Time? We'll have the world's press on our doorstep before we know it,' she snapped.

Jackman felt her frustration too, but for different reasons. The new revelations: the ransom call, the uncle, the time lapse, bothered him. He thought of the kidnapper's words, 'we will fail to meet her basic needs'.

'Maybe I should get in someone more senior.'

'Hey!' He shot her a hard stare.

'I don't mean for them to take over, just a media front, to show we're taking it seriously. Reilly's tied up with the Readman murder. That's another bloody debacle,' she said.

'I don't need a media front.' Jackman spoke through gritted teeth. 'I've worked kidnappings before.'

'This is different,' Janus said. 'We're dealing with cultural differences that span 5000 miles and parents that aren't giving anything away.'

'We can't rule out their involvement either.'

'What?'

'Well, you heard Russell. What's with all the secrecy? They didn't exactly react in the normal way to the news yesterday. What if the parents arranged this? We need to press the Embassy for their personal bank records, get a list of their business clients. Look,' Jackman continued, 'if you are going to give me more resources, put them at the college to guard the kids. It hasn't even been forty-eight hours. Give me a chance.'

She removed her glasses and rubbed her eyes. 'What about the link with the others?'

Jackman grimaced. 'It's possible, but a ransom call is a risky change of direction. More likely it's separate. How did Reilly's team get on with the restaurant?'

'Still working on it.' She sniffed and replaced her glasses. 'Will, are you sure you're up to this?'

'Absolutely.'

He watched her stand and grab her bag. 'Keep me informed.'

As Janus swept out of his office and through the incident room, his mobile buzzed on the desk beside him. He grabbed it. A message from Celia.

*Hi Dad, Hope you're having a good day. Love you. x*

A warm feeling filled his chest. It would have been so easy to let go of the world after his wife's accident; to drift through the days, weeks, months that followed, skydiving through a weightless eternity of nothingness. The only thing that stopped him, that pulled him out of his depression in those early days, was Celia.

After Alice's diagnosis he'd all but convinced himself she was going to die. But Celia fervently believed her mother was going to be one of the minority that made a decent recovery and refused to accept any alternative.

Even after he'd persuaded her to return to university, when that inner voice of temptation spoke with such lingering seduction — encouraging him to binge on junk food, give up work, lock the world out — Jackman resisted. He hadn't touched alcohol since the night of Alice's accident. He ate relatively healthily and he ran and cycled as often as the job would allow, usually accompanied by the ever-keen Erik, and threw himself into his work.

He looked back at his phone and smiled. She'd probably never realise how much that one text meant.

Jackman stared into the faces of Min's parents that filled the computer screen before him. The Skype meeting had been relatively easy to set up, but almost half an hour of questioning hadn't offered any new leads. He was fully aware of the eight hours' time difference and the likelihood that Mr and Mrs Li had barely had any sleep since Monday, but he was starting to feel little pinheads of frustration prick away at his skin.

Mr Li's hair was peppered with grey and spiked into a fringe that framed his weary face. In spite of the interpreter on hand, Mrs Li said nothing. Her pale face was cast downwards for the whole of the interview. Jackman wasn't sure if she was under the effects of sedation, didn't understand or was just frozen in grief. Yet they didn't look guilty. Just frightened. And immensely sad.

'I repeat, every tick of the clock is important now. You have to help us and tell us everything you know. Who are the contacts that arranged the ransom money and delivered the payment for you in the UK?'

Thick tramlines collected on Mr Li's forehead as he took an audible breath. 'I've already said, I cannot tell you that.'

He formed his words slowly and carefully and whilst Jackman couldn't fail to be impressed by his grasp and pronunciation of English, he was beginning to feel exasperated. 'There is a chance they could be involved in this in some way.'

'It's not my contacts that are the problem. All

they've done is what I asked and tried to help me. We need to find my daughter.'

'Finding them could lead us closer to Min. Even if they are not involved, they might have seen something, heard something . . . '

'They're not involved. I can guarantee that.'

'Then you won't mind sharing their details?'

A muscle flexed in Mr Li's jawline. 'I cannot.'

'Why not?'

He stared at Jackman. 'You don't know what these people are like. They work on trust. If you betray their trust, they come after your friends and family.'

'We'll get you protection.'

Mr Li shook his head. 'You have no idea.'

Jackman decided to change direction. 'You said you have a brother living in the UK. Can you describe him?'

'About five foot six inches tall, average build. His left earlobe is missing and there is a scar down the left side of his face.' He ran his finger down his own cheek to illustrate. 'Agricultural accident when he was a child. We are trying to find a photo. It's been such a long time.'

'When did you last hear from him?'

'Not for years. We were never really close.'

'He came over to work in a restaurant?'

'Yes. He was always good with people. He seemed to have a gift for learning different languages.'

'Okay, if you can find the last address you have for him and send it through to Detective Russell with a photo and anything else you can remember, that would help.'

'You don't think he could be involved?'

'We have to follow up every line of enquiry,' Jackman said gently. 'What about the money you agreed to pay for the ransom?'

Mr Li looked downwards. 'Somebody will be in touch. That's all I know.'

Jackman leaned into the screen. 'This is important. Please get in contact as soon as they do. We need to talk to them. It could help us to find Min.'

He glanced across at Mrs Li, just as a single tear rolled down her cheek.

# 22

DS Gray passed Jackman a mug of steaming black coffee and folded himself into the chair next to him. The seated position pulled the already strained shirt buttons across his belly to new limits, exposing intermittent blobs of hairy white flesh.

After the Skype meeting, Jackman deployed Davies and the rest of the team to the industrial estate where the ransom drop was made and drove straight to Birmingham's police headquarters in an attempt to track down Qiang Li. He was now seated in Lloyd House at Colmore Circus, a large highrise set in the heart of Birmingham's city centre. Jackman waited for Gray to place his coffee down on the circular mock-pine table in front of them before he spoke. 'Thanks for taking the time to talk to me,' he said. 'What can you tell me about Qiang Li?'

Gray exhaled loudly. 'Nothing much. We reckon he's an illegal immigrant who outstayed his tourist visa. After your phone call, we got a team straight out to the last address the family gave in Lever Street, just off Hagley Road, but all we found was a group of students that claimed they've lived there since September. We spoke to the landlord, a Trevor Smith. He doesn't know anyone of that name, although he said he has had a Chinese guy living there that meets the description. He's come and gone a few times over the years. Keeps himself to himself. He was there last summer, although Smith chucked him out because he was behind with the rent.'

'Did he say what name he was using?'

'He doesn't remember and hasn't kept any of the paperwork, conveniently.' Gray rolled his eyes. 'It's a three-storey terrace with individual rooms to rent. I'd say he works mainly in cash. I don't think he cares as long as he gets paid.'

'So we are thinking Qiang's using a different name?' Jackman said, almost to himself. 'What about local intelligence?'

Gray shook his head. 'He's not known to us. Mr Smith mentioned he might have worked at The Oriental Garden in the Chinese Quarter, but it's unlikely they'll have any records under his real name if he's here illegally.'

'So he's just disappeared?'

Gray took another sip of his coffee. 'He's kept off the radar for the past twelve years. No reason for him to make himself known now.'

Jackman heard footsteps and turned towards the door. Two brisk knocks were followed by the click of the handle. A female officer appeared, carrying a couple of sheets of A4. She looked across at Gray, 'Sorry to interrupt,' then turned to Jackman. 'These just came for the inspector.' Her mouth formed a thin smile as she handed them over and left the room.

The first sheet was a print-out of a message from Russell which read, 'Best photo of Qiang Li taken around fifteen years ago'.

Jackman looked at the photo. At first glance the image looked more like a mug shot than a family photo, although when he peered closer he saw what appeared to be a sparkle in Qiang's eye, as if he was deliberately pulling a face for the camera. Jackman stared at it a moment. Qiang's head was tilted slightly, held at an angle that obscured his left ear, but he could just about make out the grooved scar on the side of his cheek.

Gray sniggered as Jackman passed it across. 'Bloody hell.' He ran his finger along the broken line that ran through the middle where the original photo had been folded. 'Couldn't they find a better one?'

Jackman took a sip of his coffee and placed the mug on the round table in front of them. 'He probably looks quite different now, but at least it's a start.'

'What we really need is Ken,' Gray said, 'the local beat officer for the Chinese Quarter. He's British-born Chinese. Built up a lot of connections with the local community, even speaks Mandarin.'

'Great, let's get hold of him.'

Gray frowned. 'No can do. He's sunning himself in Greece. Flies back in the morning.'

★ ★ ★

Twenty minutes later, a thick stench of diesel hung in the air as Jackman and Gray parked up and wandered into Birmingham's Chinese Quarter. The afternoon heat radiated from the mortar in the surrounding buildings. Gray turned his head sharply as they passed a couple

124

of women in short floral dresses.

'There it is,' Jackman said. He halted on the corner of a narrow side street and pointed at The Oriental Garden. 'Let's go have a word.'

Gray took another passing glance at the ladies and reluctantly followed Jackman through the entrance. Elaborate lacquered prints of Chinese figures decorated the red walls of the restaurant. They climbed up grey carpeted steps and immediately faced an oversized, gilt-edged mirror that gave the impression of a room double the size. A family of four turned their heads from a table in the corner beside an aquarium containing a shoal of cichlids that glided around serenely.

A floor-walker grabbed a couple of menus, plastered a smile on his face and approached them. Jackman introduced them both and his smile instantly disappeared.

He made a play of replacing the menus in the nearby stand and looked back at them anxiously. 'How can I help you?'

Jackman dug into his pocket, pulled out the photo and unfolded it. 'Do you recognise this man?'

The waiter gave it a fleeting glance and shook his head.

'And you are?' Gray chipped in.

'Hui Zhang.'

'We were told he used to work here,' Jackman added.

The man glanced across at him, his face deadpan, and handed the photo back. 'Must have been a long time ago.'

Jackman sighed. 'Can we speak to the manager please?'

The man nodded and moved away, through a door behind the bar area and out of sight. He returned almost immediately with an older Chinese man in casual trousers and a checked shirt.

Jackman held out the photo and repeated his question.

The elder man cast a quick glance at his colleague. When he spoke, his words were broken. 'I don't know him.'

'Are you sure?' Jackman asked. 'Take another look. His name is Qiang Li, although he might have been using another name. He has a very distinctive scar.' Jackman pointed to the side of the face in the photo and explained that his left earlobe was missing.

Hui Zhang started to translate but the older man cut through his words. 'No.'

'What about any of your staff?'

'I don't think so. I'm sorry.'

They left the restaurant, crossed the road and entered the Arcadian precinct. Red lanterns hung merrily overhead. They paused at a shop offering acupuncture, the window inset with an ornate red Chinese dragon, and moved inside. A middle-aged Chinese woman with a bobbed hair-cut looked up from behind the dark counter and smiled, but as soon as Jackman introduced them both, her head bowed. When he showed her the photo she cast her eyes to the floor and shook her head. They tried the restaurant next door and faced the same response.

'I bet if we were ordering food they'd understand us perfectly,' Gray said as they left.

A mixture of heat and irritation was bubbling beneath Jackman's skin as they continued down Cathay Street. He halted near the end, just outside a Chinese supermarket and wandered inside.

The shop assistants behind the till were all busy serving customers. Jackman glanced around as they waited. He was just examining the wide range of different rice beside the door when Gray nudged him. He turned his head to find that the queue had run down and two of the assistants stood idle.

Jackman moved in towards the one on the end, raised his card and smiled. He held up a photo of Qiang and asked the assistant if she'd seen him.

She shook her head, short sharp shakes. A colleague peered over her shoulder and said something in Chinese and they both exchanged a look. Jackman swore he saw a flicker of recognition on their faces.

He leant in closer. 'Qiang Li,' Jackman repeated. 'He may have been using another name. Do you know him?'

The second girl looked up at him, bit her lip anxiously. 'I . . . ' Suddenly she gazed past him and froze. Jackman heard footsteps behind him and turned to see a Chinese man walking towards the tills.

He could hear shuffling behind him as the ladies dispersed. He raised his card, held up the photo.

The man glared at him and shook his head. 'The girls need to work.'

Jackman ground his teeth as he left the shop. He would come back tomorrow. Maybe he'd have more luck with the local officer or an interpreter on board. He hoped so.

# 23

All afternoon I ground the nail into the concrete, working the metal over the same line, time and time again, to deepen the groove. It was cathartic at first. I imagined it was my captor. I was carving my name into his chest, pushing the sharp edge in deeper with every mark. Even when my fingers ached I didn't stop. I couldn't. I had no idea how much longer I had and now that I'd set my mind to the task I wanted to complete it.

Finally I sat back and surveyed my work. My name stood out, clear as day, etched into the concrete. First in English, then in Chinese. It wasn't neat or tidy. The 'M' was wonky, the 'I' too long, but it was clear. A slight moment of pride was almost immediately smothered by a blanket of sadness. If I died in the pit, this would be like an epitaph on my gravestone.

My knuckles were bleeding. The earlier grazes stung as new dust became ingrained in the crevices. I looked around for some relief. I couldn't spare any water. My eyes rested on my skirt. I grabbed the corner, pulled hard. A slight rip. I pulled again with all my might, tore a strip of material off and wrapped it around my knuckles. The silk was soft and slipped through my fingers as I wound it around and around.

The skirt had cost £30.00. More than my food budget for a week. I'd seen it in a shop window in *Stratford* centre weeks ago and wandered past it several times, looking on longingly. Finally, last weekend, I plucked up the courage to go inside and try it on. The assistant told me it suited my slender figure and she was right. I loved the way the grey silk glistened in the sunshine and swished around my calves as I walked. I'd lived in my student jeans for so long, but this felt feminine, different. It cheered me up, made me feel special.

A lump filled my throat as I looked down at the torn material. A broken nail snagged the fabric as I ran my finger along the ragged edge. It had meant so much, and yet today it just looked like a grubby rag cast aside in the gutter.

# 24

A couple of hours later, Jackman pulled off the main dual carriageway and turned left into The Grove industrial estate. The car park was heaving and he had to drive up to the far end to find a parking space. He got out of the car and surveyed the surrounding area. A mechanic's garage was flanked by a factory unit that made car parts. A printing company sat in the corner.

Davies reached up and gave him a wave. She was stood outside a long metal unit with a glass front at one end and a rolling factory door at the other. The blue sign above the door read Atom Conveyors.

'Any luck with the uncle?' she asked as he approached.

Jackman shook his head. 'Nothing yet. How's it going here?'

'Okay.' She made for the side of the building and gave a sideways nod indicating for him to follow. He climbed over the blue and white police tape and paused next to three large, pink industrial waste bins huddled together, the bright livery on the side advocating the fight against breast cancer. A few scraps of paper and a sliver of cardboard indicated the space where the brown bin used in the ransom drop had stood.

Davies tucked a stray curl behind her ear. 'These bins are rented by Atom Conveyors. They have three 1100 litre bins,' she pointed her toe forward, 'for landfill waste and one for cardboard recycling which houses all the packaging that comes through this place — that's the one used for our drop. It's collected once a week on a Wednesday morning, usually between 10 a.m. and 12 p.m. We're working our way through the staff, interviewing everyone, then we'll take it wider to the neighbouring units. No potential witnesses yet. Biggest problem is the time of the drop. Most of these units shut up shop by 7 p.m. Even if somebody had forgotten something and popped back, they were likely tucked up in their bed by midnight.'

She pursed her lips in thought. 'One thing they were able to tell us is that the bin's stacked out by Wednesdays. So much so, they've even been considering ordering another.'

'It's collected every Wednesday? The collection company stick to that?'

Davies nodded.

'And it's always placed in the same location?'

'Yes.'

'So, we are possibly looking for someone local, someone who knew what the bin contained, the collection times. When they sent that demand, they knew the bin would be almost full. It'd make it easier to retrieve a package if it sat on top of something.' Another thought nudged Jackman. 'Aren't industrial bins usually locked?'

'According to the staff they were locked every night. The keys hang in the office. But we've already checked and the keys are pretty universal. There are only about three different types out there. Even the secretary said they're easy enough to source on the internet.'

Jackman glanced at his watch. It was 4.10 p.m. He looked back at the remaining bins. 'What about those?'

'They're emptied on a Monday.'

Jackman walked back towards the car park and turned around. What struck him was the complete lack of vegetation. No trees, hedging. It was like a concrete jungle. 'No cameras?'

Davies shook her head.

'What? I thought Birmingham was the home of CCTV?'

Davies chortled. 'Oh, there's plenty on the main roads. We'll get those checked. But this is a private estate. They have an alarm for out of hours and a security firm does a beat call at night. Didn't see the need for cameras. A couple of companies have their own, but they're situated further up.' She pointed along the line of businesses. 'We'll get them checked of course, but it wouldn't be difficult to avoid them. They hang off the front of the buildings like beacons.'

Min's parents had confirmed that the drop was made at 12.30 a.m. Min was due to be released half an hour later. He looked back down the row of bins. The bin in question was situated at the far end, obscured by the others. He tried to imagine someone rummaging through in the darkness. Even if a car had passed it was unlikely they'd have been spotted tucked away down there. It was the perfect location and somebody had gone to great lengths to seek it out.

Jackman wasn't sure what made him turn, but as he looked around he saw a taut, pointed face

133

at the window. He stared at it a moment before it moved back, away from the glass. 'Who's that?'

Davies followed his eye line. The outline of the figure was just about visible in the distance, although he'd turned and appeared to be having a conversation with somebody else in the room. 'Oh, that'd be Mr Lewis, the managing director. Very austere. Something tells me he'll be happier when he gets his new bin and we stop keeping his staff from the production line. If time is money, he measures every second.'

Jackman shot a fleeting glance back to the window but Lewis had disappeared completely now. He turned three hundred and sixty degrees, glanced at the surrounding area and then back at the spot that had housed the bin. 'Shame he's not so vigilant in the early hours of the morning. We'll need a background check on him and all of his employees. Check out the company that rent the bins too — the collectors will be familiar with the locality, and the security firm. Whoever organised this must have been here several times to examine the area. See if anyone spotted anything untoward over the past few weeks, or earlier that evening.'

The intermittent loud beeps of a vehicle reversing swallowed his words. He looked up to see two long metal pipes protruding from the back of a lorry's rear bed as it approached. Thick diesel fumes filled the air. A couple of men in navy coveralls emerged from the factory to talk to the driver, another hopped into a fork lift and reversed, carefully avoiding the police tape as he worked.

Jackman fished his buzzing mobile out of his pocket. Celia's name flashed up on the screen. He moved back down the side of the building, away from the drone of engine noise before he answered.

'Hi, Dad!'

The bright intonation brought an inadvertent smile to his lips. 'Hi, what's up?'

'Oh, nothing. I'm at Sam's and she's got some of the old crowd together from school. Bit of a reunion. Her parents are away so we're gonna have a BBQ over here and catch up. Just calling to say don't wait up. Looks like it's going to be a late one. Might stay over.'

He could hear the babble of chatter in the background. Celia giggled as if she was having a two-way conversation. 'No worries. You have a good time,' he said. 'See you in the morning.'

'Sir?'

Jackman turned to see Keane marching towards him as he ended the call. His yellow tie hung loose around his neck. 'How did you get on?'

'Bloody hopeless,' Keane said through panting breaths. He took a tissue out of his pocket and wiped his brow line. 'There's no CCTV at the internet cafe. I've spoken to the guy who was working the shift when the email was sent and he reckons it was really busy. He can't remember anything. The shops opposite don't seem to have cameras either.'

'What about payment records?'

'Nothing. It's a dirty little two-booth cash-only operation. I asked if he has any regulars, thinking

135

of people we could interview as potential witnesses but he said most of his customers are visitors to the area. They only come in once or twice. Sorry, sir. I think we've hit a dead end.'

★ ★ ★

He sat down on the wooden bench and propped his rucksack up beside him. A late afternoon breeze had gathered, whispering through the branches of the surrounding trees.

A family sat on a rug nearby, a blanket in front of them laden with a messy array of empty plates, half-eaten sandwiches and beakers of juice. A tin with the lid slid off exposed a collection of cupcakes. The woman was not unlike the opaque memories he held of his own mother, buried in the depths of his mind. Slender and petite, she was dressed in a white shirt and floral skirt that had risen up to expose her bare knees. As he watched, she leant forward and ruffled the hair of the man next to her.

Two boys, still in school uniform, were perched on the edge of the blanket, picking out tufts of grass and throwing them at one another, menacing grins on their faces. The man sat forward and stretched, then laid back and rested on the grass. The younger boy looked up, shouted to his sibling and they immediately ran over and jumped on their father in mock-combat. Their father roared as he rolled around with them. Their mother's white teeth gleamed as she trilled in the background.

He was mesmerised by the display. His own

childhood had been filled with an invented little world of playmates, imaginary friends who fitted in with whatever game or scenario he wished to play. He became good at it, adjusting his tone for the different characters, throwing his voice like a ventriloquist to make it real. More than once his mother had knocked on the door of his room, labouring under the misapprehension that he'd brought friends home to play.

Friends. He thought back to his school days. The boys taunted him, called him weird, picked him last for team games while the girls laughed in the background. Only a few of the plain girls showed him any kindness and that never lasted long. No, from an early age he had to satisfy himself with friends of his own making.

As he entered his teens, he learnt that the only way to gain his father's attention was through his school grades. His father pored over his reports, as if his life depended on them. So he decided to work hard at school and charm his teachers in an effort to reach out to his father. And he figured out how to sit on the periphery of friendships, so that he didn't stand out, the lone kid.

He looked back at the family. They'd stopped playing. The mother was gathering up the leftover food and packing up the basket. The boys nudged each other as they collected rubbish. The man brushed blades of grass from his trousers. For the briefest of moments they tugged at his heart strings, raising an ache that reached up through his chest and into his throat.

The man bent forward and pecked his wife's cheek. She turned and winked at him as he drew back. In that split second everything changed. And the ache that had gripped him so tightly turned his heart to stone.

# 25

By 8 p.m. Jackman was back at the station in Stratford, studying the statements from Min's friends.

DS Gray had established that Min's uncle had left his flat last summer. Where had he stayed in the meantime? And where was he now? Jackman was convinced that somebody in the Chinese Quarter knew something. DS Gray promised to call him as soon as the local beat officer landed, but that wasn't going to be until tomorrow.

He re-read another statement and cast it aside. He wasn't really sure exactly what he was looking for, just something a little out of the ordinary, or someone that Min had met or spoken about.

None of the friends' statements indicated anyone that had been hanging around, watching or bothering Min. None of the tutors remembered seeing anyone at the college. Even Tom hadn't noticed anything and she seemed to spend most of her time with him.

A thought jabbed at him. Maybe Min had tried to trace her uncle and ran into something untoward?

He shuffled the statements around and skimmed through each one lingering on the one from Lauren Tate, Min's best friend, who hadn't been at the party on Monday night.

Jackman sat back in his chair as Alice entered

his head. Many days she'd come home from work full of stories. Stories about friends' or work colleagues' lives, some that he'd never met or would never likely meet. Her capacity to care about the most intimate details of other people's lives, often strangers, always surprised him. He learnt very early on to listen quietly whilst she shared her news. She reminded him of a heated kettle that needed to empty itself of every drop of hot water before it had a chance to cool down.

He turned this over in his mind. If Min had a secret who would she be more likely to talk to? Tom? Possibly. Although they'd argued the night she disappeared. There was the pregnancy, the issues with her parents. Were there other problems? Maybe she wasn't sure she could trust him. But a best friend . . .

Jackman stared at Lauren's statement. He had to do something. He considered it for a split second before he grabbed his phone off the desk and dialled.

★ ★ ★

Lauren Tate wound her ankles uncomfortably around the chair legs. She was a short girl with broad shoulders and horsey features. Sleek brown hair hung down each side of her face like a pair of silky curtains. A fitted black t-shirt sat atop faded denims that clung to her thighs.

Lauren's mother had greeted them at the door of her modern semi on the edge of the north side of the town as their car pulled up, her face contorted into an expression of concern.

140

Jackman was glad he'd phoned ahead. A brief phone discussion with Mrs Tate had laid the groundwork nicely and she couldn't have been more obliging. She poured fresh coffee for all, then made a concerted effort to leave her daughter with Davies and Jackman in the kitchen alone. She didn't mention Min after the phone call, although he could see that the disappearance of her daughter's best friend was on her mind.

The Tates' kitchen was a large room that spanned the rear of the property. Dull sunbeams filtered through the skylight and glinted on the varnished table. The gentle babble of the television could be heard from the next room.

Jackman smiled. 'Thanks for seeing us, Lauren.'

She stared back at him with large eyes, then shifted her gaze to Davies beside him.

'Don't be alarmed,' he said with a kind smile. 'You aren't in any trouble. We are just building up a picture of Min at the moment and wondered if you could help fill in the gaps?'

She thrust a sharp nod, but said nothing.

Jackman cast a quick glance at Davies before he continued, 'In your statement you said that you weren't at the Old Thatch Tavern with Min on Monday night?'

She cleared her throat. 'No, it was my mother's birthday. We went out for a family meal.'

Jackman nodded. 'When was the last time you saw Min?'

Lauren thought for a moment. 'Monday

141

evening. I went back to her apartment for a coffee. She had bought a new skirt and wanted to show it to me.'

'What time was this?'

Lauren paused for a second. 'About five-ish I guess. I stayed about an hour.'

'So you left around six o'clock?'

'I guess so. Our table was booked for eight, and I wanted to get back and get ready.'

'How did Min seem?'

'Fine, really. It was a big night out, Tom's birthday. We chatted a while and then I left.'

Jackman smiled. 'Would you say you two are close?'

Lauren's face lit up, but her eyes looked like they were about to cry. 'Yes.'

'How did you meet?'

Lauren tugged at the silver necklace around her neck and wound it around her fingers. She stared into space for a moment as if she was recalling fond memories. When she met his gaze again, she seemed calmer. 'It was about the second week of term,' she said. 'I was walking across the campus to the canteen after class. A pencil dropped from her bag.' She gave a weak smile. 'Sorry, we've joked about that so many times since. A pencil drew us together. Sounds odd, but we just got talking and she followed me into the canteen. I already knew Tom and the others she hung out with, from secondary school. We just kind of clicked straight away.'

Jackman angled his head. 'Your mutual friends like Steph describe you as inseparable.'

She grinned. 'Min and Tom are inseparable. I

142

think I became her friend when I introduced her to YouTube. The internet is heavily monitored in China and YouTube is banned. She loved the music parodies on there. When we're not together we chat over Skype in the evenings, while watching them.' She shrugged. 'She's really very easy to get on with. Everybody likes her. And Min cares about everyone.'

'How do you mean?'

Lauren thought for a moment. 'Well, it's like the rich kids at the college. The arrogant ones who miss classes and nag you to copy your assignments? Most of us give them a wide berth. But Min still had time for them. She's nobody's doormat, but she'd still speak to them, laugh with them, lend them her books to catch up.'

'Was there anybody she didn't like?'

Lauren sat quietly, then shook her head.

'Anyone that didn't like her?'

'No.'

'What did she talk about when you were together?'

'All sorts. Girl stuff mainly. She shared stuff about her family back home. Wants me to meet them when they come over in the summer.'

She went on to talk about Min's family, but only shared facts that Jackman already knew. 'What about any other family?'

Lauren looked puzzled. 'She's an only child.'

'Has she ever been to Birmingham?'

'I don't think so. I know the overseas students have a few trips out to places like London and Bath. She hasn't mentioned Birmingham.' Her face was blank, eyes clear.

'Thanks.' Jackman gave her a small smile. 'What about Tom?'

'What do you mean?'

'How do they get along?'

'Alright.'

'Oh, come on Lauren. Your best friend is missing. We know she was pregnant.'

Lauren's eyes widened. There was a moment before she spoke. 'She was scared,' she said, her voice barely a whisper. 'He wanted her to get rid of it. But she wasn't sure what to do . . . ' She broke off mid-sentence and swallowed. 'Can I ask you a question?'

Jackman nodded.

'Do you think she's okay?'

'We have no evidence to suggest that she has come to harm,' he said diplomatically. 'But I'll feel a lot happier when we locate her.'

He watched as small tears formed in the corners of her eyes. 'I'm scared something has happened to her.'

Davies retrieved a packet of tissues from her pocket, pulled one out and passed it over. 'I know, love,' she said. 'Try not to think that. We're doing everything we can to find her. In the meantime, if you think of anything else that might help in any way, just give us a call.'

# 26

The backs of fingers swept across my cheekbone. Grandmother. I blinked, reached up. But the air above me was empty. Of course it was. She died almost five years ago.

Images of Tomb Sweeping Day filled my mind. Visiting the family crypt last year. The candles we lit in the rain as we remembered our loved ones that had passed.

I sat up, rubbed my cheek, desperately trying to regain that familiar feeling. Grandmother stroked my cheek every night when she put me to bed as a child. The memory warmed my insides.

Grandmother was at home when I left for school in the morning, there to greet me when I returned. With both parents working, she was the one who made sure I ate a cooked meal and did my homework, the person who seemed to have endless free time to play and chat with me. Sometimes we'd walk to the park, sit on the bench and stare at the clouds in the sky. Grandmother loved clouds. She said they were free to move, visit other lands and experience new pleasures.

We'd spend hours out in that park, talking about my school, my friends, the things that seemed so important in my little world. And she would tell me about her childhood. I loved to hear her talk about where she grew up in

Shandong. I never knew her age, but her face bore the deep-set lines of a long hard life. She told me stories about her childhood, how from an early age they shared in the household chores, worked the land with their parents. Her community still practised some of the ancient Chinese customs, ignoring the bans and restrictions applied by wider government. Her earliest memory at home was watching her sister being led away to a room upstairs, then hearing her cries as each toe was broken, all apart from the big toe, her foot folded back and bound in the coveted lotus shape. They were told that it was good for girls, especially the eldest in a family — the secret to making a good marriage. For days after that she watched her sister weaken. The local women had rallied around, administering herbal medicines as red spikes shot up her sister's legs. A week after the binding she died from an infection.

I was never sure whether it was being exposed to such raw experiences so early in life, or just a blunt stubbornness that imbued Grandmother with a staunch sense of individuality. Outwardly she respected the strict regime. Inwardly she fought hard against it. Through Mao's rule when everything from her reading material to the music she listened to was controlled by the government, then later as Deng introduced economic reform and the communist reigns relaxed a little she saw opportunities: pushing for an education and career for her daughter, supporting her son-in-law in his quest to run a factory, then later for me.

'I feel your sense of adventure, my little Lan Hua,' she would say. 'You are like a little caged bird: fed, watered and nurtured. One day, the cage door will spring open so that you can spread your wings and fly. And when that day comes, you must fly high and never look back. And you will experience new opportunities that the rest of us can only dream of.'

New adventures. I looked around me, swallowed hard.

I wanted to scream back at her, 'But Grandmother, the clouds aren't free, they are governed by the wind. A wind that can get angry and whip them up into a frenzy. A wind that can wipe them clean from the sky. And you didn't tell me what to do when they get angry, when they disappear. You taught me to take advantage of every opportunity, but you didn't tell me what to do when it all goes wrong.'

At that moment desperation like no other clawed at me. I fell to the floor, hunched like a child, and wept.

Time stood still. Slowly, exhaustion wrapped around me, pulling me back to my slumber. It was too hot. Don't sleep. Don't sleep. My mind spiralled. How much longer would I be kept here? My eyelids felt heavy. Just for a moment . . .

# 27

Jackman leant against the edge of the desk at the morning briefing and cast his eyes across the board in front of him. A spider diagram filled the area with Min's photo in the centre and lines leading out to Tom, Qiang Li, the ransom note. Min had been missing for over two days and, as far as he could see, they were no closer to locating her. 'Any news on the motorbike?'

Keane nodded. 'I sent the photo over to a dealer. They think it's a DRZ Suzuki. A popular dirt bike, sir. Easy to steal. We're working through the reports of missing bikes. Nothing yet.'

'What about the helmet?'

'Nothing significant. Forty-six refers to the race number of Valentino Rossi, nine times world champion. The stickers are easily available online.'

'There's been a huge response to the public appeal,' Davies said hopefully. 'We're prioritising the messages, eliminating the time-wasters. It's a mammoth task.'

Jackman nodded. 'Good. Any sightings of the van?'

'We're struggling on that one,' Davies said. 'We've trawled the police cameras over the past three weeks and checked the sightings of the number plate with the owner in Coventry. We can't find any movements he can't account for. It could be that they're changing the plates.'

'Any news from the family?'

Russell shook her head. 'Her father's been talking to people in their local community, trying to locate anyone that may have kept in contact with Qiang Li. Nothing yet. They're panicking,' she added, 'I can hear it in her father's voice. Talking about coming over to help with the search.'

'What about the phones of the people that made the ransom drop?'

'All pay as you go and not registered,' Keane said. 'They used a different SIM card every time they contacted Mr Li. Can't trace them.'

'And the money?'

'Paid.'

Jackman raised a brow.

'His contacts over here arranged it,' Russell said. 'He borrowed from local associates, several different sources and passed it to the man he met who organised everything.'

'The man whom he can no longer reach?'

Russell nodded. 'So he says.'

Jackman shook his head wearily. He stared out into the sea of faces. 'What about the uncle, Qiang Li?'

Davies spoke up, 'His details have been distributed nationally and internationally. If he's known to the police, somebody's bound to holler.' She cleared her throat. 'What time are you due back in Birmingham?'

'I'm meeting the local beat officer in the Chinese Quarter at 4.15 p.m.' He blew out a sigh. 'Let's hope we have more luck than yesterday.'

Jackman checked his watch. 8.45 a.m. 'Right, I need to get going. I'll be back in a couple of hours. You can reach me on my mobile.'

* * *

Davies pulled off the main Campden Road, past the New Inn Hotel and into Clifford Chambers, squinting through the morning sun that bounced off her windscreen.

As she drove down the main drag she found herself in the midst of middle England at its finest. A plethora of detached houses and quaint cottages lined the street, all surrounded by rolling rural countryside.

She turned at the bottom by the wrought-iron gates that led down the drive to the Manor House, doubled back and parked up on the right, just past the old church. The group of stone, terraced cottages were situated directly on the pavement and she guessed they would have once been owned by the Manor House.

The twitch of a curtain at the second house from the end caught her attention. She cut the engine wearily. The influx of calls from the press appeal was stretching resources to the limit and with the DI out of the office this morning, the last thing she needed was another time-waster.

By the time she'd exited the car and walked along the cracked concrete pavement, the door was pulled open to reveal an elderly man with a slight stoop. He was dressed in grey trousers and a beige knitted cardigan over an open-necked cream shirt, in spite of the soaring temperatures outside.

Davies raised her badge. 'Mr Graeme Ward? I'm DS Davies. You called us with some information?' He reached up and scratched the

150

wisps of hair that barely covered the liver spots on his head.

'Yes, do come in.'

She wandered past him into the narrow hallway. 'Go on through,' he added, 'first door on the right.'

She could hear the sound of a dog barking in the distance as she opened the door into a sitting room. A green sofa decorated with floral cushions stood next to a reclining armchair opposite a seventies-style electric bar fire. An old-fashioned box television sat on a cabinet in the corner. A sideboard against the far wall was covered with a mixture of painted porcelain figurines and photographs of children at various stages of growth. The air smelt musty and thick, like an old oven that hadn't been cleaned in years.

Graeme Ward shuffled in behind her. 'Do sit down,' he said, then turned towards the closed door at the end of the room that Davies guessed led out to the kitchen. 'That's enough, Flick!' he commanded, although the dog showed no sign of abating.

'Now, what about tea?' The man's voice rasped as he attempted to raise it another decibel.

Davies managed a smile. 'No, thank you.'

'Oh, I insist!' Graeme raised a single hand and turned to the door at the end. No sooner had he pressed down the handle than a small dog rushed out bellowing louder than ever.

Graeme turned. 'Don't mind Flick. She only wants to be friendly.'

The dog looked anything but friendly,

151

hovering well within biting distance and emitting rolling growls through its teeth. Davies watched it warily, relieved when Graeme returned with cups and saucers jostling together on the tray as his hands shook. Flick rushed to his side.

'Let me help you with that,' Davies said and eyed the dog carefully as she stood and relieved him of the tray which was now slopped with tea from the metal pot. She placed it on the small coffee table between them and proceeded to pour the tea.

'You live here alone, sir?' she asked as she passed him a cup and sat back down on the sofa.

'Graeme, please.' He widened his eyes. 'Yes, since my Vera passed, six years ago.'

She nodded. 'When you called the station you said you had some information that might be relevant to our enquiry?'

Graeme relaxed back into his armchair. 'Yes.' He paused for a moment to take a sip of tea. 'I saw a van, like the one they mentioned on the radio.'

'Can you describe it?'

'A white Volkswagen van. Quite distinctive it was, with blurred marks on the side where the sign had once been, and a rust circle around the diesel cap.'

Davies sat forward. 'This is very important, Graeme. Where did you see it?'

Graeme placed his cup on the saucer. 'Hmm, let's see. I was out with Flick.' He glanced at the dog. 'We walk for miles around here every day, don't we girl?' The dog immediately stood, cocked her head and wagged her wiry tail. Graeme winked at Annie. 'Keeps me young.'

Davies could feel a sense of irritation ripple beneath her skin, but said nothing.

Graeme looked up at the ceiling. 'It would have been on the main road, earlier this week. Monday or Tuesday.'

'What time?'

Graeme didn't answer. His eyes crossed to the side, deep in thought. 'You know, I think if she's here, I bet they've got her in the old wood.'

'I'm sorry?'

'The girl you're looking for? That's why you're here isn't it? There's some water tanks in the old wood on the hill, haven't been used in years. Perfect place to keep a body, I'd say.'

'What makes you say that?'

Graeme shrugged. 'It makes plain sense to me. Go down to the old Manor House gates and turn right. You'll have to take it on foot from there, but you'll see the wood directly ahead of you up the hill.'

Davies felt a stir of alarm. The ransom note hadn't been released to the press. The last thing they needed were the ramblings of an old man to spark interest and get the public speculating. 'Of course we'll look into it, but at the moment this is only a missing person enquiry.'

She thought hard. Clifford Chambers was practically a hamlet. The main stretch was a dead end for vehicles beside the hall. One way in, one way out. Surely too risky for a kidnapper to consider using?

Graeme stared into space as he continued, 'Always comings and goings down here just recently. This used to be a quiet place.' He

153

turned his head from side to side. 'Things have changed . . . '

'How do you mean?'

Davies stared at him perplexed, and was just about to press him further on the van when she heard the slam of a door. Flick jumped up. The kitchen door opened and a younger man with a shaved head marched through. 'What's going on here?'

Davies rose from her seat as the dog rushed to the intruder. But instead of barking, Flick wagged her tail and bounced around his ankles. Graeme looked up as he spoke. 'Ahh, Carl. Nice to see you.' He turned back to Davies. 'This is my son, Carl. He's a fine-looking lad, isn't he?'

Carl was an intense forty-something in dirty combat trousers and a navy polo shirt that clung to his muscular chest. He wiped a rough hand across his sweaty forehead and viewed Davies suspiciously as he spoke. 'Who's this?'

Davies felt it necessary to flash her card.

'Was always very popular with the ladies,' Graeme rambled on. 'He'll like you. Got a real eye for the dark-haired ones.'

'We're investigating the disappearance of a student in Stratford,' Davies said. 'Your father called us with some information that might help our enquiries. Do you live in the village, sir?'

Carl looked taken aback. 'No. I grew up here. I live in Stratford now.'

'Carl's a plumber,' Graeme said, puffing out what little chest he had left.

'I'm just fitting an outside tap down the road,' Carl added.

Davies tried to question Graeme more, but his answers were vague and he seemed distracted now that his son had arrived. She placed her tea cup on the tray. 'Well, I think we have everything we need for now, Graeme. I'll send a colleague around to take a statement. Thanks for your help.' She stood, held out her hand and Graeme shook it. Her hand juddered inside his. 'If you think of anything else, don't hesitate to give us a call.' Davies gathered her bag. 'Thanks for the tea.'

Carl followed her out to the pathway. When they reached the car he spoke again. 'There's something you should know.'

She rounded to face him.

'My dad.' He shot a furtive glance back to the house. 'I'm not sure how useful his information will be.'

'And why is that?'

'He's got dementia.'

'Has it been diagnosed by his GP?'

Carl pulled a face. 'It's only in the early stages. But he often sees things, hears things that aren't really there. And he gets confused.' Davies raised her eyebrows as Carl continued. 'The other week he called me out because he'd heard an intruder downstairs. Two in the morning it was. I came all the way out from Stratford and there was nothing here. The house was locked up — no sign of a break-in. Even Flick wasn't barking. And he puts things away in the wrong cupboards. He couldn't find his milk yesterday. We searched high and low and he'd put it in the bin. A full carton too.'

Davies stared down the road at the gates to the

Manor House. The heat of the day was really kicking in now, leaving a soft haze in the air around them. She looked back at Carl. 'Thank you. We'll certainly bear that in mind.'

But as she climbed into her car, a wave of uncertainty washed over her. Were these the ramblings of a senile man? Or had he seen the van? She quickly fished her mobile out of her pocket. Whatever it meant, she couldn't afford to ignore it.

# 28

I woke to the sound of crackling from above, like dry kindling tossed into a flame.

I lunged forward, held my breath. Almost immediately silence filled the air, punctuated only by the rustle of leaves in the distance. I sat back. Maybe it was the rats. But they scratched and scuttled. This was different. I shook my head, to disperse the paranoia nagging at my brain. I'd been here too long. I was imagining things.

The rough concrete had left gravelly indentations on my forearm. I rubbed the loose pieces of dust and stone away.

The slice of light that seeped through from the outside world indicated daylight. I looked back at the rough concrete beneath me, around at the walls and thought back to last night: the depression, the desperation. Grandmother. I couldn't even picture her in my mind today. Even my memories were starting to desert me.

I moved forward and then froze. There it was again. Not crackles. I strained my ears. It was more like . . . shuffles. Shuffles on powdery, old concrete. Footsteps.

The shuffles became louder and more frequent, scratching at times like sandpaper on plaster. I stared up at the grill. The movements flashed intermittent shadows into my den.

Suddenly a thought struck me. What if it wasn't him? What if it was someone else?

Someone that had stumbled across the area. Someone that didn't know a woman was kept captive in the darkness, only metres below.

'Help!' My voice was weak, barely a whisper. I coughed, tried again. 'Help me, please!'

The sound stopped. My stomach lurched. I shouted again at the top of my voice, 'P-Please, h-e-l-p me!'

A shock of sunlight tore at my pupils as the cover was lifted away. I squinted, shielded my eyes. I could see the battered remains of an old roof above. I must be in an old house or barn. Sporadic gaps stood out where slate tiles were missing, exposing bare patches of rafter.

I'd just lowered my hand when something pounced into the pit.

I gasped, jumped back. Dark eyes peered through slits in a black hood.

The man dropped to his knees. I shrunk back into the corner.

There was a bag beside him. I glanced from one to the other. I needed to jump up, fight, escape. But my limbs felt as though they had been turned to stone.

In a flash, he reached for the holdall, rummaged inside and retrieved a roll of tape.

He grabbed my arms and pulled them roughly together in front of me. The duct tape made a loud rip as he released it from its roll and wound it around them. I pulled back my legs in a feeble attempt to resist, but he quickly reached up and secured them.

'Please . . . No . . . ' I squawked the ailing words out. Tears spilled over. He leant forward,

158

his breath hot on my cheek. Trepidation turned my stomach, round and round.

A gloved hand reached out to my face. I braced myself.

It cupped my chin. A finger from his other hand gently swiped the tears away. For a moment he paused, stared at me.

In desperation, I narrowed my eyes, tried to peer through the slits in his hood. Instantly, he jolted back. Then, as if he had never stopped, he again reached for his bag. I could smell the glue as more tape adhered my lips together. Finally he pushed my head forward and tied a piece of material around my eyes. And the world turned black.

I started to shake, every muscle trembling in unison.

The blindfold was uncomfortable. Specks of dust made my eyes itch. It wasn't tight though. In some strange way he went about his business with the deftness of a mother carefully but firmly dressing a toddler.

But this was no dressing. He bound my hands in front of me and my feet together.

I felt him move away. Scratches and shuffles as he cleared up his bag.

I became aware of space around me. I was alone once more. I sat, still hunched in the corner, waiting for the familiar sound of the grill being replaced, the chain being locked.

I wasn't going to die. Not right now. Relief swamped me. The muscle spasms subsided into a million questions. Why tie me up now? How was I supposed to eat? What did he have planned?

159

Time stood still as a deluge of thoughts swam around my mind. Fear mingled with confusion.

At that moment my bladder kicked in. I needed the toilet. That's the last thing I wanted, trussed up like a pig in an abattoir. I was just wondering how I would manage it, how I would attempt it, when I heard another noise.

A thud. A presence beside me. Thick breaths came fast and quick. He was back. The tearing of more duct tape. I listened hard trying to make sense of what I could hear in the background. Grunts, murmurs. But no fixed words.

Movements around me. Swishes of air oscillating as he worked.

A crash — soft this time. Was it his bag being bundled out? I strained my ears. Finally, the grate of the grid being replaced jerked my head up. The jingle of the chain. Then nothing. Silence pervaded the room. Apart from the sounds of slow rasping breaths, closely followed by a gentle picking. Almost like drips falling from a tap. I realised then that I was not alone.

# 29

Situated in the quaint village of Milcote, just outside Stratford, Broom Hills Nursing Home was a red brick Georgian structure set within six acres of sculptured gardens. Jackman and Celia navigated the long driveway in silence. The main house sat majestically on the peak of the hill, the Wisteria that snaked around its entrance a dazzling carpet of purple in full bloom. Yet any beauty it held was lost on Jackman, clouded by the memories of what it represented: a prison for his sick wife.

Jackman's shoes squeaked on the parquet flooring as they entered the lobby. Gilt-framed Monet prints decorated the walls and floral curtains were tied back over the leaded windows. A pretty blonde receptionist with hair coiffed into a tidy bun looked up from her computer and smiled a greeting as they signed in the visitors' book and moved into the main building.

They passed a library with floor-to-ceiling bookcases and leather easy chairs, a residents' lounge that was filled with floral comfy sofas, chintzy cushions and elegant china figurines, and took the lift to the third floor. Alice's room, the room that had been her home these past eight months, was just out of the lift, second on the right. Her window overlooked rolling country-side to the rear of Broom Hills.

Alice was sat in a green easy chair beside her

bed. Blue straps, just visible beneath the hands folded into her lap, were clipped together to keep her from falling forward. At first glance she looked asleep. Her head was laid at an angle on her chest; a line of spittle had collected in the groove beside her mouth. But as they drew nearer they could see her blue eyes hung open.

'Mum, you'll get a bad neck if you sit like that,' Celia said cheerfully. She pulled her satchel strap over her head, leaving it to fall beside the bed and lifted her mother's head back before wrapping her arms around her.

Jackman hung back and swallowed. It wasn't the lack of response that bothered him. Over the months he'd grown accustomed to that. It was Celia's voice. The fact that she managed to remain upbeat and positive in the face of so much adversity choked the hell out of him. He waited for Celia to move aside, then stepped forward and embraced his wife briefly.

Jackman watched his daughter retrieve a tissue from her bag and wipe her mother's mouth before she emptied a pile of cards onto the bed, then sat beside them and proceeded to open each one and read the contents out loud. It had been a while since they'd visited together and her actions saddened him. He perched himself on the other side of the bed and, as Celia chattered away, let his mind wander.

Having joined the Royal Marines at seventeen, Jackman had been set on a career in the armed forces. But five years in, on home leave, he met Alice, a microbiologist, originally from Denmark and two years his elder. She was different to any

162

woman he'd ever met and shared his passions for the great outdoors, camping and hiking. For a while they squeezed their relationship into his short periods of leave. At first it had seemed exciting, almost clandestine. But as the intensity grew and the relationship deepened, it soon became obvious to Jackman that the long periods they spent apart distressed them both, more and more.

It hadn't been an easy decision to leave the Marines, affecting almost every aspect of his life but, almost two years after their initial meeting, they married and Jackman, lured by a job that boasted the excitement of daily challenges, joined the Metropolitan Police Service.

He recalled how they spent their early days, languishing on the sofa during their evenings together, making plans to visit the Pyramids, trek to Machu Pichu, skydive over the Grand Canyon. It wasn't exactly that they made a pact not to have children, more that their dreams simply didn't allow the room. It was an exciting time of new beginnings, dreams and adventures.

But within a year of their wedding, Alice's hormones had made a U-turn that took them from a B-road to a dual carriageway overnight. She suddenly started cooing at babies they saw in the street, waved at toddlers in shops and restaurants, bought magazines on nursery design and layout.

Pregnancy agreed with Alice and she wandered around the house singing like a dawn chorus over the months that led up to the birth. In contrast, Jackman was wracked with a mixture of excitement, apprehension and dread at the turmoil that was about to be inflicted on their lives.

But as soon as Celia was placed in his arms the love he felt for the pink, wrinkled bundle with the tiny fingers and full head of white hair was instant and, what's more, so powerful it was frightening. And in the days, months and years that followed, that protective urge developed into an all-encompassing shell.

He recalled the moment when he taught her to ride a bicycle, her little voice squeaking, 'Please don't let go, Daddy,' as he ran alongside her clutching the back of the saddle, the small of his back protesting angrily. He remembered when he went to her first parents' evening and looked through her school work to find a picture she'd drawn of her best friend with the words written beneath in her disjointed handwriting, 'my daddy'. The little girl who gripped his hand tightly in crowds and, even as a young teenager, was too shy to order her own food in a restaurant.

He looked across at her now. She'd retrieved a brush from the bedside cabinet and was gently pulling it through her mother's hair. A year ago, Celia had been a normal, confident nineteen-year-old, home from her first year at university. The accident that summer changed her life forever. Yet, she coped with Alice's condition so much better than he did.

Part of Jackman hoped that Alice would have some recognition, something that would incite an improvement in her condition one day, maybe even bring some of her old self back. But, as awful as it was to admit, another side of him wished she had died that night. He switched his gaze to Alice. Her eyes were pointing absently in the direction of the window as Celia continued to tease the brush through her hair. He wondered if she dreamt, and hoped that if she did, her dreams were visited by happy memories. Because that was all she had left.

Jackman excused himself and headed down to reception to get them coffees. While the machine was pouring what resembled dirty water into a cup, he reached for his mobile. The X in the corner indicated no signal. He waited until the coffees were made, emptied a sachet of sugar and a couple of mini-cartons of milk into Celia's, then placed them on the side.

He nodded at the receptionist who was tapping away at her computer, ventured outside and checked his phone again. Still no signal. Frustrated, he wandered around to the side of the main house. A line flickered for a split second, then disappeared. Broom Hills might offer excellent views and a beautiful rural setting, but when it came to mobile signals it was hopeless. Jackman turned, glanced up at the house. He could see the birthday cards that lined Alice's window ledge from here and the sight injected a twinge of guilt. He paused, inhaled deeply, then pocketed his phone and headed back inside.

Celia almost pounced on him as he walked back into Alice's room. 'Dad, Mum just moved her eyes.'

He steadied himself, relieved he'd placed lids on the coffees.

'I asked her if she wanted the blinds turned down because the sun was coming through and she shifted her eyes to the right!'

He looked at his wife. Her eyes were fixed straight ahead. 'That's great, honey,' he replied with as much enthusiasm as he could muster.

Celia's smile melted. She moved around to the other side of the bed, sat beside her mother and grabbed her hand protectively. 'You don't believe me.'

He passed a coffee across. 'Of course I do. It's just, well . . . ' He sighed. He'd lost count of the number of times he'd watched Alice at the hospital, asking her questions, willing some sort of reaction. It was easy to make a gesture and mistake an errant blink or eye movement for some sort of recovery, then repeat the process and get nothing. 'Don't get your hopes up. It could have been a coincidence.'

Celia took a mouthful of coffee and swallowed. 'I wasn't imagining it, was I Mum?' she implored.

Jackman approached the window. 'It's going to be another beautiful day,' he said.

A movement behind him made him turn back. Christine, one of Alice's carers, had entered the room. 'Good Morning, Alice,' she said in her cheery Irish tone. 'How are we today?' She nodded at Jackman and Celia. 'And you've got your family come to see you on your birthday. How nice!'

Jackman moved to the bedside. 'How's she doing?'

166

'Very well, thank you,' Christine said.

'Have you noticed anything?' Celia said. 'Any recognition?'

Christine rested her hands on her hips. 'Can't say I have, but it's early days.'

Celia explained what she thought she saw.

'Did she, now? Clever girl,' she replied and patted Alice's arm affectionately. Christine, with her smile that lit up her ruddy face, was just the sort of person that Alice would have liked. Jackman was glad.

Christine bustled around the room, smoothing Alice's bedclothes, fluffing up her pillows and commenting on her array of cards. Jackman moved across and sat on the armchair in the corner.

'Can we put a book beside the bed?' Celia asked. 'To keep a note of when Mum shows some recognition? So that we can see if a pattern emerges.'

'Well, I shall put it in her notes in the office,' Christine said, 'but of course you can keep a book yourselves. Nothing wrong with that.'

The thought of Celia's optimism formed a lump in Jackman's throat. It was easy to imagine something, cling onto a tiny thread of hope, only to find it snap off in front of your face.

He suddenly felt a warm hand on his shoulder and looked up to find Christine staring back. 'We never lose hope,' she said.

# 30

I sat there, huddled in the corner listening to the staccato of 'picks' beside me. The noise was disconcerting. Pick, pick, pick, interspersed, every now and then, with an intermittent throaty tear.

My new company was bound. Just like me. And somehow they were working on their tape, gradually pulling at the adhesion of the glue.

Another tear, then a rip. A shuffle. More picking. Though different, louder this time, as if there was more control. Another rip was followed by coughing and spluttering.

I shrank back. Terror pressed down, suffocating me.

There was more fidgeting next to me. It seemed to go on for ages.

Eventually a voice spoke out, 'Min, is that you?'

Goose pimples skittered down my arms. I concentrated hard. The inflection in his voice betrayed his roots. He was Chinese, although not from my province and he spoke in English. Why was he here? I tried to grunt back, but the sounds merged together into a muffled din behind the tape.

'It's me, Min. Lonny.'

Relief choked my voice. I let out a huge whimper. It was somebody I knew, somebody from the college.

I felt him reach forward. 'I'm just going to remove the blindfold.'

Again in English. But this time I knew why. Lonny was from Hong Kong. His native language of Cantonese couldn't be more different to my own Mandarin. My mother always said that I shouldn't have put all my efforts into learning English at the expense of other languages closer to home.

Threads of my hair felt his presence as he moved around to the back of my head. Strands snagged as he nudged the material this way and that. I flinched, but remained silent. Suddenly, the material was pulled away. I took a moment to focus. A thin layer of daylight illuminated the pit.

I glanced up at Lonny. He was one of the richer kids, the ones with parents who gave them generous allowances, the ones who hired vehicles and took off to explore the country. We shared a couple of classes. But I knew him well enough to see how different he looked today. His usually immaculate hair was dishevelled. Spots of glue blotted his face around the mouth. His clothes were dirty, as if he'd rolled in a dust bath.

He gave a weak smile, held a palm to his temple. 'My head's killing me,' he said.

I glanced down and spotted a pile of duct tape on the floor. From the moment he'd been left here, he'd set to work on removing the tape, spindly fingers working back on his wrists, then his face. I raised my eyes to meet his gaze.

He pointed at my mouth. 'Shall I remove the tape?'

169

I nodded.

'It's gonna hurt.'

I nodded again. It was all I was capable of.

Slowly, he pulled at the edge of the tape. I felt a tiny sting as he grasped enough to give him leverage. 'Ready?'

I blinked acknowledgement. He pulled back, short and sharp. The tear of the glue travelled like a burn across my cheek. I recoiled. Twice more, he repeated the actions, each time checking that I was ready to brace myself for the pain that was about to follow. When I was finally free, I gulped in huge mouthfuls of air before I mouthed, 'Thank you.'

He sat back on his heels and set to work on the binds around my hands. 'Are you okay?' He looked up as he spoke. His eyes were soft and full of concern. 'Everyone's been looking for you.'

For a moment I couldn't speak. I'd sat here on my own for so long, contemplating my fate, loneliness squeezing every ounce of energy from me.

'What happened to you?' I eventually said. My words were rough and brittle and my throat hurt as I pushed them out.

'I'm not sure exactly,' Lonny said staring into space. 'It was around nine in the morning, I was walking down Alcester Road. Felt a bang on the back of my head,' he reached up and rubbed his crown, 'must have blacked out.'

I absorbed his words slowly. I wanted to hear every minute detail, every second of his capture, in the faint hope that his experience would

170

answer some of the questions that had plagued my brain these past couple of days.

My hands freed, I rubbed the area around my mouth and sat forward as we worked on the tape around our ankles in unison. 'Maybe somebody saw you?'

He paused, thought for a minute, his eyes searching the space in front of him, then shook his head. 'Maybe. I don't remember seeing anyone.' If he noticed my hesitation, the shadow of disappointment that crept across my face, he ignored it. 'When I woke up, I was in the back of a vehicle.'

'What kind of vehicle?'

'I don't know, my eyes were covered. I could hear the engine. I wanted to call out but I was gagged and my hands were tied. At first I thought I was dreaming. It seemed like ages until he parked up, the engine cut, and the door opened.'

'That's when you arrived here?'

He looked across at me. 'Yes. He pulled me out of the vehicle. Then, as soon as I was upright, I felt a sharp point through my t-shirt.' He leant forward and winced as he fingered the small of his back. Thin threads hung loosely where the material had been snagged. The area was circled with specks of blood, where the top layer of skin had been scratched beneath. 'He didn't speak, just led me here. But the knife didn't leave my back. I remember being pushed down onto my knees, the jingle of metal . . .'

'The chain.' I raised my eyes to the roof. 'I think it locks the grid in place.'

Lonny wavered as he stood to examine it.

'Hey, careful.'

'My head feels like it's full of cotton wool,' he said.

'I felt like that too. I think he drugged me. Had a massive headache afterwards.'

Lonny rubbed his forehead and looked around at the walls, then reached up towards the grill. 'This the only way out?'

I nodded and watched him grab the bars. 'It's no use. I've already tried.'

His shirt flapped as he gave it a quick shake. The chain rattled like a snake in the background.

'There must be a way,' he said.

'There isn't.'

Lonny rubbed his hands up and down his face, covering his eyes. He wobbled again.

'You'd better sit down. I felt very dreamy at first. Like a hangover I had to sleep off.'

He sat and rested his head on the concrete wall. Silence filled the pit for several minutes. Finally, he looked across at me. 'What about you?'

'What do you mean?'

'How did you get here? We all know you disappeared after leaving the Old Thatch Tavern on Monday evening. It's been on the news, the radio. Everyone's talking about it. The police are crawling all over the college. What do you remember?'

'What day is it today?' I asked, ignoring his questions.

'Thursday.'

Thursday. That meant I'd been cooped up in

this hell hole for three nights now.

I looked across at Lonny. I wasn't sure what I'd expected. Of course the police would have been alerted to my disappearance. But being encased in this dark cell for the past couple of days had played tricks with my mind. There were times when I felt so alone, like I'd been forgotten, as if the world had pushed me aside and moved on without me. In a way it was heartening to think that they were looking. But why hadn't they found me? And why was he here now?

I relayed the story of how I arrived here and, as I mouthed the words, I was reminded just how little I knew about our captor.

Lonny listened intently, waiting for me to finish before he spoke. 'They thought you'd been murdered like that other girl.'

I jerked my head to face him. 'What do you mean?'

'Well, she disappeared for a week before they found her body. People thought you might be another victim.'

A shiver slipped down the back of my neck. We sat quietly for a while and I became aware of how thick the atmosphere of the pit had become, now that two people vied for a lungful of air.

'Why do you think we are here?' I eventually asked.

He took a deep breath and thought for a moment. 'Ransoms? Both our families might be considered wealthy.'

'Mine aren't. Their money is tied up in the factory.'

He shook his head, his face blank as if he'd run out of ideas.

'And even if it was kidnap, as you suggest,' I raised my arms wide, 'why put us together? It doesn't make any sense.'

'I don't know,' he said. 'Maybe he thought if we were tied up and gagged we wouldn't be able to communicate.'

The thick air was mingling with the heat now and the dual effect was stifling. I fixed my gaze on the wall in front. 'He.'

Lonny twisted his head. 'Sorry?'

I returned his gaze. 'You said, 'he'.'

A few seconds passed before Lonny spoke. 'Well, I presume he must be male. To have the strength to lift me into the vehicle and manoeuvre me across to here.'

I glanced back at the grid above us. 'Yes,' I said, as if I was speaking to myself. 'That's exactly what I thought.'

# 31

Jackman slowed right down as he passed the Volkswagen parked in Clifford Chambers' main street. The white van with yellow and blue signage read 'C Ward Plumbing Solutions' next to a blue water droplet. Dots of yellow painted vapour sat above the symbol. He looked at the petrol cap — no rust circle. But he'd seen that symbol before somewhere.

He pushed the thoughts aside, continued to the end of the road and pulled up beside a police car. It was parked behind two police-issue Land Rovers, a Transit van and a black Audi. The sight of the Audi puzzled him. What the hell was Reilly doing here? He slammed the car door behind him and headed up the track that led out of the village and into a farmer's field.

Jackman had picked up Davies' excited voicemail after he'd left Broom Hills and dropped Celia back home that morning. 'A possible lead to the victim in the woods just above Clifford Chambers'. He'd tried to call her back, but when the line went to voicemail, he sped straight here. Keane updated him from the incident room as he drove: Davies had responded to a call this morning, a potential sighting of the white van near Clifford Chambers village. A search team had been called out to examine some disused water tanks in the nearby woods.

Jackman raised his badge to the uniformed

175

officer guarding the gate to keep unwanted dog-walkers and nosey villagers away, and looked up at the wood as he climbed the uneven hill. Having walked Erik over these fields in the past, he knew this area well. Halfway up he paused and glanced around dubiously. A racetrack was situated behind the wood, a road beyond that. It was well-frequented by dog-walkers and children played up in the woods in the summer. To store a body here seemed a risky plan.

He was about to continue when he spotted Davies in the distance making her way down the hill. The gradient was such that her step quickened and she almost appeared to be running, out of breath by the time she reached him. 'False alarm, sir,' she said.

Jackman looked past her to see Reilly emerge from the wood, mobile phone glued to his ear. 'What's he doing here?'

Davies rolled her eyes. 'No idea. He arrived at about the same time as the search team.' She cut off as Reilly reached them.

'Ah, Jackman,' he said just as his shoe caught a rogue clod of earth that set him off-balance momentarily.

'You organise this?' Jackman lifted his head towards the direction of the wood.

'Yes,' Reilly said as he steadied his footing. 'I was with Superintendent Janus when the call came through. Thought I'd lend a hand. One of the tanks had been disturbed recently, we needed cutting gear to get into it.'

Jackman gave a short nod. 'Anything there?'

'It appears not.'

176

Jackman looked back up at the wood. 'How did you get on with the restaurant?' he asked, changing the subject.

'In the Readman case?' Reilly shook his head. 'So many people pass through there. My detectives have tracked down the staff who worked on the nights when the girls were meant to be there, but they don't remember them specifically.'

'Mr Ward was really talkative until his son arrived,' Davies said. Her face was confounded, as if she had been working it through in her mind and hadn't heard a word of their conversation. 'He seemed quite insistent he'd seen a van, and mentioned the rust mark around the petrol cap too. Then his son arrived and he seemed to get sidetracked. Went on about what a ladies' man he was and how much he liked girls with dark hair.'

Davies prattled on, relaying her interview with Graeme Ward, but Jackman was no longer listening. The image of the water droplet symbol had crept back into his mind. He was turning the symbol over and over. Suddenly he felt a strange sense of foreboding as he remembered where he'd seen it before.

'That van down the road,' Jackman said. 'The plumber's van. Does that belong to Ward?'

Davies looked taken aback at the interruption. 'Yes. Well, not Graeme Ward. It belongs to his son, Carl.'

'And his son's a plumber?'

Annie nodded.

Jackman switched his gaze to Reilly. 'I've seen

the symbol on the side of that van before.'

'Where?'

'It was on a fridge magnet at the house Ellen Readman shared with her friend. I'm almost certain of it.'

'And Ellen Readman had dark hair,' Davies interjected.

Jackman faced her. 'What?'

'Mr Ward said his son was a ladies' man, likes girls with dark hair,' she repeated.

'Get some urgent background checks done on Carl Ward,' Jackman said. He turned to Reilly. 'I think we need to have a word with Mr Ward junior.'

Reilly stepped back. His voice faltered as he spoke. 'I'll get the checks organised.'

Jackman gave him a hard stare. 'Annie's got it in hand. Come on!' He pulled on his arm, forcing him into a reluctant jog.

They raced down the hill leaving Davies behind. Jackman sped up as he reached the gate and headed for the village, leaving Reilly to stumble along behind. A couple of dog walkers deep in conversation eyed him suspiciously as he passed them and headed up the main street.

Jackman's mobile buzzed as he approached the plumber's van, still parked on the main street of Clifford Chambers. 'Davies' flashed up on the screen. He paused to catch his breath and clicked to answer. 'What have you got, Annie?'

'Plenty of intel, sir.' Her voice was puffed as if she was rushing. 'Ward has previous — assaulting an ex-girlfriend in 2006 and in 2009 he was arrested for rape, which the complainant later

178

dropped. Last year uniform were called to a domestic at his home in Stratford. His wife refused to press charges, but there's still a 'violent' marker on his file.'

'Right, thanks.'

Jackman ended the call, slipped his phone into his pocket and rapped the front door of the cottage. Reilly had reached him now and was bent over holding his knees, gasping for breath.

The chain on the back of the door rattled as it opened. A tall man with dark eyes and a bald head appeared. He raised his eyebrows at Reilly who immediately hauled himself to a standing position.

Jackman held up his card and introduced them both. 'Carl Ward?'

'What is this?' Ward said. 'Your lot have already been here today. My father needs to rest.'

'I wondered if we could have a word with you this time, Mr Ward?' Jackman said.

'What about?'

'Could we come inside?'

Ward looked from one detective to another. He then stepped outside, closing the door behind him. 'We can talk out here.'

Ward folded his arms across his chest as he vehemently denied any association with Ellen Readman. When given her address, he recalled being called out to mend the heating system at her housemate's home earlier that year, but claimed that he had never actually met Ellen. His manner was calm, he spoke with ease. But there was something about him that made Jackman edgy. He looked back at the van. 'Do you mind if we take a look inside?' he said.

Reilly shot him a warning glance and he knew why — he had no warrant and no grounds to search. In fact, all he did have was a tenuous link with the victim through work and Ward's father's line about his son liking girls with dark hair.

Carl Ward hesitated for the briefest of seconds. 'I've nothing to hide.' He dug into his pocket, retrieved a bunch of keys and sorted through them. Jackman exchanged a look with Davies who had now joined them as he unlocked the back doors and flung them open.

The smell of bleach assaulted Jackman's senses as he climbed inside. He felt Ward's thick presence beside him as he stood and looked around. Apart from an array of tools that hung on a rack on the inside wall and a large toolbox in the corner, it was empty.

Jackman noticed Davies look from the scruffy stature of Carl Ward to the inside of the van and back. 'Do you always keep it this clean?' she said.

He blinked contemptuously. 'I like my work ordered.'

Jackman could feel Ward's gaze on him as he scanned the area and was aware of Reilly staring in from outside. A sense of urgency filled the air. He was desperately searching for something but he had no idea what it was.

'Right.' Ward checked his mobile phone. 'If you're finished, I need to get back. I've got another quote to do this evening.'

With much reluctance, Jackman followed him to the door. He was about to climb out when he turned at the last minute, just as a flash of gold caught his eye. He moved back, approached the rear of the front seats and bent down. Something was wedged between the seats. He poked it. It felt like a tiny line of plastic. He leant in a little closer.

'Oi! That's enough.'

Jackman ignored Ward's call, pulled his torch out of his pocket and shone it on the area. A gold spot glinted back.

'I said that's enough!' The sound was followed by a thud and suddenly Jackman felt a weight crash into him as the raw edge of Ward's anger exploded. A fist was thrust into his gut, a hand gripped his neck, pressing hard on his vocal cords. As he fought to pull the hand away, he looked up to see a wrench moving toward his forehead. Jackman summoned all his energy, ducked back, the hand still around his throat, and kneed Ward in the groin.

The clatter of the wrench crashing to the floor of the van reverberated around the whole area. Jackman heard shouting and felt a force yanking Ward away. He recovered himself and looked up to see a couple of the search team had now joined them and secured Ward, helped by Davies.

He stood and rubbed his neck as Ward was dragged out the back of the van. 'Get out of there!' Ward cried. 'You've got no right.'

Jackman stared at him, moved forward and jumped down onto the pavement. 'I'll see you at the station.'

Curtains twitched, windows were flung back and doors opened as the commotion quickly attracted the interest of local residents. Within seconds, it seemed a crowd had gathered near the van, heads at the back craning their necks for a better view.

It wasn't until several officers had wrestled Ward into handcuffs, Davies had officially arrested him and they'd pushed him into the back of the car that Jackman returned to the van, donned his gloves and managed to retrieve the thin piece of plastic from between the seats. He smiled inwardly as he peered down at the SD memory card.

\* \* \*

Jackman heard the door click closed behind him as he entered the interview room. The eyes of Carl Ward, his solicitor and even Keane who was poised over his notes, were on him as he pulled out a chair, placed the pink envelope file tucked underneath his arm carefully on the table and restarted the tape.

Reilly had initially wanted to postpone the interview until his own team arrived from Leamington. But Jackman didn't want any more delays that might cost another life. If there was any possibility that Ward might be linked to Min's disappearance, that he might be able to reveal something about her whereabouts, he needed to start now. And when the chief constable phoned Reilly direct for an update, he'd reluctantly agreed.

The first hour had, as Jackman expected, gone in Ward's favour. Ward had recovered his composure, claimed to be a happily married man, refuted any idea that he knew or had even met Ellen Readman, Katie Sharp or Min Li. He even hinted at being singled out by a desperate police force who had been guided by the words of a senile old man in their desperation to make an arrest.

Jackman folded his hands together on the table and said, 'Earlier you told me that you have no knowledge of either Ellen Readman, Katie Sharp or Min Li.' He unfolded his hands and allowed them to rest on the file in front of him.

Ward's solicitor, who had barely spoken a word throughout the interview, immediately sat forward. 'What is this?'

Jackman ignored her and drew two sheets of paper out of the file. He kept his eyes on Ward as he turned over the first, a selfie picture of Ellen Readman and Carl Ward, cheeks pressed together, beaming back at the camera. They looked like they were sitting in the back of Ward's van. He turned over the second, a bare shot of Ellen.

'For the purposes of the tape, the woman in the photos matches the appearance of Ellen Readman,' Jackman said. 'Mr Ward, how do you account for these images that were retrieved from the SD memory card found in your van?'

'That's not Ellen,' Ward said. 'Her name is Emma. Well that's what she told me.'

'I need some time with . . . '

Ward held up a hand to silence his solicitor. 'It's okay.' He looked down briefly before he spoke again. 'Look, I'm a married man. We did have a brief fling, for a few weeks, but it was over months ago. I haven't seen her in ages. And I definitely don't know any of the other girls.'

'Are you sure?'

Ward sat tall, nodded.

Jackman sat back in his chair and gave Ward a moment. 'Are you absolutely sure?'

Ward glanced at the file and then back at Jackman and said nothing.

Jackman pulled a police exhibit bag out of the file. A mobile phone sat at an angle inside. 'Is this your phone, Mr Ward?'

Ward peered closer, nodded.

'Would you explain to me why the call records show calls and texts from this number to the phone of Ellen Readman, the last being on the day that she disappeared?'

Ward jerked forward. 'It's not true. Her number's not in there.'

'No, because you deleted it from the handset. But you can't delete it from the billing records.'

His solicitor immediately stood. 'I want some time with my client. Now.'

A knock at the door made Jackman turn. He was beckoned out into the corridor by Russell. Her face was red, as if she'd been rushing.

'What is it?' Jackman asked. He closed the door behind him.

'Ward has an alibi for Min's disappearance. We've spoken to his wife. They were in London for the weekend, didn't get back until Tuesday morning. We checked with the hotel and they confirmed the booking. The receptionist remembered him, apparently he was very suggestive.'

At that moment the door at the end of the corridor swung open and Reilly appeared, mobile phone stuck to his ear. His face shone like a kid at Christmas. 'Okay, no problem. I'll let you know as soon as it happens.'

He clicked off as he approached. 'Anything new?'

Jackman shook his head. 'He's having some time with his solicitor. I suggest putting him back in his cell afterwards. Give him a chance to think things over.' Jackman handed him the file. 'Right, I'm off. Need to get back to the kidnap.'

Reilly stared at him, astounded. 'What? We're almost there.'

Jackman sighed inwardly. 'You have a suspect who has had an intimate association with one of the victims, phone records and photos. The van is being forensically examined. By the morning you'll have their preliminary report which will hopefully give you enough evidence to charge on the Readman case. I'm meeting the beat officer for the Chinese Quarter in Birmingham at 4.15 to help me track down Min's uncle.'

Reilly looked bemused. 'Min Li has dark hair and disappeared into thin air. Just like the other two victims. How do you know they're not connected?'

Jackman stared at Reilly. 'He was in London with his wife when Min disappeared.'

Reilly snorted.

'We've checked it out.' Jackman sighed. 'Look, this has the makings of a love triangle that went wrong. Perhaps he never meant to kill her. Perhaps she threatened to tell his wife. The bottom line is that he had a motive. Northampton are checking out any possible connection

185

with Katie Sharp, but we've found no association with Min Li and her situation is different — we have a ransom call.'

'Maybe he got greedy? He could be working with someone else?'

'The ransom note was sent in Mandarin. There's a Chinese element somewhere even if they are connected. I'll leave Keane with you. He knows the Min Li case well. If anything crops up he'll spot it straight away.' Jackman held up his phone as he approached the door. 'I have my phone if you need me.'

Jackman heard Reilly grunt as he closed the door and strode down the corridor. He turned the corner and almost collided with Davies, bustling towards him.

'Ahh, thought I'd missed you,' she said.

'I can't stop, I'm already late.'

'I know. I'm coming with you.'

Jackman narrowed his eyes. 'Are you sure? I've a feeling it's going to be a late one.'

'No problem. Popped home at lunchtime and John's got it all under control. Between you and me, I think he's hankering to give up work and become a house-husband.'

Jackman chuckled. For some reason he couldn't imagine the sporty John spending his days feeding babies and changing nappies. 'Okay, if you're sure?'

A smile spread across Davies' face. 'Just try and stop me.'

# 32

Ken Yang looked cool and calm in dark trousers and a white linen shirt, leaning up against a shop window opposite the entrance to the Arcadian. His face broke into a creased grin as Jackman and Davies approached. 'Good to meet you,' he said and shook both their hands.

'How was your flight?' Jackman asked.

'Noisy. I have a six-month-old baby girl.' He grimaced. 'The altitude played hell with her ears. Screamed the whole time.'

'Well, I appreciate you helping us out,' Jackman said. 'I take it DS Gray's filled you in?'

'You're investigating a kidnapping. Trying to trace the victim's uncle, a Qiang Li?'

'That's pretty much it.' Jackman explained his frustrating experience the day before. 'Think you'll be able to help us?'

'Possibly. We'll start with the Red Dragon. Follow me.'

Jackman was just about to suggest that The Oriental Garden may prove more successful when Ken crossed the road and strode off through the Arcadian. He exchanged a look with Davies as they both followed.

Ken paused outside the Red Dragon acupuncturist. 'Do you have a photo of the uncle?' he asked.

Jackman handed him the old picture. He looked at it, thanked him and pushed open the door.

A welcome blast of air conditioning hit them

as they moved across the threshold. Jackman recognised the same lady from yesterday seated behind the counter as they entered, although there was a marked difference in her reaction today. Her face lit up as it rested on Ken.

They had an animated conversation in Chinese, accompanied by lots of nods and smiles before he pointed at Jackman and Davies who she had completely ignored until that moment. She nodded, bowed her head to them and scurried away, around the long curtain that Jackman guessed covered the entrance to the back of the shop.

The shop area felt smaller than yesterday somehow and for the first time, Jackman noticed a small, black leather sofa against the far wall, next to a low table with glossy magazines fanned out on top. As if she'd read his mind, Davies wandered over to it and pressed the seat with her hand, a cheeky grin on her face.

At that moment, a Chinese man with grey hair and a curved moustache emerged. He greeted Ken like an old friend and smiled at Davies and Jackman. More words were exchanged in Chinese. The photo was passed about. If there was any recognition in the Chinese man's face it didn't show, although he spent some time studying it. Jackman looked from one to another, trying to glean an ounce of their conversation. He was starting to feel frustrated when Ken lifted his mobile phone, nodded and gestured for them to follow him out of the shop.

A wave of thick heat hit them outside. Jackman loosened his collar. 'What happened back there?' he said.

Ken faced him. 'Jian Zhou is what they call a community leader in this area.'

'And he doesn't speak English?'

Ken smiled briefly. 'He does, but only with his customers. He prefers to speak Mandarin. We can go to The Oriental Garden now. They'll speak to us.'

Jackman tugged at his arm to slow him down. 'You seem to know him pretty well?'

Ken turned. 'His son was involved in a racial attack. I helped the family through the trial. He's always been grateful.' He moved on, heading in the direction of the restaurant.

As they crossed the main road Jackman had to shout to speak over the engine of a passing lorry. 'We're not going to do all of this in Mandarin, are we?'

Ken hesitated a moment. 'It's okay,' he said. 'Tao Chén at The Oriental Garden speaks good English.' Then, sensing Jackman's concern, he added, 'Don't worry, Inspector. I've been working this area for three years now. You get to know the locals. They learn to trust you.'

'I suppose it helps if you speak the language.'

'It's all about following protocol really. They come over here and form their own little cultural organisation. There's a hierarchy. Unless you have agreement from the person at the top, nobody will speak to you.'

Jackman nudged his head back towards the acupuncturist's shop. 'He runs the show?'

Ken nodded. 'Nothing happens without Jian's backing.'

'Does he know Qiang?'

'The photo looked familiar. That's all he would say.'

They paused as a car indicated and turned in front of them, then crossed the side street and headed to the restaurant. 'In fact, he thinks he might still be around.'

A different waiter met them at the door of the restaurant today. He opened it, smiled and exchanged pleasantries in English, much to Jackman's relief, as he guided them through with an open arm.

'We're here to see Tao Chén,' Ken said.

'He's expecting you.' The waiter bowed his head slightly. 'Follow me.'

They walked in formation behind the bar and through a beer cellar then out into the back of the restaurant. In contrast to the opulent décor inside, the walls here were painted cream and bore black and grey scratches, nicks and scrapes where things had been carried through and caught them over the years.

The waiter made a fist, gave a single knock and opened the door. He moved aside for them to enter, nodded and retreated without speaking.

Expecting to see the man from the day before, Jackman was surprised to see a younger man stood at the window. He could have been no more than forty, Jackman guessed, with short hair and a square jaw. He was dressed in a pink open-necked shirt and dark trousers and smiled at them as they entered.

'Tao Chén.' He walked around the desk as he introduced himself, shook their hands in turn, and indicated for them to sit. 'I hear you are looking for a Qiang Li?' he said as he returned to his own side of the desk. 'I'm not familiar with that name.'

Jackman sat forward in his chair. 'Yes. We came in yesterday and asked, but were introduced to another man?'

Tao nodded. 'The restaurant supervisor. He's not here today.' He smoothed out the green blotter on the desk in front of him. 'I'm not sure what I can say to help you,' Tao said.

Davies passed over the photo which was looking crumpled and dog-eared around the edges now.

He shook his head. 'I don't recognise him, although we get so many people come here. Some stay a few weeks, others longer.' He rambled on for a moment but Jackman was no longer listening. His eyes had fallen on a double-page cutting from a local newspaper that hung beside him on the wall in a clip-art frame. The heading read, *Local Restaurant Celebrates 25 Years*. A group of staff were huddled together in front of the bar smiling with Tao in the middle. In the background there was another figure, just on the edge of the shot, standing behind. His head was twisted to face the audience.

Jackman stood and pointed at the frame. 'Who's that?'

Tao looked briefly taken aback at the interruption. He quickly recovered himself and moved around the desk to Jackman's side. 'It was our twenty-fifth anniversary celebration,' he said.

'I can see that,' Jackman said. He pointed at

191

the figure behind the bar. 'Who's that?'

A flicker of unease travelled across Tao's brow. He swallowed before he spoke. 'His name is Peng Wu. He's . . . helped us out a bit in the past.'

Jackman paused before he spoke, retrieved the photo from the desk and held it up next to the cutting. Both men held their heads at a similar angle that obscured their left ear. He peered in closer and just caught the thread of a scar on the left side of his face. 'Well if I'm not mistaken he has a very similar disfigurement to the man we are looking for.'

Tao dug his hands in his pockets and buried his eyes in the press cutting.

'What can you tell us about this man, Peng Wu?'

'He helped us out for about three years, waiting tables in the restaurant. He was a good waiter. People liked him.' He gave a single head shake. 'But he finished last summer.' Tao turned and eyed Davies suspiciously as she retrieved her notebook and pen. 'Not officially, you understand?'

Jackman raised a flat hand. The last thing he needed was for Tao to clam up over an immigration issue, just when he'd managed to get him talking. 'It's okay,' he said in his most reassuring voice. 'We are here to investigate a missing girl and we think that Qiang Li or Peng Wu might be able to help with our enquiries. That's all. Why did he leave?'

'He was constantly late. Came mostly in the evenings as he seemed to cope better with that but still the lateness. We couldn't rely on him. Then some nights he didn't turn up at all. We had to let him go.'

'Have you seen him since?'

'Not personally, although I believe he's been in a few times. His brother-in-law works in the kitchen — he does have a visa,' he added rather hastily.

'Can we see him?'

Jackman watched him make a quick phone call which was followed a moment later by a knock at the door. A wiry man in a white chef's hat and long black apron appeared.

Tao introduced the officers. 'This is Jie Wang. His sister is married to Peng Wu.' He tapped Jie on the shoulder. 'Tell them anything they need to know,' he said. 'Excuse me. I'm needed in the restaurant.'

'Please, sit down,' Jackman said, after Tao had left the room.

Jie sat in the chair behind the desk, the only one available, where he looked smaller than before and distinctly uncomfortable.

'When did you last see Peng?' Jackman asked.

Jie looked from one officer to another. 'What is all this about?'

'We just need to speak to him in connection with an enquiry,' Jackman said. 'We think he might be able to help us.'

The answer did nothing to curb the suspicion on Jie's face.

'How long has your sister been married to him?' Jackman asked.

'There are not officially married. We just tell

people that because they have a daughter and it sounds better.' He squirmed uncomfortably in his seat. 'They've been together for about three years. Although for the last year they've been living separately.'

'Do you know where?'

'She and their eighteen-month-old daughter live with me. Peng?' He shook his head. 'No idea. He only visits once a week to give her money and he doesn't always come. He's a very bad man. Spends too long in the casino. Owes people money and they come looking for him.' Disdain coloured his face. 'He should have come last night. The baby needs milk.'

'Does he come to your house?'

Jie nodded. 'My flat is above here.'

'What time?'

'It could be any time. Usually at night time or in the early hours of the morning. Never in the daytime. He's almost nocturnal.'

Jackman eased forward. 'Why don't you tell us everything you know about Peng Wu?'

# 33

Jackman tore open a sachet of sugar, added it to his espresso and looked up at Ken as he stirred the coffee. 'I'm impressed. You've achieved more in fifty-five minutes than we managed in a couple of hours yesterday.'

After the restaurant they'd walked back through the Arcadian and into the supermarket. The same girl was behind the counter today. They were joined by her protective manager, although today his manner was much more convivial when they approached and, after a quick exchange, he allowed her a few minutes away to talk to them. In a mixture of broken English and Mandarin, with Ken translating, she was able to confirm that the man that fitted the description of Min's uncle had been in there shopping on Tuesday evening. Her eyes searched the photo. She said his hair had thinned but pointed to the scar just visible on the left side of his face. She was in no doubt it was him. He was a regular customer at Kitzy's Casino around the corner where she worked night shifts as a cleaner. She also knew him as Peng.

Ken smiled. 'It's all about how you ask the questions. You have to be direct. Make it clear what you want. None of this skirting around the issue and trying to catch people out like we do in our interviewing. If you try that, they just clam up and you get nowhere.'

'We've certainly struggled to get any background information on the family from the Embassy and when the report did arrive it was scant at best. No information on Mr Li's business.'

Ken nodded. 'When it comes to dealing with authority the Chinese are naturally suspicious and very wary of their regime.'

Jackman ran through his Skype meeting with Mr and Mrs Li, how they had paid the ransom and avoided all contact with the police until absolutely necessary and even now wouldn't disclose the details of who helped them or how they raised the cash.

'That's not surprising,' Ken said. 'Many Chinese people grow up to distrust the police in their country. They are not governed like we are in the UK. In China anyone in authority represents fear. People work hard to stay on the right side of them. If they had a complaint they might share it with their closest, trusted friends, but never openly in public for fear of what might happen to them. They build up a support network of people around them. If something goes wrong they would more likely use these people to help them resolve the situation, rather than go to the authorities. Many immigrants form pockets and emulate this by building their own little communities when they come over here, which is why they have someone in charge. It can have its benefits, as long as they are on our side.'

'How do you mean?'

'They don't want any trouble. They want their businesses to make money and thrive. When there's an element that threatens the system, theft for example, they deal with it. We just need to make sure it's done legally. Like I said, I've worked this beat for almost three years and you get to know some of the residents really well. They share stuff. Building up contacts and learning to speak to the right people has been really useful with managing the crime rate. If you lose their confidence, they'll monitor it themselves. And that's not always pretty.'

'How would the Li family have managed to raise the money and find contacts here to help them?'

'There are many community groups here in the UK with links to China that could make those arrangements. It wouldn't be difficult to find someone to help, especially when there's money involved.'

'You mean organised crime groups like Triads?'

'Triads are one of them, yes. There are others too. We know it goes on. But if you're looking for something on that level, you're unlikely to get any answers. When it comes to organised gangs or Triad activity, everybody shuts down. They are a law unto themselves. We've a little intelligence, but it really is the interminable brick wall.'

Davies looked up from her coffee. 'Where are your family from?' she asked.

'Tianjin, on the eastern side. They came over before I was born.'

'What do they think of you being a cop?'

'It took them a while to get used to the idea.' He flashed her a smile. 'But they're okay with it now.'

Jackman and Davies paused to read the signage outside Kitzy's Casino. *Open 24 hours. Live entertainment every night. Private functions catered for.*

It was almost 6.30 p.m. Ken had excused himself to enjoy the last evening of his leave with his family.

Cars, lorries and vans buzzed past them on The Broadway. A motorcyclist weaved in and out of the traffic. Jackman took a deep breath, pushed open the door and held it back for Davies and himself to enter the reception area.

Jackman wasn't a great fan of casinos. He'd played a few slot machines, dabbled at roulette and blackjack when he and Alice visited Las Vegas for their tenth wedding anniversary, but his job had exposed him to the darker side of gaming, the addictive side that, much like a drug, turned the most amiable person into the worst kind of hunter in pursuit of their dream.

They signed in at reception, flashed their ID cards and passed through mirrored double doors into a large room with low-level lighting and a round bar at the centre, surrounded by booths of leather chairs and sofas curled around small walnut tables. Glasses of every size and description glistened under the chandelier lighting on open shelves above the bar; bottles of spirits lined the walls behind.

This seemed to be some kind of central area. Several sets of glass double doors edged with gold were dotted around the perimeter of the room. He read the signs above them: restaurant, cabaret, games room, card games. Davies excused herself to go to the ladies' and Jackman followed the signs for the games room. The doors opened automatically as he approached and he crossed the threshold into what seemed like another bar area. A single blonde waitress clad in a clingy red dress with matching lipstick looked up and smiled as he approached. It seemed that twenty-four-hour opening meant twenty-four-hour party wear.

'I'm looking for the gaming room,' he said.

'Of course, sir.' Her accompanying smile showed off a set of straight white teeth an orthodontist would have been proud of. 'Just through the double doors at the far end.'

Jackman smiled back at her and her eyes glistened. 'Is there anything I can get you?' she said.

'You might be able to.' He held up his badge.

The woman leant her elbow on the bar and rested her chin on her hand, as if this was some sort of game. The position exposed a generous amount of cleavage.

'I'm looking for somebody. He's a customer here.' Jackman placed a hand in his pocket and realised that Davies had the photograph. He looked up in time to see the woman run her tongue along her teeth. A smile tickled her lips.

Suddenly he became aware of a presence beside him. 'Were you looking for this?' Davies asked and handed over the photo, rolling her eyes.

The woman stood back, stared at Davies a

moment and glanced at the photo he'd placed on the bar.

'Can I help you?'

Jackman turned to the direction of the voice and was confronted by a stocky man with heavy-set features in a creased black suit and open-necked white shirt. Jackman lifted his badge and introduced them both.

The man proffered a hand. 'Sam Chapman, I'm the manager. What can I do for you?'

'We are trying to trace a Chinese man by the name of Qiang Li. He also goes by the name of Peng Wu. I believe he is a customer here?'

'We have lots of customers.'

The lady behind the bar snorted and moved back to checking the spirits.

Chapman's mouth curled into a grin. 'Just a joke. You'd better come into my office.'

They followed him to a black door in the corner with a gold sign that read *Private* on the front and waited as he entered a code into a keypad on the wall beside. A bleep sounded and he pushed the door open.

Much like the restaurant earlier, the back corridors of the casino lacked the inside opulence. They followed the manager into an office where he moved behind a chipped laminate desk and clicked a few keys on his keyboard. Jackman and Davies sat on plastic chairs in front. A row of grey filing cabinets lined the wall behind him.

'All our customers are required to register and sign in, part of gaming regulations,' he said. 'No, we don't have a Qiang Li,' he said. He clicked a few more buttons. 'But we do have a Peng Wu registered. That's assuming he's the same one of course.'

'Would you recognise him?' Jackman asked.

Chapman shook his head. 'I doubt it. Do you have a picture?'

Davies pulled the photo out of her pocket and handed it over.

He shook his head. 'Looks like this was taken a few years ago,' he said and moved to pass it back.

'Take another look,' Jackman said and pointed out the scar on his face.

Chapman rubbed his chin. 'Hmmm. I might have seen him here.' He looked up. 'Honestly, can't remember. I don't spend a huge amount of time out in the main casino.'

'Do you know when he was last here?' Jackman asked.

Chapman clicked a few more buttons. 'Over the weekend. Several times on Saturday and Sunday by the looks of it. I can have my staff email you the digital footage if you want to take a look?'

'As soon as you can. I'll need a hard copy too.'

# 34

I glanced at Lonny. He was gently banging his head against the concrete wall behind him as his eyes surveyed the pit.

Eventually he stopped and sat there motionless for a second, his eyes staring at the grill above. 'Where do you think we are?' he said.

I took a deep breath, rested my head back. 'In the middle of nowhere.'

'What makes you say that?'

I sighed. 'Listen.' We sat in silence a moment. A bird chirped twice in the distance. I turned back to him. 'No people, no car engines, not even the sound of the trees today. I've tried shouting, screaming and no one comes. But I can smell vegetation, trees, leaves, soil. I'd say we're stuck in the middle of the countryside. In the middle of nowhere.'

I could feel the pithiness rise in my words as my temper came to the fore, not helped by the sticky heat that showed no promise of abating.

'Who'd build a concrete pit below the ground in the middle of nowhere?' he asked.

I looked around at the dirty, cracked walls. An old spider's web hung like a used fishing net in the corner. The floor was uneven and equally cracked, with a powdery finish. 'I don't know, for storage maybe? Looks old though. Like it was built years ago and forgotten.'

'Must have been something secret.'

'What do you mean?'

'Well you wouldn't go to the trouble of building a room like this below the ground if it hadn't concealed something secret.'

His words washed over me a minute. I'd never considered it a room. A room had soft flooring, painted walls, comfortable furniture, family photos or memorable pictures on the wall. A room was somewhere you chose to go, somewhere you relaxed, somewhere you spent time with friends and family. For me that simple word conjured up warm images of sitting on sofas around the fire back home. Yet he was right. I'd arranged it — a toilet in one corner, a drinks store in another, used the blankets as a makeshift bed and folded them back like a futon in the mornings. Somehow this semblance of order made it feel more like a dwelling, a room. The very idea brought tears to my eyes.

'I'm sorry.' He reached out, touched my shoulder.

'It's okay.' I swallowed, shook his hand away.

'No, it must have been awful for you to have been stuck here for so long on your own.'

It was true that the feeling of fear and sheer desperation was tempered slightly by the presence of another human being beside me. But uncertainty and a strong sense of disquiet still clawed away at me. 'What's going to happen to us?'

'I don't know, but I don't like it. Why keep us together? And for so long?'

Tears meandered down my cheeks. My eyes immediately became hot and swollen, I'd cried

203

so much over the past few days.

Lonny cleared his throat. 'Let's talk about something else.'

I wiped my fingers across my cheekbones. 'What?'

He didn't answer for a moment, as if he was trying to think of the right thing to say. 'What will you do when you finish this year?'

The optimism in his voice caught me. 'If we ever get out of here?'

He blinked a nod.

I took a deep breath, slowly exhaled before I answered. 'I have a conditional offer for Bristol University to study accountancy.'

'That's what you want to do?'

I stared at the floor. 'That's all I ever wanted to do. What about you?'

He shrugged a single shoulder. 'No idea. My father wants me to sign up to another course, continue my education over here. I'm not so sure.'

'You've not applied for anything yet?'

Lonny shook his head.

The disorder in his life surprised me. Having such an ambition from an early age meant my life had been governed by a strict schedule of routine. Every course was another stepping stone in my plan. I couldn't envisage last-minute decisions, a life left to chance. 'What will you do when we finish?'

'Go home for a bit. Or maybe I'll look around then. Haven't planned that far ahead.'

'It's only a few weeks away.'

He shrugged again. 'How do your parents feel

about you doing a degree over here, spending another three years away from home?'

'I'm sure a part of them feels sad. My mother especially. We're very close. But there are so many more opportunities in England. I like the idea that you get a job on your merit over here. It doesn't matter so much who you are or who you know. If you have the qualifications and the ability, you get a chance.' The sigh that followed caught in my throat. 'I grew up back home watching my parents fawn and pander to the authorities. Sitting quietly around the table at dinner parties, smiling sweetly at people I hardly knew. It was never-ending. And just like that,' I clicked my fingers, 'it could all disappear. Upset the wrong person and the rug is pulled from beneath you. It's all so precarious.'

Recognition spread across Lonny's face. 'So you want to stay over here permanently?'

'I did.' We sat in silence a moment. When I looked back at him, he was staring at me intently, as if he was examining every contour of my face.

'Don't you miss anything about home?' he asked.

I twisted my mouth. 'Of course. I miss my parents. I miss the way it all seemed so easy, the way they always looked out for me.'

'You surprise me.'

'Why?'

'You always seemed so happy on campus, so confident in class.'

I wasn't sure how to answer. 'What about you?'

'Me?'

'What do you miss about home?'

He gave a half-smile. 'I thought I'd miss the food, but in the end I didn't really. I'm pretty surprised how quickly I adapted. I do miss being beside the sea though.'

'There's sea here.'

'Yeah, if you want to take a road trip.'

'What about your family?'

'I don't think that makes much difference. I rarely saw my father. He was always at work. And when he was at home he was working, or entertaining. I just got in the way.'

'Your mother?'

'She died when I was nine.'

'I'm sorry. I had no idea.'

He stared into the open space in front of him. 'You weren't to know.'

An awkward silence followed. I wanted to probe more, ask him about his life back in Hong Kong, but his face looked far away, stuck in a different moment. Now wasn't the time. Although the mood that he'd so effectively lightened had now grown dark again.

I was beginning to feel breathless, cocooned by the rising levels of humidity. A crash in the distance caught my attention. I tilted my head, switching from Lonny to the grill at the top.

The noise came again, like the rumble of campus wheelie bins on refuse collection day.

'Thunder,' Lonny said. 'Good, at least it'll clear the air.'

# 35

Jackman took a deep breath and arched his back. They were now ensconced in the narrow side street just up from a painted black door, set back from the pavement slightly, which marked the entrance to Jie Wang's flat. From this position they could see past the overflowing bins beside the kitchen and down to the glamorous entrance lights of The Oriental Garden restaurant.

After the casino they'd visited Na Wang, Jie's sister, inside the flat they now watched. She was a petite woman, a mirror image of her brother but with softer features. Although her English was very clear, she'd been less than forthcoming on the whereabouts and habits of Min's uncle, claiming they'd had an acrimonious break-up and she knew little about him when they were together and even less now they'd parted. She didn't even flinch when Jackman mentioned his real name was Qiang Li. It was almost as if nothing to do with her former partner could surprise her anymore.

He thought back to the casino. The last address they had on file for Min's uncle was Lever Street, just like Na. Qiang had obviously gone to some trouble to carve out a new identity for himself under the name of Peng Wu. Until last summer he had a regular address and a job of sorts. Jackman heard the ring of Davies' mobile and watched as she fished it out of her bag. She mouthed the word 'Keane' as she answered.

It was after eight and low clouds had moved in, painting the air around them with premature brush strokes of grey, bringing in an early dusk and with it the threat of heavy rain.

'Hold on, I'll put you on speaker,' Davies said.

He watched as she pressed the screen and held it out at an angle in front of them. Keane's voice filled the car. 'What do you know?' Jackman asked.

'Mixed bag. Nothing more from Ward. After he discovered that we had accessed his phone records he's gone 'no comment'. Forensics have been in touch though. They've found some strands of hair down the side of the seats, seemingly pulled out at the root, and tiny spots of blood on the inside of the roof. They're going to put them through on a fast track for DNA. Hopefully we'll have some results by the morning.

'Excellent.'

'That's not all. We've been in touch with Northampton. Apparently Ward's firm installed a new central heating system at Katie Sharp's home last year.'

'Interesting.'

'Yeah. Nothing to link him with Min though. We checked the CCTV at the hotel in London. He was definitely there. Any luck with the uncle?'

'We've established he's still around the Chinese Quarter,' Jackman answered. 'Although he appears to be lying low. He was seen in the supermarket on Tuesday and he visited the casino last weekend. We're going to hang around to see if we can spot him tonight.'

'Okay, just one more thing. Reilly's been lording it up on BBC national news this evening. I'll send you the link.'

As Keane rang off, Jackman watched Davies run her fingers over the screen on her phone, then wait as it loaded. A newsreader in a red jacket filled the screen talking about the heat wave that dogged the nation, and predicted thunderstorms. Davies turned down the volume. 'Hold on, I need to run it forward.'

She fiddled with her phone a bit more, then nudged his arm. 'We're on.'

Jackman stared at the tiny phone screen as Reilly appeared. His hair was slicked back and his face freshly shaved.

'Looks like he's picked out his Gucci suit for the occasion,' Davies said.

Reilly lifted the notes in front of him, although didn't refer to them as he shared the fact that they had made important inroads into the investigation into Ellen Readman's murder. He called the arrest today 'a significant development'.

The journalist asked him about the activity in the village of Clifford Chambers that morning. 'That's a line of enquiry I've had my team looking into for some time. I can't share any of the details right now, but I'm fairly confident we are moving in the right direction and will be in a position to charge very shortly.' His words were as smooth as chocolate with just the right

209

measure of reassurance, his face conveyed the perfect level of gravitas as he continued to say how they'd worked around the clock to solve this case and to thank everyone involved in seeking to make Stratford safe once more.

'Urrrgh! Where does he spew that from?'

Jackman glanced across at Davies. Her jaw was hanging at an awkward angle. He looked back at the screen to watch Reilly give one more sincere nod, then retreat.

Davies put her phone back in her bag. ' "That's a line of enquiry I've had my team looking into for some time . . . " God, he's full of it.'

Jackman shook his head. 'Don't let it bother you.'

She turned to face him. 'I wouldn't if the powers that be didn't think he was so marvellous.'

'What, Janus?'

'No! The new bloody chief constable. Apparently they're always on the golf course together. He thinks the sun shines out of Reilly's arse.'

They sat in silence for a moment.

'Is that what we've got to look forward to now? Political policing?'

Jackman shrugged.

'Roll on the next ten years,' she said. 'If that's the case my thirty can't come soon enough.'

Jackman opened a bottle of water and took a glug. Even with the windows wound down the car felt stuffy. He glanced at the entrance to Jie Wang's flat.

Davies followed his eye line. 'Are we sure

there's only one entrance?'

Jackman nodded. 'Only one accessible from the street. The other is through the back of the restaurant and we'd spot him going in from here. I think we're pretty much covered.'

The rain came down gently at first, blurring Jackman and Davies' view as small spots littered the windscreen. Within a few minutes it had changed force to huge blobs falling from the sky at breakneck speed that clattered as they hit the vehicle.

A flicker of lightning in the distance was followed by the rumble of thunder. Jackman tucked his elbow inside and raised the window. He couldn't imagine who would want to come out in that weather.

★　★　★

Hours later, Jackman rolled his shoulders and checked the clock on the dash. It was 3.53 a.m. He shifted his gaze to the seat next to him where long tendrils of black curls hung down, tumbling across Davies' shoulders and the surrounding seat.

He stared at her a moment, listening to her soft raspy breaths as she slept.

They'd sat and watched people trailing in and out of the restaurant for hours. Cars crawled, then later spun by on the main road at the bottom as it thinned out. Finally, the restaurant lights turned off. The staff filed out.

Jackman loved covert work. The thought that something could happen at any moment excited him. It represented the hands-on policing that he'd joined the force for, all those years back, although apart from an urban fox and the odd cat nothing had appeared tonight.

Glints of first light were already filtering through the darkness. The sun would come up soon. He'd watched so many sunrises this past year that he was accustomed to the gentle brightening of the air around him, the warmth of those first early-morning rays on his skin.

The birds had already started jostling in their roosts, twittering together, warming their voices up for the morning chorus.

He sat there for several moments, lost in the expanse of his mind. Slowly, his thoughts dissipated into the dust motes that gathered in the surrounding air as the sun's rays struck through stronger. Here it comes, he thought, that warm hue of weariness that never failed to strike in those waking hours when everyone was rising, fresh for the day. It was a constant battle, a curse of insomniacs across the globe. And he fought the sleep that evaded him so resolutely every night.

# 36

I woke suddenly to the sound of dripping. A small puddle had collected beneath the gap above and was rapidly expanding, just inches from my feet. Instinctively I drew them in slightly.

A silvery darkness swamped the pit. The storm had cleared the air, but sent the temperatures plummeting. As my gaze rested on Lonny, I jumped.

He lay propped up next to me, eyes wide open, his whole body juddering.

'You alright?'

He looked back at me. 'Bloody hole. Goes from sticky heat to freezing in the course of a few hours. Are they the only blankets?'

I swallowed. I knew what I should do, but it felt wrong somehow. I hesitated for the shortest of seconds then lifted the corner of the blanket and looked at him tentatively. He gave a juddered nod, uncrossed his arms and sidled across. It felt strange, having a man that wasn't Tom beside me. But Lonny wasn't a complete stranger. Not now.

Time stood still as we laid there in the darkness together until his breaths steadied into a gentle rhythm and I found myself falling into a deep sleep.

# 37

Jackman yawned. Cars were beginning to pass through the main road at the end of the street as he knocked on the door of Jie Wang's flat. The sound of soft footfalls on carpet were followed by the turn of a key in a lock. The door opened swiftly. Jie's hair was spiked around the crown area as if he'd just rolled out of bed. He rubbed his eyes.

'No luck,' Jackman said. 'Any calls?'

Jie shook his head.

Jackman dug his hand into his pocket and passed over a card. 'Give us a call the moment he gets in touch, please?'

The car rocked slightly as he climbed back inside and shut the door. Davies awoke, sat up abruptly, rubbed the side of her neck and glanced at the clock on the dash.

'Wow, 7.13? Is it that time already?'

Jackman nodded. 'Afraid so. Sleep well?'

Davies pulled a face. 'Best night's sleep I've had in ages.'

'I wondered why you insisted on coming.' They both chuckled.

She reached up and tied her loose hair back behind her neck. 'Any visitors?'

'Nothing. I think we'll call it a day.' He reached for the ignition, just as his mobile buzzed.

'Jackman.'

Keane didn't bother to introduce himself. 'Sir,

there's been another kidnapping.'

A sharp pain spiked Jackman's lower back as he jerked forward. 'What do you mean?'

'Twenty-year-old male student from Hong Kong, name of Lonny Cheung, also studying at Stratford College. His father received a ransom demand yesterday. He alerted the college this morning, who contacted us.'

'How long has he been missing?' Jackman asked.

'Not sure, but the email is the same as Min Li's, practically a carbon copy. It seems we have a double kidnapping on our hands. Janus is gathering everyone together and looking for you, sir. Briefing's here in an hour.'

Jackman thanked Keane, rang off and immediately redialled Janus.

'Will, where the hell are you?' She didn't attempt to hide the annoyance in her voice.

'In Birmingham. We stayed over on the off-chance of running into . . . '

'Well, get back here,' she interrupted. 'Now. Reilly needs your help.'

The line went dead. Another kidnapping. Another student from the college.

Jackman recalled Janus' words, 'Reilly needs your help.' What did that mean? There was no reason for Reilly to be involved. Surely he was tied up with the new leads on the Readman case?

He could just imagine the smile that wormed its way onto Reilly's face at the thought of taking over another high-profile case straight after claiming to solve the Readman murder. A positive result would probably be enough to

215

whisk him through the next promotion board. Jackman ground his teeth. Some people would go to any lengths for an ounce of glory.

★ ★ ★

The M6 was thick with traffic that Friday morning and they crawled out of Birmingham, not managing to pick up any kind of speed until they'd cleared Spaghetti Junction. The sun had risen early and the storm that cleared the air last night now seemed a distant memory.

As they passed the Dunlop building on their left, the traffic slowed again. Jackman turned to Davies. 'This is bloody hopeless. Give Keane a call and see if they've anything back on forensics.'

Davies rummaged through her bag, retrieved her phone and waited for it to dial.

Within seconds Keane's voice filled the car.

'Morning,' she said. 'You're on speaker. We're held up in traffic. Anything back on forensics?'

The phone line crackled and scratched. 'I keep losing you,' he said.

Davies shook the phone. They crawled forward another couple of metres. 'Looks like we're back in signal,' she said. 'What do you know?'

'Hold on. Forensics are just back. There's a match on the hair samples with Ellen Readman and,' he paused and they heard the sound of a page turning, 'that's interesting . . . '

Jackman leant closer to the phone. 'What?'

'Looks like they found a DNA match on the blood with her too. Nothing on Katie Sharp yet, but looks like enough for us to charge.'

# 38

A blast of warm air tickled my ear. I wriggled. The concrete scratched at my skin as I edged a few inches away. Again.

I turned awkwardly, stretched around and looked back at Lonny. A stripe of light illuminated his face which was pointed towards me, his breaths slow and deep, relaxed in sleep. He was close enough for me to feel the heat that radiated from his body, watch the rise and fall of his chest.

It was different waking up with somebody else in the pit. Almost comforting. I stared at him a moment.

He lacked the traditional round face and angled eyes of many Chinese people. His face was long and framed with dark eyebrows. A shadow of stubble was just forming across his chin. His eyes, still glued shut, were shaped like teardrops. Quite handsome, really.

I watched him awhile. His face was relaxed, peaceful, the lips slightly parted. His cheek flinched. Maybe he was dreaming.

Back home I dreamt a lot. They weren't full stories or scenarios, just snippets of scenes, most of which I forgot within minutes of waking, although one was very set in my mind: I was in an exam room. I turned over the paper and my pen wouldn't work. I picked up my spare and that didn't work either, nor did the invigilator's whose eye I managed to catch. I seemed to try

217

pen after pen and nothing made a mark on the page.

I looked back at Lonny. I hadn't dreamt in the pit. My nights in here were filled with snippets of shallow rest, where I jolted awake intermittently. I knew the rats were close by, lurking in the shadows.

A definite line of light brightened the pit today. It was like sunshine bursting through the crack in a pair of thick shades. The warmth beckoned me like a seductive finger. I imagined it was a lovely day outside, the storm having washed the plant life clean, the air cleared with freshness that only rain leaves behind.

Was there a field above? I knew there were trees, I'd heard their branches bending and creaking during the storm. Maybe there was a meadow too? I could see it in my mind. The leaves lush and extra green, blades of grass swaying in the morning breeze.

I skimmed the concrete walls. It was like living in a parallel world, a microclimate. Down here we got to experience the smells, witness when day turned to night, were fed and watered. Our whole lives controlled. We were aware of the natural changes in the outside world but prevented from experiencing or enjoying them.

I glanced back at Lonny and a thought struck me. That was the first time I'd slept all night with another man. Tom and I had spent time together in my room, but he only ever stayed until the early hours. My apartment was small, my bed narrow. Tom was so tall that I felt squashed when he joined me in my little bed.

218

I couldn't help but wonder what Tom would think of my being here, like this with Lonny. I told myself that it didn't matter. We'd simply edged together to keep warm, prompted by self-preservation, but it still felt oddly strange to be so close to somebody, yet feel so far away.

What was Tom doing now? Did he miss me? I missed his warm smile, his sharp wit, his ability to lighten the load and make me laugh. I felt torn though. Meeting up with Tom again would raise the whole abortion issue, force a decision, and I still didn't know what to do.

Instinctively, I rubbed my stomach. Although I hadn't felt my baby move, I knew it was there even before the pregnancy test had confirmed it. I just felt different. Protective and wholesome. My stomach grumbled back at me. I needed to eat something. My child needed feeding.

As I scrambled towards the food we'd pushed to the corner to make room for Lonny, I heard a distant scratch. I glanced back at Lonny. He was still fast asleep. My eyes darted around the pit. All was quiet.

I edged forward and it came again. I reached back and grabbed an empty bottle. Pity the rat that wants to take my food.

I approached slowly, grabbed the bag containing bread and biscuits, and raised the bottle in my other hand as I whipped it away.

A squeak made me jump. The baby rat stared up at me for a split second, wide-eyed, then bolted up the wall.

*I'd let my guard down since Lonny had joined me in the pit. I'd slept deeply. I couldn't afford to do that again.*

# 39

Jackman felt a rivulet of sweat trickle down his back as he stared at the photo that filled the screen. Lonny Cheung was leaning against the side of a car, one ankle wrapped over another, hands pushed deep into the pockets of his jeans.

'God, can somebody open a window?' Janus said. She wafted her face with her hand. 'It's like an oven in here.'

Russell squeezed through the bodies that filled the briefing room and undid the latch. The window creaked as it opened. 'What do we know about him?' Jackman asked.

'Lo Cheung, known generally as Lonny,' Keane said. 'Son of Chinese shipping magnate, Miu Cheung, from Hong Kong. Twenty-year-old student, came over here to study the access course at Stratford College last September.'

'I've spoken to the college principal. He's one of the so-called lazy rich kids, given a generous allowance from his father to get him out of the way. Drives around in a Subaru Impreza, attends just enough lectures to ensure he's not kicked off the course. Hence he wasn't reported missing. First we knew about his disappearance was the contact from his father.'

'What about friends, relatives over here?' Jackman asked.

'Nothing. Seems he's a bit of a loner. Rents a

flat off campus, lives alone.'

'Off campus?'

'Yeah, apparently the rich kids prefer to organise their own accommodation. Means they don't have to share.'

'We need to find out everything about him,' Jackman said. 'Get back out to the college, interview everyone who knows him and everyone who's ever taught him. What's he doing when he's not at college? Take a look at his flat. Find his mobile number and run a check on his calls. See if you can site his phone. Who is he associating with? Who was the last person to see him? We also need to find out about his life in Hong Kong. Has anyone spoken to his father?'

'Keane took the initial call,' Russell said, 'and I called Mr Cheung back when we'd got an interpreter. His English is sketchy, but he's going ballistic from what I can make out. Talking about sending his own investigators over here.'

'That's all we need!' Janus said.

Jackman ignored her. 'Okay,' he nodded to Keane. 'Talk us through what we know so far.'

'It seems he disappeared yesterday. Didn't turn up for class, but nobody suspected anything, as that's not unusual. The first alert was an email to his father's business at 4.30 p.m. our time.'

Keane pressed a button on his laptop and the image of Lonny was replaced with a typed message in Cantonese. He read the translation below it:

*DO NOT CONTACT THE POLICE OR THE PRESS, EITHER IN CHINA OR BRITAIN, IF YOU WANT TO SEE YOUR SON ALIVE.*

222

*We have Cheung Lo. He is safe and unharmed at the moment.*

*If you want to see him again, follow these instructions:*

*We require £40,000 in used bank notes. The notes should be tied together, wrapped in an orange supermarket carrier bag and taken to the waste bin in the lay-by on Bracken Ridge Road, Turnley Industrial Estate, BIRMINGHAM at precisely 12.30 a.m. on 23rd of May. Cheung Lo will then be released.*

*At present Lo has food and water and is in good health. If you do not pay we won't kill him. We will fail to meet his basic needs and he will die a slow death of starvation in captivity.*

'Same town, different industrial estate,' Jackman said. 'Practically doubled the ransom. And no picture. Do we know where it was sent from?'

'Another internet cafe in Birmingham. Different one this time.'

Jackman sighed. 'And nobody alerted us.'

'Same as last time, sir,' Keane said. 'Mr Cheung got in touch with a contact to raise the cash and make the drop. Apparently located them through a business associate. A contact he won't disclose.'

'What about the drop location? Was that changed again at the last minute?'

Keane scratched his chin. 'Doesn't seem so. I asked the father if the people that made the drop saw anything, but he said the location was too open. They were afraid to hang around in case the kidnapper might see them and be scared off.'

It was a risky move to keep the drop location

the same as in the ransom note. If Mr Cheung had contacted the authorities they could have staked out the place, or watched from a distance. Jackman thought back to his conversation with Ken yesterday. How suspicious the Chinese were of their own authorities, how they preferred to police themselves wherever possible. 'So, we have two students taken from the same college. Same method of contact, both ransoms met and nobody released. Where are they? Did they know each other?'

'Could be a love pact they cooked up to enable them to elope?' Russell said.

Jackman considered this. 'At least that gives them more chance of still being alive.'

'I've already sent a request to the Embassy for information on the family,' Russell said, 'although I'm not holding my breath. If past experience is anything to go on, we'll hear back by the end of next week.'

'Have you tried International Liaison?' Jackman said. 'They might be able to help us speed things up a bit. They don't have a presence for China, but they might still have a desk for Hong Kong. If not, they might have some old files or contacts. See what you can find out. We need to know if the parents' businesses are linked in any way. And see what you can dig up on the Cheung family.'

'Any news on tracing Min's uncle?' Janus asked.

'He's very elusive,' Jackman said. 'We know he's still around the Chinese Quarter. He was spotted in the supermarket a few days ago, and he's been in the casino. We're still working on it.'

Jackman thanked his team and glanced around the room as they retreated to their desks. His eyes landed on Reilly who was stood at the back beside the window. He'd been conspicuous in his silence during the briefing. Jackman was just wondering why Janus had brought him in when he felt a presence beside him and turned to see her staring up at him.

'Will, I . . . '

'We need to decide how to handle the media with this one,' he interrupted. 'Take it national. That way we can appeal for witnesses at the drop locations.'

'Sir?'

Jackman looked across to see Russell calling him. 'Excuse me,' he said, but Janus caught his arm as he moved forward.

'Meet me in the conference room in ten minutes,' she said, then walked out of the room.

* * *

A mixture of frustration and fatigue pummelled into Jackman as he climbed the stairs to the conference room. He couldn't understand the need to meet in there when they could easily have discussed the press strategy in the incident room downstairs. He knocked on the door and waited several moments before he pushed it open to find Janus sitting alone. He glanced around the empty room. 'Where is everyone?'

'Sit down, Will,' Janus said. She opened her arm to indicate the chair beside her, although

225

there was a definite tightness in her voice.

Jackman sat gingerly. 'What's going on?'

Janus rubbed her lips together before she spoke. 'Will, I'm a little concerned for your welfare.'

'What?'

'You've missed your last three counselling sessions.'

'We spoke about this the other day. I've got one tonight.'

'Good. But I'm very aware that this is a high-profile case and you've had a lot on this past year with Alice's illness. I want you to take some time off. We can call it compassionate leave.'

'I don't need compassionate leave. I just need to do my job.'

'Well, take today at the very least. Go home, rest up, attend your counselling session and come back tomorrow when you're fresh.'

Jackman could feel his patience dwindling. 'It's not . . . '

She raised a hand to silence him. 'That's an order,' she said, and then her voice softened. 'Will, take a look at yourself. You're unshaved. You look like you're still wearing yesterday's clothes.'

'I've been up all night staking out Min's uncle. Of course I'm unshaved. He's still our best lead.'

Janus shook her head, gave a short cough. 'Anyway, I have to go away for a few days. Back to Aberdeen. My father is ill.'

'I'm sorry to hear that.'

Janus nodded. 'Now that Reilly has charged

on the Readman case, he can leave his team to build the file for the CPS which frees up his time. So I've asked him to chip in and give us a hand.'

'I don't need a hand.'

'Look.' Janus removed her glasses. 'Nobody is doubting your ability to do your job here, Will. It's just, with another kidnapping we could certainly use the help. And the powers that be feel that Reilly has the confidence of the press.'

'I don't believe this. Are you saying I don't?'

'I didn't say that, but we do need to change strategy. And some of the decisions you've made over the past few days have been questioned.'

'Like what?'

'It's felt that by not releasing details of Min Li's kidnapping, other students were put at risk.'

'It's felt? By who?'

Janus rubbed her forehead, but didn't answer.

'I was following protocol! Preserve life. Shut down the press. Isn't that what we're taught?'

Janus took a deep breath. 'It's a judgement call. You made the decision you felt was right at the time.'

'The kidnappers were explicit — no police involvement. You can't say that decision led to another kidnapping!'

'Maybe not. But sharing the details may have made the college students more aware, more vigilant . . . '

'They were all told to be extra careful, to go out in pairs, look out for one another. You were at the press conference with me when we pushed that one home.'

Janus ignored his interruption. 'All I'm saying is that the chief constable feels if we'd been a little more transparent with the media, there is a possibility that parents would have been alerted and more cautious.'

'No.' Jackman shook his head. 'I'm not with you. I'm sorry to hear about your father. I really am. But we're never transparent with the media. We tell them what we want them to report, what we feel can help us progress a case.'

'Look, Will, I'm getting pressure from above. They seem to think it's likely that if Lonny's father had known about the other kidnapping he might have come to the police when he received the ransom email, given us a chance to monitor the drop and try to find out who's behind this.'

'That's just speculation. So I'm your scapegoat now?'

Janus sighed. 'Nobody is a scapegoat. You did what you thought was best. But now we need to make some changes, to bring the press back on side.'

Jackman clenched his teeth.

Janus reached forward and gathered up the papers in front of her, feeding them into a pink envelope file. 'Right, we're in agreement then.' She stood. 'I'll see you after the weekend. You'll need to work with Reilly until then.'

The door clicked shut behind her. Jackman stood up and walked to the window. If they were so concerned for his welfare, why did he feel like he was being stitched up?

His thoughts were interrupted by a babble of raised voices outside. He peered down and

228

recognised a few members of the local press gathering outside the staff entrance below. That was all he needed, an encounter with the media. If they were gathered for a press conference, he certainly didn't want to catch Reilly mid-flow. He'd have to find another way out.

He scooted past the incident room, down the stairs and along the corridor until he found the door that linked the station to the neighbouring Magistrates Court building. Relieved to find it unlocked, he moved through the corridors until he reached the entrance and cast a cursory glance towards the steps outside. Empty. He slipped out, walked across the adjacent gardens and over into Chestnut Walk.

Jackman marched down the street, past numerous parked cars and an overflowing skip, but he didn't really see any of them. Right now he wanted to get as far away from the station as possible. He needed time to think.

He passed the preparatory school and continued into Old Town. He could see the spire of the Holy Trinity in the distance. A car whizzed past, followed by a cyclist in fluorescents.

As he entered the wrought-iron gates that led into the churchyard, a squirrel scurried past him, stopping him in his tracks. He glanced up at the imposing stone building. Jackman wasn't a religious man. He'd attended church years ago; Alice had thought it would be good to introduce Celia to Christianity when she was young, 'so that she could make her own mind up about religion'. But there was something about the ancient stonework of this particular church that he found strangely calming.

He skirted around the perimeter of the churchyard and paused at the bottom. This was one of his favourite spots. The vista looked across the River Avon and into the open fields of the recreational ground beyond with its trimmed willows. A couple of ducks quacked noisily as they moved across the water in front of him.

Jackman sat on a bench beneath the yew tree and allowed his mind to wander. How dare Janus express concern at his decisions. She would have done the same in his shoes, he was convinced of it. But then he remembered her words, 'The powers that be feel . . . '

This was the first case he'd managed alone. Janus was covering her back by ordering him to take the rest of the day off, inviting Reilly to step in. If the investigation took a turn for the worse, if the two students were found dead, or the case management was criticised by a review team she and Reilly would turn this on him.

He considered them both for a moment. They made a good team, their shared obsession with budgets, management meetings and figures dominating their careers. Neither of them concerned for the welfare of anyone but themselves.

Jackman thought back to the homicide unit before Reilly. His former DCI, Ernie Stiles, had been an old-school, hands-on detective. He had a wealth of experience behind him, but was always willing to listen to the views of others. When he retired, Jackman applied to the board to take his job.

He'd filed the papers, attended the assessment

day, not because he was ambitious in the traditional sense, more because he knew that he would never be able to completely manage his own homicide team as a DI. The role of senior investigating officer, heading murder and major incident enquiries, was given to DCI and superintendent rank and it largely depended on which SIO you had, as to how much freedom you were given.

But then Alice had the accident.

The interviews came a month afterwards and although he attended, he would be the first to admit that he wasn't himself. But what really stuck in his throat, what riled him to the core, was that Reilly had attended the same board. And passed.

# 40

The light was fading slightly; evening was drawing in. 'You hungry?'

Lonny nodded.

It didn't matter so much that all the meals were the same, more that they were eaten regularly. Not just for me, but for the baby too. By now I recognised when the sun was at its brightest as lunchtime, and when it dulled in the evening as tea time. The routine served to break up the day, provide intervals in between the long stretches of boredom. And right now I needed that.

I pulled a slice of bread out of the bag, balanced a biscuit and apple on the top and offered them to Lonny. The tiny ration looked unappetising and dry, something we'd have dressed up with meats and condiments in the real world. But down here, it was all we had.

I passed him a bottle of water and was suddenly reminded of playing house as a child. Being seated beneath a table covered with a cloth whilst my friend served me pretend meals on plastic plates.

I collected my own food and sat down beside Lonny. We ate in silence, first the biscuit, then the bread, which clung to the top of my mouth, and finally the apple to wipe my teeth clean. The acidity probably did them more harm than good, but at least they felt fresher.

The memory of playing house faded, replaced by a picture of home. Meal time. Sitting around the table together when there were no visitors and it was just the three of us. These were rare moments I cherished. My father would fill our minds with stories from the factory. My mother would smile, her face fulfilled and wholesome at sharing a meal with her family.

A sudden pang of homesickness hit me.

Lonny crunched into his apple. 'What you thinking about?' he said, his words muffled through the food.

'My parents.'

'You miss them?'

I faced him and nodded. 'I didn't too much. Not before. Life at the college was so busy. But now they feel so far away.'

He pressed his hand on my wrist and stared at me with such sincerity that it startled me slightly. 'Must be nice to be so close.'

'You're not?'

He withdrew his hand, finished his apple and slung the core into the rubbish corner. I watched it nestle down into the leaves.

Lonny shook his head. 'My father was always at work.'

'So were my parents really. My mother taught at the local school, my father spent most of his time at the factory. My grandmother was the one who took me to school, helped me with my homework when they weren't around. What about you?'

'Nannies mostly.'

A bird was singing in the distance, something

we probably wouldn't notice in the real world, but down here senses were heightened. It made me realise what a beautiful sound it was. My eyes caught a kink in the corner of the blanket and as I reached forward to straighten it, I felt his eyes glance behind me.

'What's that?'

I turned. He was running his finger along my name carved into the stone. 'Oh, just wanted to do something.' I could feel the heat rise in my cheeks.

'It's a good idea.' He moved in closer and squinted at my name written first in English and then in Chinese.

A shower of powdered concrete scattered across the edge of the blanket as he brushed his hand across the wall. I cleared my throat. 'I just thought it might be a clue, you know, for someone.'

He nodded, although his eyes didn't leave the words. Slowly he turned to face me. 'It's missing a date.'

'What?'

'There's always a date. Think about it. We don't know who will discover it and when it will be discovered. If there's a date, they can link it together with your disappearance.'

I stared at the writing. He was right, but the prospect of a date made it seem all the more like an epitaph. Like we were carving out our own gravestones. I drew a sharp breath, pushed the notion to the back of my mind.

'What date should we use?'

'Monday, I suppose. The date you disappeared.'

'What about you?'

'We'll worry about that later. Let's get this one finished first. Do you still have the stone?'

'It was a nail.' I reached down and passed it across to him. 'It's a little blunt now.'

Dust skipped into the air as he pulled back the blanket, leant forward and began to grind the nail into the wall. The sound of the metal working into the old concrete, going over the same area time and time again was strangely comforting. Like those noises that emit from apartments nearby while you are sitting around the dinner table or watching television.

As I watched him, I was struck by how lucky I'd been. In spite of them both working, my parents still seemed to make time for me. Even at the age of five or six my father would sit on the floor and play with me. My mother and I would cook together. I was never showered with material items, but I always felt loved.

'It must have been hard,' I said.

His head twitched, but he didn't face me. 'What?'

'To have been brought up by nannies.'

'No choice. My mum died.'

'I'm sorry.'

'Was a long time ago. I was only nine.'

'What was she like?'

The air thickened between us. It was a while before he spoke and when he did his voice sounded distant. 'My memories are a bit vague.' He sat back on his heels and scratched the side of his neck. 'I remember cuddling up with her on the sofa, I must have been about five I guess,'

235

his mouth formed a gentle smile, 'and she would read to me. Peter Pan and The Lion, The Witch and the Wardrobe. Stories by great British authors, she called them. We used to have picnics in the park, huge picnics with every type of food you could imagine . . . ' His words trailed off.

'Was it sudden?'

His face tightened. 'I found her in the kitchen, sitting in a pool of blood.'

'She killed herself?'

'Slashed her wrists. Didn't even say goodbye.'

My hand flew to my mouth. 'I'm so sorry.'

'Apparently she'd suffered from depression. Nobody told me that though. Took me years to work it out.'

I wanted to say something more, something comforting, but the words caught in my throat.

'I didn't speak for months afterwards. And when I finally did, it was in English.' He turned to face me. 'My mother was English so my father hired British nannies to encourage me. As time passed I did speak in Cantonese too, but I've always preferred English.'

'That's why your accent is so good.'

His mouth formed a smile that didn't reach his eyes.

'So you can stay here as long as you want?'

'What do you mean?'

'British mother. Chinese father. You get the best of both worlds.'

'No such luck. My passport says Chinese. Don't you know, we're not allowed dual citizenship?'

A shiver slipped down my spine. It reminded me of Lauren — she always said that happened when someone walked across your grave. Suddenly I felt very sad. 'Do you think they'll fly us back?'

'What?'

'We're Chinese citizens. If we die down here, do you think they'll fly our bodies home to our families?'

# 41

Jackman stared at the magnolia walls around him and sighed inwardly. The high ceiling, wrought-iron fireplace, large sash window and polished floorboards were akin to his front room. But that's where the similarities ended. The bookcase in the corner was filled with modern classics, the sort you bought in bound collections out of Sunday newspaper supplements and never read; the circular coffee table in the centre gave off a permanently unused sheen, the single painting on the wall of pink roses in a vase was flat and lifeless. Everything in this room had been meticulously arranged to afford basic comfort whilst discouraging distraction.

He cast a fleeting glance at Doctor 'call me Richard' Stephens who sat opposite him, hands folded on top of an A4 pad resting on his lap, a biro poking between his fingers. They were amidst one of those long silences where Richard would stare at him, angle his head if he made eye contact. It was tedious.

Jackman used the 'silence technique' and 'open questions' to incite conversation during interviews. In fact, when he thought about it, this part of their jobs was quite similar. Jackman worked hard to make his witnesses and suspects feel at ease, create an atmosphere whereby they were comfortable, encourage them to talk. He too broke down the barriers to find the truth.

But that's where the similarities ended. Once he had gleaned the facts, the justice system took care of the victim, witness, suspect. Richard picked away, peeling back each layer and rummaging through the emotions beneath until, eventually, there was nothing left.

Jackman's eyes rested on the box of tissues on the sideboard in the corner, just within reach of Richard's chair, and wondered how many times he'd stretched across and passed them over, or even whether he'd counted. Richard adjusted position. The pen rolled off his lap and rattled as it hit the floor. Jackman watched him reach down and retrieve it, sit back and cross one leg over the other, making him appear at a strange angle. His mind switched back to the investigation. He wondered how they were getting on at the new drop site. Whether they'd heard from the Embassy, or got a new lead on Min's uncle.

Richard sniffed and pushed his glasses up his nose. 'I'd like to talk about the night of the accident,' he said.

'Why?' Jackman asked.

'Because we've never gone into it in any detail. I think it might help.'

You or me? Jackman thought. But Janus' words were still at the very forefront of his mind. 'Just go along and keep the appointments. At least it'll keep welfare off our backs.' He bit back his frustration. 'What do you want to know?'

'Why don't you talk me through it?'

Jackman paused and shifted in his seat as if he was trying to recover some distant memory from the filing cabinets buried deep inside his mind.

Problem was they weren't buried deep. These were the memories that suffocated the suggestion of sleep and haunted his every waking hour.

Jackman cleared his throat. 'I'd been to a retirement party in Leamington. My old boss. I didn't intend to drink, but I got pulled into the joviality of the evening. In the end, I couldn't drive, so I called Alice to come pick me up.'

'What was Alice doing?'

'Pardon?'

'When you called her?'

Jackman struggled to see the relevance. 'She was in bed reading.'

'And how did she react?'

Jackman shrugged. 'Wasn't best pleased. She asked if anyone else could bring me, but there wasn't anyone, so finally she agreed to come out.'

'And what time was this?'

Jackman thought for a moment. 'The accident happened at 12.49. I remember looking at the clock on the dash. She must have left around midnight and arrived with me half an hour later.'

'And how did she seem?'

'A bit snappy, but that was quite understandable.'

'The alcohol didn't impair your memory?'

'I said I'd been drinking, not that I was drunk. I knew exactly what was happening.'

'What do you mean by snappy?'

'She was tired. Grumpy at being pulled out of bed. We bickered a little. I'd promised to be home early, said I wouldn't drink.'

'Can you recall the conversation?'

Jackman shook his head to hide the lie. He

could remember it, the exact words, as if it was yesterday, but he wasn't about to share that with Richard.

'What happened next?'

'Not much. We drove in silence for a while. Then a car crossed the carriageway. It came from nowhere, hit us head-on.'

It was a moment before Richard spoke. 'Can you remember what happened next?'

'I remember a pain in my head like my skull splitting in two. The car lay on its side. Alice was unconscious. I couldn't get her to wake up. I just kept thinking: get her out of the car.'

The sound of a siren passing outside broke the stillness that saturated the room. Jackman suddenly realised that he'd become lost in his memories. He took a deep breath, regained his composure.

Richard sat back in his chair. 'Will, who do you think is responsible for the accident that caused your wife's condition?'

Jackman looked back at him. 'The idiot that was driving too fast and lost control of his car, of course.' But his words were tainted with a soft sadness. The idiot was a young lad in his new car showing off to his mates. He had lost his life that night before he'd even reached his nineteenth birthday. It was a cruel injustice, an accident, just like Alice.

Richard surveyed him for some time. 'Is there anyone else you feel was responsible?'

Jackman's voice came out in barely a whisper. 'If I hadn't been drinking she'd never have been on the road that night.'

# 42

I felt Lonny's eyes on me.

'Do you know what I'd really like to eat now?' he asked.

My eyes rested on the bread and biscuits in the corner. All that was left were the remnants of those nibbled by the baby rat. I shook my head.

'McDonald's fries. Large.'

A weak laugh escaped me. I was expecting him to come out with something deep and meaningful, or a Chinese dish he treasured. Not McDonald's. I could feel him laughing next to me and giggled quietly. Suddenly, I realised I hadn't laughed for so long. Even before the pit, all the problems with Tom and the baby. A dark cloud had prevailed over my life for what seemed like ages. I indulged in the loose feeling now and the release of those happy pips of endorphins shooting around my veins felt like a medicine.

'What about you?' he eventually asked.

I rested my head back on the concrete. A week ago I'd have probably said chocolate. Cadbury Dairy Milk. Many a dark evening I'd sat in my apartment, poring over my laptop, craving its velvety texture and rich sweetness. But now, oddly, I craved the crisp freshness of pear, papaya, lychee, banana.

'Fruit salad.'

He laughed. 'You're so boring.'

'What about you, fries? Must be the British side of you.'

'Maybe.'

'I think it's great. You get the best of both cultures.'

'Or you never quite fit in either.'

Just as I twisted to face him, he grinned. 'You're so gullible.'

I nudged his shoulder. A lukewarm heat filled me. It was nice to have Lonny. He was good company. For a short moment, I forgot where I was.

I stretched out my legs and felt a sudden stab of pain that made me gasp and grab my stomach. The baby.

Lonny's face dropped a little. 'You okay?'

I didn't answer. Another stab, harder this time, I drew my knees in. I wrapped my arms around my stomach and stared at the pockmarked concrete in front of me, trying to regulate my breathing.

'Min, what's wrong?'

The pain eased a little, but I still couldn't answer. Instead I concentrated on my breathing, slowly in and out.

'What is it? Are you sick?'

I huddled into myself. What was happening? And in that moment I knew. I couldn't let my baby die, it was too much a part of me to let go. It wouldn't be easy, but I'd have to find a way.

'Min, please? Talk to me?'

I turned to face Lonny. I'd almost forgotten he was sat next to me. I opened my mouth to say something, then closed it again like a fish out of water.

'You're scaring me now.'

I cleared my throat. The pain had lessened to a simmer, just beneath the surface. 'I . . . I think it's nothing really. Just a little indigestion. I need to sit quietly for a bit.

He stared directly at me. The look in his eyes told me he didn't believe a word I'd said. And why not? It wasn't true. Something had stopped me from telling him the truth, but I had no idea why. He'd confided in me about his mother. Yet a little voice inside my head told me this secret was better kept. For now.

# 43

Back home later, Jackman took a deep breath and eased back into the sofa.

Alice's presence oozed from every room in the house. Not the mute, glassy-eyed shell that lay in Broom Hills. The real Alice. The vibrant Dane with the quirky nature, wicked sense of humour and smile that could light up a room. If he concentrated hard enough he could still feel her presence here — curled up with Erik on the sofa, feet tucked beneath her, chuckling at her beloved American sitcoms; in the kitchen, hair pulled back into a messy half-ponytail as she lifted a flapjack out of the oven; laid flat on the floor of her study, eyes clamped together, Bach playing in the background. Alice loved Bach. Whenever she had a research problem, she laid in the dark with her music, allowing the rhythms to concentrate her mind.

Jackman had never been keen on classical music himself. She laughed when he hiked up the volume on the radio to listen to the Foo Fighters, the Red Hot Chili Peppers or Kings of Leon. But right now, he felt a yearning to listen to Bach. He pulled the long curtains together shutting out the evening sunshine, laid prostrate on the hearth rug and pressed play on the iPod. Erik wandered over and slumped next to him as the soft ripples of music began to play. The case gently filtered into his mind.

He could see Min Li leaving the Old Thatch Tavern, her heels tapping the pavement as she moved in the direction of the police station. The black BMW appeared, the car whose occupants had spoken to her. Were they the words that encouraged her to move back to the pub? What would have happened if she hadn't turned there, if she'd have continued down the road? Was she heading in any particular direction or just walking off a rage?

Jackman sighed. The music became louder, the tension growing. He imagined her reaching the pub. Did she hesitate, consider going back inside? He knew she'd continued, the camera footage showed she turned the corner into Greenhill Street. Yet she never reached the end of the street. She was taken somewhere along that stretch.

The music continued to work up to its crescendo as more thoughts crashed through his mind. Her kidnapper had picked her out, researched her family background, organised a location to store her, watched and trailed her for some time. Ready and waiting. What he didn't understand was why she hadn't been released. A business transaction. The ransom had been paid. So, where was she now?

The white Volkswagen with false plates, cloned from a similar van in nearby Coventry, passed through Greenhill Street just before her. It must have picked her up as she walked along that stretch. Where did it go next?

Track after track played as his mind kept going over and over the facts that were laid before him.

Extra protection had been placed at the college, yet amidst all that activity, Lonny Cheung had also been taken. The ransom note indicated he was taken by the same abductors. What was the link?

Eventually the room became silent. The music had played out. All he could hear were Erik's soft breaths next to him. He reached out and stroked his neck. The dog's tail beat the floor, but he didn't move.

Jackman jumped up and pressed repeat play before he resumed his position on the floor. Dusk crept in and slowly enveloped them in darkness. Alice used to tease him that he 'lived' his cases and she was right. He could already feel this one seeping through the pores in his skin until it sat beneath the surface. He'd joined the police force to make a difference, to help people in their darkest hour of need. But to live a case meant working it: interviewing witnesses, pounding the streets, visiting scenes; not sitting in an office, reading statements and setting strategy while delegating investigative actions to your team.

Jackman couldn't believe the cruel twist of fate that befell him when Reilly landed the position as his boss. Yes, he might be adept at managing the press, convincing the politicians, his superiors even, but he had no interest in, and certainly no flair for, investigation. In the short time they'd worked together, he'd made it quite clear he was there to serve his time and move upwards.

A tense anger hardened inside Jackman. He sat up. Erik raised a sleepy head as he rose and headed out to the kitchen. There was only one kind of solace that he sought this evening, only one antidote to the leaky tap that dripped icy drops of loneliness into his chest. Whisky.

He rummaged through the cupboard under the stairs, his hands moving urgently, pushing aside a mop bucket, shopping bags, a sack of dog food. Finally he found it, sitting proudly against the wall at the back. Half a bottle of Glenfiddich. A crusted line of dust had gathered around its rim. He pulled it forward, gave a short blow, which did nothing to remove the sticky dust, reached for a glass and poured.

The first gulp made him cough, the rich liquor caught in his throat, searing his chest as it rippled down into his gut. He wiped the back of his hand across his lips and took another. It was stronger than he remembered and it burnt like a ball of fire. Good. That was just what he needed right now.

He lifted the bottle and glass, moved back into the lounge and sunk into the sofa. Erik climbed up and thumped his body down beside him. The cushions juddered causing the drink to slosh out of the side of the glass onto his trousers. In normal circumstances he'd jump up, curse the dog and reach for a cloth. But frankly these weren't normal circumstances and right now he really didn't give a damn.

He looked down at the dog who'd nestled his head into Jackman's lap. He was oblivious to the glass, the bottle now resting on the coffee table beside him, the strong aroma of Scotch filling the air. Jackman filled the glass again and drank.

Then another. They were starting to slip down easier now. Heat rose through his stomach into his chest, up his neck and into his face. Slowly the thoughts in his mind blurred along with the room around him.

★ ★ ★

A spasm in his calf wrenched Jackman from his deep sleep. He jerked forward and clutched the cramped muscle, then jumped up sharply, hopping around the room on his good leg. Short spikes of pain set off an array of fireworks in his head, forcing him to ease up. The cramp started to melt away, but simultaneously the pain in his head reached new heights. He sat on the edge of the sofa in the darkness and tried to focus. Suddenly the room began to move like a paddle boat riding a wave. The sweats followed, then the nausea, and finally the rush of bile to his throat. He raced up the stairs, his head pounding, and only just reached the bathroom in time.

The stench of vomit filled the air as he hung his head and retched. Sweat coursed down his back. Finally, when he was well and truly spent, he laid back on the cold tiles. His stamina ate away at him. What a lightweight. He'd only polished off half a bottle of whisky and he couldn't even do that right.

His mouth felt dry. The aroma of sick caught his nostrils. He should have jumped up, taken a shower, drunk a pint of water, but his body was laden with self-loathing. If Alice could see me now.

A wave of fatigue washed over him and he invited it until it swaddled him like a baby and gave him a brief respite from his thoughts.

★ ★ ★

His eyes pierced the darkness that flooded the room. The wind had dropped to a whisper, as if the trees outside were sharing a million secrets just out of earshot.

He sat up. The air inside smelt thick and pungent now that the heat of the day had passed. Stage two of his plan had proved more difficult to execute than he could possibly have imagined. His back was sore and his shoulders ached. And very soon it would be time to change things again. But there was a part of him that was enjoying the raw thrill of the chase. A wry smile curled the corner of his mouth as he pictured the detective and his team scrabbling through bins in Birmingham, searching for clues. Now it was only a matter of time.

# 44

The sound of crows cawing in the distance pulled me out of a deep sleep. My eyelids were stuck together, my body glued to the bed. I hadn't slept so well in ages and I wanted more. Tom's body was curled around mine, his paunch pressing into my back. It felt warm, comforting. His arms encased me, swaddling my body like a blanket. I tried to return to my slumber, but the crows were insistent this morning — their calls echoing around the walls. I slowly opened my eyes. And started.

I was still in the pit. The damp smell of the puddle, which sat barely inches from my feet, filled my nose. I'd done it again, in spite of all my efforts — I'd slept. And it wasn't Tom's arms wrapped around me. It was Lonny's.

Instinct screamed at me to jump forward, release myself from his grip. But that was instinct in the real world. And nothing felt the same down here. This wasn't a romantic gesture. It was purely for the warmth. The rationale made me feel better. I tried to wriggle forward, but his embrace was vice-like, holding me rigid.

A wave of compassion hit me. He'd been so kind to me over the past couple of days. Listened to my stories, shared food with real generosity, covered his eyes and ears when I'd had to use the makeshift toilet in the corner. I didn't want to wake him. But I needed to find a way out.

251

Suddenly, I felt a deep inhalation, and the exhalation of a sigh trickle down my neckline. He nuzzled into my hair. Then a hard lump pressed into the back of my thigh.

I froze, frantically working through my options, listening to the regularity of his breaths, feeling the rise and fall of his chest. The lump expanded.

Summoning every ounce of might, I pushed forward, instantly releasing myself from his grip. His breaths halted. I watched him smack his lips together a couple of times, turn and rest once more.

Relief sunk into me as I sidled out from beneath the blanket, sat forward and scratched the back of my neck. Day five in this hellhole.

# 45

A sharp glint of light warmed Jackman's forehead. His cheek was pressed into the groove between the cold tiles, arms and legs splayed across the hard floor. A million clocks chimed in unison inside his head as he raised it.

He recognised the toilet in the background, the sink, the bath. The smell of vomit filled the air, although he no longer felt sick. Right now he was thirsty. Desperately thirsty. He hauled himself up, blinked one eye to shut out some of the pain, then turned on the tap and wedged his head underneath, glugging down the water as if he'd just discovered an oasis in the midst of a desert.

He stood, wiped his mouth down his sleeve and glanced towards the window. Luminous strips of sunlight pushed through the gaps down either side of the blind. What time was it?

Just at that moment he heard the sound of hefty paws moving around on the laminate flooring below. He ran the tap again, splashed the cold water over his face and made for the stairs.

Erik greeted him in the hallway like a long-lost relative.

'Hey, boy.' Jackman caressed his ears affectionately, entered the lounge and glanced at the clock. Almost seven. He'd slept right through.

Jackman crossed to the French doors, flung

253

them open and took a moment to inhale the air while Erik plodded around the garden. It had rained overnight and tiny drops of water glistened across the lawn in the morning sunlight. The freshness cleared the smog in his mind. And sharpened the pain. He moved into the kitchen, switched on the kettle. What he needed now was strong coffee and strong medicine.

By the time Erik wandered in Jackman had popped two paracetamol and was seated at the breakfast bar sipping black coffee. Erik nudged the side of his thigh and looked up expectantly.

Jackman stared into his eyes. 'Want to go out?' The tone of his words whipped the dog up and he wagged his tail enthusiastically.

Jackman placed his mug back down on the bar and raised a wry smile. 'Come on then, mate,' he said. 'Let's go for a run while this cools down.'

The park opposite Jackman's home was quiet that Saturday morning. In a couple of hours it would be filled with local lads, fashioning their jumpers into makeshift goalposts as they played football, and young children crawling over the climbing frame in the play area, swirling on the roundabout. Yet, right now, the only other person in the park was a man pushing a toddler in a pushchair. It felt peaceful and inviting.

Jackman let Erik off the lead and stretched his calf muscles. His head was thick, a burgeoning ache filled his skull. His right leg was stiff and sore from sleeping at a strange angle the night before and he gave it a quick massage. But nothing was going to stop him running.

It wasn't that he enjoyed it. Not like he used to. The competition of it, the sense of achievement, those wonderful endorphins that sizzled through his veins afterwards and the satisfying fatigue of worked muscles. He felt none of that anymore. It was more of a routine, the last bastion of his previous life that he couldn't bear to leave behind.

The first lap of the park was more laboured than usual. He had to stop a few times to rehydrate, the after-effects of the alcohol from the night before still draining the juices from his body. Erik raced around happily, stopping momentarily to sniff and cock his leg, before returning to his owner's side.

The second lap felt slightly easier as his body loosened, but the third was tortuous as every tendon cried out. Weakness was to be expected today, especially after half a bottle of whisky. By the time he'd completed the fourth he was almost spent. His hair was wet and his t-shirt clung to him. But instead of stopping, he stepped it up a gear, sprinting between two of the aged willows beside the canal, almost fifteen metres apart. Back and forth he went, time and time again. Erik, quite accustomed to the habit, laid down just out of the way and watched as Jackman continued to run at full pelt until sweat coursed down his back and his lungs were raw.

Finally he halted, rested his back on a tree trunk and slid down, paying no heed to the abrasive bark as it scraped at his skin through the thin t-shirt. For some time he sat there, glugging from his water bottle, staring into space. As his breaths started to even the words from the counsellor the night before crept into his mind: 'We need to find a strategy to deal with that guilt'.

He looked across the park. The man had let the toddler out of the pushchair and was chasing her across the park. She turned her head and squealed with delight as he scooped her up in his arms. The simple gesture triggered a moment of sadness. A year ago, he was happily married. He lived for his girls, his sport and the job. Right now he'd all but lost his wife and best friend, his job was hanging like a loose thread and his daughter was away at university. Sport was the only thing he had left and even that wasn't much fun anymore.

He thought about Janus' comment the day before, the suggestion that he'd made the wrong judgement call in Min's case. He recalled his meeting with Richard, when it was suggested that he was consumed with guilt. Was it true? Had he plunged himself into a life of guilt, a mood that coloured his decisions at work and tainted his judgement? He couldn't deny that he felt guilty over Alice's condition. But no, he wasn't wrong about the press coverage with Min. In the event that she was still alive, he'd made that decision to protect her safety. There was no way that decision caused a second kidnapping.

As Jackman gathered his stuff and started moving back towards home, Richard's words continued to grate away at the back of his mind. His life may have been turned upside down this past year, but he was a good detective.

Problem was he'd only ever be able to sidestep the Reillys of this world if he ran his own investigation. He needed this job, not just in a financial capacity to supplement his wife's care, his daughter's studies; but also for himself. It was all he'd ever known since leaving the forces and it fitted like a second skin. Perhaps it was time to transfer, move to another station, another area, where his background and memories didn't follow him around and haunt his every move. Somewhere he'd be judged on his merit, gain promotion and lead his own cases. Maybe now it was finally time to make that move.

# 46

'Is that all we have left?' Lonny said.

I followed his eye line to the bottle in the corner, only a third full with water. A couple of breakfast bars spilled out of the box next to it, a single apple sat on the top. I nodded and as I did so a pain shot through my head.

'When does he normally come?'

I glanced across at Lonny and shrugged. My limbs felt weary, every muscle in my body ached. My stomach cramps had returned too. I should have been worried, thought of the baby's safety, considered my options. But I didn't have the energy. I suppose it was inevitable really. Being stuck down here with a poor diet of biscuits, dry bread, apples and water. Thrust into a pit with little natural light, a pile of faeces in the corner, rats lurking in the shadows. Maybe that was the plan all along, to leave us to starve to death.

I tried to conjure the images of my parents, those dear pictures that I clung to in my mind, but even they were growing hazy. I cleared my throat. 'The first time was at night.' The words were an effort to speak. I closed my eyes. 'The second when he brought you here.'

'He hasn't been for days.'

I shook my head, felt him stand beside me.

'We need to find a way to get out of here.'

I rubbed my hands up and down my face.

'No, I'm serious. When he returns, we'll rush at him. Two to one. If he's armed I'll go for the weapon, while you try to climb out and get help.' He spoke like an excited child and his plan sounded like a bungled escape from a war film. 'Well?'

I thought back to my own earlier plan of escape. When it came to it, when I finally had my chance, my limbs had let me down, paralysed in fear. It was hopeless. Now I no longer had the energy nor the enthusiasm to fight or argue.

'You're giving up?'

The desperation in his voice pulled my gaze to him. 'I'm tired.'

'We can't give up. We have to find a way.'

I took a deep breath. The plan made one huge assumption. 'Maybe he's not coming back.'

'What?'

'Maybe he's been caught.'

# 47

Jackman had just stepped out of the shower when he heard the knock at the door. He groaned, ignored it and pulled the towel across his torso. The sound of a fist on glass followed.

His robe flapped around his calves as he navigated the stairs and pulled the door open.

Davies stared at him, head angled. 'Not answering your calls then?'

'Morning to you too.'

He stepped aside to let her through and followed her into the front room just in time to catch her eyes flit down to the bottle leaning up against the side of the sofa.

'Don't worry. Most of it's down the toilet.'

She lifted her head in acknowledgement, said nothing.

Jackman glanced about awkwardly. 'Coffee?'

'Thought you'd never ask.'

Back in the kitchen, he checked his mobile. Three missed calls from Davies, two yesterday and one this morning. He could hear the thud of her feet pacing the room as he popped some more painkillers, ibuprofen this time, and made the coffee. She'd be no good undercover, he thought. Like a baby elephant.

By the time Jackman returned the front curtains were drawn back. The French doors at the rear were once again flung open and she was standing beside the aquarium in the corner, staring into the glass. Steam rose from the mugs in his hands and swirled into the air as he approached.

'Don't you ever wonder what they're thinking?' she said, not taking her eyes from the tank.

He handed her a mug. 'Where their next meal's coming from probably,' Jackman said. 'They're very simple creatures.'

He stood next to her a moment and watched the fish glide gracefully around the tank.

Davies drew the mug to her lips and flinched. 'No milk?'

'Ran out.'

She lowered the mug, said nothing.

He turned to face her. 'What are you doing here?'

'You left your car at work yesterday.'

Jackman had completely forgotten about his car that still sat in the car park at Rother Street station, although he wasn't about to admit it right now. 'Fancied a walk.'

She ignored his comment and instead looked across to the French doors. 'It stinks in here.'

After a brief silence, Davies finally made eye contact. 'You okay?'

He gave a short nod. 'Any news on the students? Sightings, contact from the kidnappers?'

'Nothing. The van's left the radar too by the looks of things.'

'You brought me any good news?'

She rolled her eyes.

'You'd better bring me up to date on the new kidnapping.'

He tipped his head towards the sofas. They moved across and sat, one on each, as Davies continued. 'Lonny Cheung was last seen by his English tutor walking past the college around nine yesterday morning. His phone was switched off in the vicinity of the college around the same time.'

'What about his car?'

'Still parked outside his flat. You obviously heard about the ransom note and the drop, this time on another industrial estate.' Jackman nodded as she continued, 'Well, I pulled a few strings and spoke to our friend DS Gray in Birmingham who agreed to get their forensics to lift the bin. I also sent some of our detectives across to scour the estate and organised a separate team over to search the surrounding area.'

'Any luck?'

'Nothing from the industrial estate; whoever planned this has chosen their drop locations very carefully. The search team didn't find anything, although we didn't really expect them to. But we did establish that the money was never collected. It still sat in the bottom of the bin.'

'Really? You'd have thought Lonny's father's contacts would have checked.'

'You heard Keane, it was an open area.'

'And they didn't change the location at the last minute.'

'I know. It's a strange one. As if something went wrong. I did get to the internet cafe though. They used a different one this time, must be getting sloppy because they have cameras. We've trawled through. There were only three people in there around the time the email was sent.'

'Can we get an ID?'

'Not sure. But I had another word with Gray and emailed the footage over. He said he'd take a look and see if it rings any bells.'

'Good.' Jackman felt a smile stretch across his face for the first time in what felt like days.

Davies beamed back at him. 'You're welcome.' She took a sip of her coffee. 'That's disgusting,' she said, pulled a face and placed the mug on the coffee table beside her. 'Reilly's driving us mad. All he does is stride around talking budgets and press releases.'

Jackman rubbed his forehead. The extra painkillers he'd taken earlier had dulled the drum that was pounding the insides of his skull. 'Okay, give me ten minutes.'

# 48

A low-bellied roar filled the incident room as Jackman entered that morning. He smiled and held up his hand. 'Okay everyone. Settle down.'

Russell spoke up from the back of the room. 'The DCI can't be with us for briefing. He's at a meeting with the assistant chief constable in Leamington.'

'Then we'll bat on without him,' Jackman said and perched himself on the edge of a desk.

Davies moved to the front of the room, switched on her laptop and pointed to the stills of three men that appeared on the white screen in front of them. They all looked similar: dark hair, Caucasian, no distinguishing features that he could see. Two wore jeans and t-shirts, the other a navy polo shirt and beige trousers.

Davies pointed to each of the men in turn. 'One of these men sent that email,' she said. 'Who are they? What are their backgrounds? Why were they in the cafe?'

Jackman turned to the rest of the room. 'Any news from the industrial estate?'

Keane moved in and provided a brief update.

'No witnesses, no cameras . . . ' Jackman summarised. 'Same old story. What we need to establish is why the money wasn't collected. Did something go wrong?'

'Maybe they were interrupted?' Keane said.

'If so, there should be a witness. What do we

know about Lo Cheung?'

'Twenty-year-old student from Hong Kong,' Keane said. 'Known to most as Lonny. Studying the same course as Min. Nothing so far to suggest they were friends. Son of Hong Kong-born father and British mother, although she died when he was nine. Suicide.'

Jackman tilted his head. 'Does he still have family over here on his mother's side?'

Keane shook his head. 'Doesn't look like it. She was an only child. Parents moved to Geneva years ago. We managed to trace them but they lost contact with Lonny after his mother died. Apparently his father wasn't very helpful when it came to access.'

'Interesting. Keep on it. Check for extended family too. What about friends?'

'Not much there either,' Keane said. 'Apparently he only turns up for the minimum lectures to pass.'

'What did he do in his spare time?'

'No idea. We've been through his flat. Once you get past the piles of takeaway boxes and dirty washing, there's not much left. Nothing to indicate where he might be.'

Jackman drummed his fingers on the desk. 'What about bank statements, phone records?'

'Bank statements have just come through. There's a substantial amount deposited each month from an account in Hong Kong. We think it's from his father but we're getting that checked. Just working our way through his transactions. He withdrew a lot, seemed to like to work in cash, but no pattern immediately comes to light. Phone has been off since Thursday morning. He didn't make a lot of calls.'

'Any luck with International Liaison?'

Keane shook his head. 'It's almost seventeen years since China took Hong Kong back. There's nothing there to speak of, and all the contacts have either moved on or retired.'

Jackman thought for a moment and turned to Russell. 'Anything from the college?'

She shook her head. 'We've re-interviewed the tutors. They shared a couple of classes. That's all.'

Jackman stared up at their board. A photo of Lonny was now positioned next to Min. He exhaled loudly. 'Why those two students? There has to be a link with the college somewhere. Go through the statements again and re-check with witnesses. Look again at the two victims' families and speak to both parents to see if you can establish a connection.'

He moved back into his office, opened his laptop and trawled through his emails. A message from Sam Chapman caught his eye. He'd been true to his word and sent across the camera footage from the casino the weekend before. Hours of film to be checked. He'd also given DS Gray a hard copy to be logged. Jackman looked up through the open blinds. The incident room was a hive of activity as the team followed up the earlier leads. Phones were ringing in harmony. He glanced back at the email. Right now he simply couldn't spare the resources to wade through the tapes, especially as the new kidnapping had taken them in a different direction.

Jackman let his mind wander. The thought of waiting several days to get the Embassy file on Lonny's background incensed him. And the weekend was bound to delay matters further. A thought struck him — he'd attended a retirement party for an old colleague, DS Dave Benton, a couple of years ago. He remembered something in his speech about him being seconded to the Hong Kong police just before the switch-over in 1997, long before they'd been acquainted. He grabbed his phone, scrolled through the contacts and pressed dial, more in hope than expectation, and was surprised when it was answered on the fourth ring. And even more surprised when he recognised his old pal's voice at the end of the line.

'Dave? It's Will. Will Jackman.'

The former police sergeant seemed pleased to hear from Jackman and talked at length about life after retirement. The long days taken up with the gym and the golf course. Jackman politely let him ramble for a few minutes before he interjected. 'Actually I was wondering whether you might be able to help me?'

By the time Jackman had given him a brief rundown on the case he could almost feel Benton puffing out his chest at the other end of the line as it filled with a sense of self-importance. 'You were seconded to the Hong Kong police for a couple of years before China took them back, weren't you?' he continued. 'I just wondered whether you still had any contacts out there and could do a bit of digging for me? You know the sort of thing. Background stuff on the Cheung family. Any previous dealings with the police. Doesn't have to be strictly on the record.'

Benton's tone became imbued with a sense of excitement, as if this was the first interesting thing to happen to him outside of the golf club in the last year. He said he would see what he could do. Jackman ended the call suitably satisfied that his old friend would be back in touch with him soon, at the very least before the Embassy.

He cast his phone aside, opened his drawer, pulled out his policy log and began to record their findings from the morning's briefing, outlining his current strategies and priorities. Almost an hour passed before the door of his room suddenly opened and Davies burst in catching her breath.

She slipped her phone into her pocket. The dimple was fixed hard in her left cheek. 'That was Gray,' she said. 'They've ID'd the guy who sat at the computer when the ransom email was sent.'

Jackman felt a rush of adrenalin. 'What do we know about him?'

Davies waved her pad in the air like a winning ticket. 'Forty-eight-year-old British divorcee by the name of Richard Whittaker. Currently unemployed. He's got previous. Petty stuff: handling stolen goods; a couple of counts of shoplifting. Gray said their intelligence suggests he's a small-time cannabis supplier. His name's come up a few times from informants, but it seems he's very careful, skulks around avoiding

268

being seen with the wrong people.'

'Any links to China?'

'Nothing we know of.'

Jackman frowned. 'Kidnapping seems a far leap.'

'That's what Gray thought. But we have him on camera, and the techies have confirmed that he was using the PC that sent the ransom email. Nobody else used it within ten minutes either side. In fact he was in there for less than five minutes although he paid for a full half an hour.'

'What about associates?'

'Not much to go on there. Gray's going to check with some of the local officers. But he did give me an address!'

Jackman's phone buzzed again. He glanced at the screen, sighed inwardly as Reilly's name appeared, then looked up at Davies. 'Well done. Give me two minutes.'

It took less than thirty seconds for Jackman to update Reilly. He finished up, 'I think we should consider putting some observations on Whittaker. We know he's involved. The kids are still missing. If we watch him, there's a fair chance he could lead us to them.'

Reilly was silent a moment. 'Pick him up now. Bring him straight here. We've enough to make an arrest, the rest we can drag out of him in interview.'

Jackman took a deep breath to soothe his frayed patience. 'Our first priority is to preserve life. We could lose any chance of finding the victims, dead or alive, if he refuses to cooperate.'

'Not necessarily. We'll search his house. That

could give us what we're looking for.'

'You heard the intelligence. He's a small-time petty thief. It's possible he's not working alone. If we follow him he could lead us to them.'

'What we need is an arrest. I'm sure your team can get the rest out of him in questioning.'

Jackman chucked his phone across the desk and cursed as the line went dead. Reilly had absolutely no idea. He reached out, hovered over the phone. For a split second he considered going over his head, until he remembered Davies' comment in Birmingham about Reilly and the new chief constable on the golf course together. And cursed again.

# 49

Jackman craned his neck as they turned off the Hagley Road into Richardson Street. Two rows of plain brick terraces faced each other across a road lined with cars parked nose to tail on each side. It seemed most of the residents were home this Saturday morning. Davies slowed to a crawl as they reached number eighteen. Cream net curtains that looked in dire need of a wash veiled the windows. She continued on, took the next left and parked curbside.

As soon as Jackman was out of the car he saw the rotund figure of DS Gray climbing gingerly out of a green Volvo two cars up. He was followed by three uniformed officers, two of them carrying thick gloves and helmets.

Gray beamed a greeting as Davies and Jackman wandered up to meet him, and introduced the other officers standing nearby. He placed his hands on his hips and looked around. 'I know this area pretty well. Covered it for a while as a beat officer in my early years. Many of the properties have been converted to bedsits and flats. Whittaker's is still a house, which is better for us because it means one point of access at the front. I've put a plain clothes officer on the corner of both ends of his street in case he is out, spots us on his way back and does a runner. That lane there,' he indicated diagonally opposite, 'provides rear access to the back of the properties. We'll cover that. Otherwise, unless he climbs over neighbours' gardens, we've got him.'

'We think he's home?' Davies asked.

'Can't be sure, but,' he patted the battering ram that his colleague was holding, 'Doris is going in whatever.'

'Okay, I say we break straight in,' Jackman said. 'There's still a possibility that the victims are housed in there somewhere. We don't want to give him a chance to injure them. What's the layout of the property?'

'Two up, two down really, plus bathroom and kitchen,' Gray said. 'There'll be loft space, of course, but none of these houses have cellars. Back garden is laid to paving. No shed.'

'Do we know anything more about him?' Jackman asked.

Gray shook his head. 'Intel is all petty stuff. Local officers say he rubs shoulders with the big guys but never a sniff of firearms or anything like that.' He looked around the team. 'I think we're good to go as we are.'

Jackman nodded and set the team into motion. He sent Gray and another officer around the back. The two with helmets followed him and Davies to the front. He felt a rush of excitement as they moved into position.

Jackman issued the command. The officers rushed forward. Two loud cracks later and the door swung open. The uniformed officers charged into the house. One rushed upstairs, the other through the ground floor.

Jackman and Davies followed. The front door opened directly into a living room. A brown sofa

272

with frayed arms faced a flat-screen television on an old table in the corner. A huge open space occupied the other end of the room. A dirty oval mirror hung over the fireplace. Jackman moved towards it and, as he lifted the photo that sat on the mantel beneath, he dislodged a hairbrush full of matted wisps of dark hair tucked behind. It fell to the floor. He bent down to pick it up and stared at the photo. It was a young boy, around seven he guessed, dressed in shorts and a t-shirt. He was grinning broadly, showing off a wide gap in his front teeth.

Jackman replaced the photo and wandered over the grey carpet. It was threadbare in places, exposing bobbly underfelt that scrunched beneath his feet. He looked around him. Apart from that single photo and the clock in the corner, there were no pictures on the walls, no ornaments on the side. No cupboards or bookshelves for storage.

As he pushed the door open into the kitchen the rancid odour of chip fat and nicotine greeted him. He stopped beside a pile of dirty clothes that sat in front of the washing machine and pulled out a drawer that contained knives, forks and spoons. Another was filled with hand towels and tea towels. Another with used receipts, a water bill, a mobile phone bill, and a couple of store loyalty cards. He pulled them out, made a mental note to get them bagged up and worked his way through the cupboards until he felt a presence beside him.

'Nothing upstairs, sir.' Davies grimaced. 'Although his bedding could do with a bloody good wash. Looks like it hasn't been done in months. The guys are just checking the loft.'

Jackman felt a sense of disquiet as he stood and glanced out of the window at the bare paving below. No sign of any motorcycle gear so far, nor any clues regarding the victims.

Suddenly he became aware of a commotion in the distance. Raised voices, one edged with anger. He followed the sound to the front door where the two officers in helmets were holding back a dark-haired man dressed in a green t-shirt and denims. His face was tomato-red. The plastic carrier bag in his hand slid to the floor as he looked up at Jackman, eyes burning. 'Who are you?'

★ ★ ★

Richard Whittaker was a small bony man with a thick head of wiry dark hair. He hadn't said anything on the drive back to Rother Street station and had only answered what was absolutely nec-essary as he was fingerprinted and prepared for interview. Even when they'd arrested him for the kidnapping, he remained silent.

Jackman dragged the chair out from under the table and took a seat. 'Give me an account of your movements on Thursday afternoon,' he said.

Whittaker flashed the briefest glance at his solicitor before he spoke. 'I was walking down the Hagley Road on Thursday. When I passed JJ's internet cafe on the corner of Dover Street a man stopped me and asked if I wanted to make some quick cash. I thought he was gonna offer me something at first. You know, maybe drugs.' He paused, looked momentarily affronted, before he continued, 'But then he said if I sent an email for him he'd give me fifty quid. All I had to do was to log in to a Hotmail account, retrieve an email from the drafts folder, press send and logout. I wasn't sure at first, but he waved the notes in front of me. So I thought, what have I got to lose?' Whittaker sat back and rested his hands in his lap.

Jackman watched him for a moment. The only sound was the gentle scratch of Keane's pen on the pad beside him. 'What did the email say?' he eventually asked.

'Don't know. It was in a foreign language. Chinese or Japanese. Something like that.'

'Can you describe the man who asked you to send it?'

'White, about five foot ten. Wore dark trousers and a black hoody. Couldn't see his face.'

Jackman retrieved two photos from the brown envelope file in front of him and placed them on the table. He watched closely as Whittaker's eyes worked from one to another, then back up at him.

'Have you ever seen these people before?'

Whittaker shook his head.

'For the purposes of the tape I am showing the suspect photos of Min Li and Lonny Cheung. Can you confirm your answer, please?'

Whittaker leant in closer, appeared to examine Lonny's photo again. 'My answer is no. I haven't seen them before.'

Jackman continued to ask him about his

275

movements on Monday and Tuesday. Whittaker claimed he was at home alone. He went through a list of dates — when Lonny's ransom request was sent and the money was collected for both kidnappings. Each time Whittaker claimed to be at home, the belligerence in his tone increasing with each answer.

Jackman pulled a photo of Qiang Li out of the envelope. It squeaked between his fingers as he placed it on the table in front of him. 'What about him?'

Whittaker leant over the photo and hesitated a moment, as if deep in thought. Finally he drew back. 'No.'

'Are you sure? Take another look,' Jackman said. He tapped the corner of the photo twice. 'He has a distinctive scar down the left side of his face. His left earlobe is missing.'

Whittaker shook his head.

'For the purposes of the tape, the suspect indicated he has never seen Qiang Li, also known as Peng Wu, before.'

If Jackman had blinked he would have missed it. But it was definitely there. As soon as he mentioned the name, Peng Wu, a muscle flexed in Whittaker's jawline.

He stared at Whittaker a moment. His skinny frame was swamped in the navy police-issue jogging suit he'd been given when they'd asked him to remove his clothes for forensic examination.

'You see I've got a problem with that,' Jackman said. 'While you were at home alone, these two students disappeared.' He pointed to

Min and Lonny. 'Less than twelve hours later, emails were sent to their parents requesting a ransom for their safe release. We know you sent the second email. We have you on camera. Yet you claim not to know who they are.'

Whittaker stared back, unruffled.

'Are you a parent?'

Whittaker shrugged a single shoulder, nodded. 'I have a son. His mother and I are separated. She doesn't let me see him.'

'Is that why you kidnapped somebody else's?' Jackman didn't pause for him to answer. 'Is that why you sent the ransom demands? So that you could raise some cash, impress your ex so that she'd let you see your kid?'

'It's got nothing to do with me.'

'Really? Do you make a habit of sending strange emails?'

Whittaker looked away, didn't answer.

Jackman leant forward. 'Who asked you to send that email?'

Whittaker stretched his neck back before he answered. 'I told you. I don't know.'

Jackman pointed to the photo of Min Li. 'This student has been missing since Monday evening. Every minute she is out there could mean a minute closer to death. Or maybe she is dead already?'

Whittaker's gaze brushed back over the photos. Jackman could see a flash of fear in his eyes.

'You really need to start talking, Richard,' Jackman continued. 'Because we will find them and, dead or alive, the footage means that you are clearly implicated in their disappearance.'

Jackman gathered up the photos and put them back in the envelope. 'One more question,' he said. 'When was the last time you rode a motorcycle?'

# 50

As much as I tried, I couldn't ignore Lonny's banging and clattering in the background. He was wrestling with the grate, jiggling it about, this way and that. And every movement, every clang juddered right through me. I held my head, willing the noise to go away, until I could bear it no more.

'Please, stop!'

'I can't.' His voice was peppered with excitement. 'I think it's coming away.'

I heard the rattle of the chain in the distance, the jingle of metal.

'Look Min, it's moving.'

I stood gingerly, just as he gave the grill one last loud heave and pushed it up sideways.

'I don't think it's locked properly.' Lonny was shaking with excitement now, his tendons visibly trembling. 'Come on, if you get on my shoulders you could crawl through that gap.' He straightened his arms, cupped his hands together.

I looked at him a moment, still doubtful. 'You go. You're so much taller than me, you'd get up there easily without any help.'

'Not without you. Come on!'

I lifted my foot and pushed up on his hands, steadying myself by holding onto the shirt around his shoulders. I heard a rip, wobbled and grabbed a handful of skin.

'Owww!'

'Sorry.'

The weak, sickly feeling had dissolved, driven out by a rush of adrenalin. My mind focused on freedom. There was no room for anything else. I reached my hands through the gap and pushed back the wooden board at the top.

A surge of sunlight gushed down.

'Jesus!' Lonny cried from below. The weight in his body shunted to the side. I felt myself wobble as he steadied himself.

I tried to look up. After days of living in a soft grey, the incandescent light pierced my eyes. But I knew I didn't have long. I needed to open them, focus. This could be our only chance. I grabbed at the ridge of concrete, and began to haul myself up.

I was almost through when my hand slipped. My chin hit the metal. I screamed as a pain seared my jaw bone and kicked out, desperately trying to gain a foothold. My foot collided with Lonny.

'Arrgh!'

'You okay?' My voice was splintered, my energy divided between my pulling myself free and speech.

'My ankle!'

I scrambled forward and pulled myself through the narrow gap, my kneecaps scraping and burning against the concrete as I moved.

Out of the hole for the first time in days I paused, glanced about. I found myself in a battered old barn. Piles of rubble littered the floor. Daylight spilled in from a bare opening which must have at some point housed a door. The walls were a shoddy mixture of bricks and mortar. Wooden rafters hung precariously from above. Splinters of light slid in from a roof, which was in dire need of repair.

I crouched at the side and glanced back in. The pit looked strange from this angle, like peering into a different world. 'Are you hurt?'

Lonny was sat in the corner rubbing his lower calf. 'I think I pulled my ankle.'

'Do you think you'll still be able to jump up?'

He stood carefully, but as soon as he put any weight on the leg he cried out. He looked up, face crumpled in pain. 'I don't think I can do it.'

A scratching noise jerked me back into the shadow of the corner. I pressed my body against the cold brickwork. The noise stopped almost immediately. After a few moments, I edged towards the exit and craned my neck around the side. A pile of rubble sat in front of me, intermingled with a grassy mound that had been growing over and consuming it for what looked like many years. Beyond was a patchwork of fields stretching down the hillside to what looked like a road at the bottom. The air smelt clean, fresh, free.

I moved back to the pit. 'Lonny?'

'What can you see?'

'We're surrounded by fields. There looks like a road in the distance. If we can get you out . . . '

'No!'

'I can't leave you here!'

'I'll just delay things with my ankle. You go, get help.'

'I can't . . . '

'You have to, Min.'

I hesitated a minute.

'Step back.'

I moved away from the hole just as a trainer found its way through. It bounced off the wall beside me, followed by another.

'Take my shoes,' he said. 'They'll be too big, but at least they'll protect your feet.'

My heart was in my mouth. What if our captor returned and found Lonny alone? I was torn, torn between helping Lonny, finding a way to get him out, or running to get help.

'Go! Quickly!'

The urgency in his voice kick-started me into action. I pushed my feet into the trainers. He was right, they were too big, like paddle boats around my feet but I tightened the laces as much as I could and stood.

'I'll be as quick as I can!'

I moved forward tentatively, listening hard with every step.

The sun flexed its muscles from its central position in the clear blue sky. I had to raise a hand to shield my eyes, although the instant warmth on my skin felt blissful. A quick scan of the area showed I was up high. There was a concrete path, wide enough for a single-track road to my right, beyond the mound of concrete and rubble. I shuddered. This was the likely route of our kidnapper. I couldn't afford to use that. To my left a myriad of patchwork fields tumbled down into the valley below. In the far distance I could see a road. One, two, three cars whizzed past. I turned and headed down the field towards it.

I swayed and tripped as I navigated my way down. Lonny's trainers became heavy and clumsy. After only a few minutes, my legs ached, my mouth was parched.

I passed a copse to my right, moved over the brow of the hill and came face to face with a hawthorn hedge at the bottom. My heart sank. There was no gate, no stile, no way through. I turned and glanced behind me. Perhaps there was a natural opening further back, into the copse maybe? But the thought of retracing my steps back up there, even if I had enough energy in my weary limbs was overwhelming.

I moved down the hedging, searching for an area where the branches that intertwined together to form a natural wall were less dense. Finally I reached a small gap. If I curled up and moved through on my knees I could just about make it. Armed with a thick stick from nearby I batted the surrounding area in an attempt to increase the size of the hole. Finally, I was through.

Then I heard a noise.

It sounded like a loud snort. I turned. A herd of black and white cattle crowded in the far corner, less than two hundred yards away. Fear engulfed me. I'd seen cows before in photographs of the countryside back home, but having lived in a city for all my life, I'd never seen them in the flesh, and certainly never been in a field with them. Primal fear flushed my veins. I kicked off the shoes that were slipping and sliding around my feet, and ran as fast as I could. Through another hedge. Stones snagged at my feet, the sun picked at every inch of bare flesh. My vision blurred, my knees weakened, my stomach ached, but I couldn't stop.

Another noise. The sound of an engine. I could barely see now, but my ears were sharp. It was in the field, closing in on me. And that's when I realised the game was up.

# 51

Back in his office, Jackman shoved his hands in his pockets, leant against the side of the window frame and stared out into the evening. The interview had been frustrating. Whittaker knew the score — it was up to the police to find proof of his direct involvement in the kidnapping. And without witnesses or camera footage on the stretch of the Hagley Road where he claimed to have met the stranger that persuaded him to send the email, they could neither prove nor refute his account.

So far, background checks showed no association with Min Li or Lonny Cheung, let alone Stratford College. But Jackman could tell by Whittaker's reaction to the photo of Min's uncle that he'd seen him before. Suddenly a flashback from the Skype interview with Min's parents skipped into his head. Mr Li had said that his brother was good with languages. The ransom notes were sent in Mandarin as well as Cantonese. Did Qiang draft the notes for Whittaker to send? He needed to find the link between them and fast.

The door creaked as it opened behind him, breaking his concentration. He turned as Reilly entered.

'Ahh, Will,' he said as he seated himself in the chair opposite. 'Good to see that we are finally making some progress. Any news on the victims?'

Jackman shook his head and shared the details of the interview.

'A likely story,' Reilly replied.

'I don't think it's him,' Jackman said.

'We know he sent the email.'

'Yes, he sent an email. But I think someone else did the kidnapping. I think he had help.'

'What makes you say that?'

'Something about the whole situation doesn't ring true. The ransom demands are written in grammatically correct Mandarin and Cantonese. What's his link to the Chinese community? We've checked with the DVLA. He doesn't own a car, a motorbike and he doesn't even hold a licence. How would he get over here to Stratford? How would he make the ransom collection?'

'Half the criminal fraternity of Warwickshire doesn't have a licence. It doesn't stop them.'

'That doesn't answer the Chinese link. I'm still wondering whether we should release him.'

'What?'

'We can only keep him until tomorrow morning and, right now, unless he gives us a name or CSI find something at his house, we haven't enough to plant a charge on him.'

'Forensics might come up with something. We'll get an extension.'

'On what grounds? That he sent an email? That makes him an accessory, but if we charge him with that and he doesn't talk we're no closer to the truth. The victims are still out there.' Jackman paused, weariness was creeping into his voice. 'Look, we know that he's involved in this in some way. If he is the driving force, the very fact that we've tracked him down is going to scare him. Even if they are dead, he may still need to dispose of their bodies, clothes or other evidence he might have stashed somewhere. And if he's not in charge, then it's likely he's going to try to make contact with whoever is. I don't think we can miss a chance like this.'

'Oh, come on Will, I'm not sanctioning surveillance on Whittaker when I see absolutely no benefit. We've spent a small fortune on this case — tracking the boyfriend for twenty-four hours . . .'

'He was a strong lead with motive . . .'

Reilly cut through his words, 'Search parties at Clifford Chambers.'

'You organised that!' Jackman could feel his fatigue gradually being replaced by anger.

'We just need to work him over a bit harder. Chuck him in a cell for the night. That'll give him a little clarity of mind.' Reilly checked his watch. 'Right, I need to be off. Got another press conference at 5 p.m. Be good to share the developments.'

Jackman seethed as he watched him stride out of the room.

He looked back at his notes. Relying on questioning was a risky strategy, especially since Whittaker wasn't giving them anything. They needed a new lead, some fresh evidence. He reached for his phone, dialled Gray and requested that they step up the search for Min's uncle.

Davies' face appeared around the door as he replaced the receiver. 'Sir.' Her face was sombre. 'They've found a girl they believe to be Min Li. You need to come now.'

★ ★ ★

Jackman turned left off the A3400 and onto a single-track road that passed a collection of industrial units on the left before it became rough and uneven. He followed the track up the winding hill until he reached a couple of police cars parked at an angle, next to an old Land Rover. A cluster of uniformed officers stood beside them, one of them speaking into his radio. Blue and white chequered police tape cordoned off the area which included a nearby rubbish tip and two adjoining barns beyond.

The first person Jackman recognised when he climbed out of the car was PS Barby, the duty sergeant. He approached him and shook his hand. 'Thanks for getting everything set up here,' he said. 'What do we know?'

'The farmer, Mr James Edwards, was fencing three fields away,' he paused to point to a patchwork of fields that stretched down to the road, 'when he saw the girl who matched Min Li's description. She appeared from a gap in a hedge. She was weary and almost immediately lost consciousness. When the ambulance arrived she came around for a few seconds. Just kept uttering the same name: Lonny.' They took Min to hospital. We searched the area and found these barns. There's a pit in one of them, covered by a grate. Lonny Cheung was still in there. He said they were trying to escape when he sprained his ankle.'

'Are they both okay?'

'The paramedics said Min Li's suffering from

a mixture of exhaustion and dehydration. They've taken them both to hospital.'

'Great. Get a full search team out here, will you? I want this whole area examined.' He looked up at the sky, which had now darkened into patches of blues and purples like a nasty bruise. Heavy rain was threatening. 'As soon as you can.' Jackman thanked him and moved across to the Land Rover. The tall figure of Mr Edwards in an open-necked green shirt, jeans and wellies leant against it. He was twirling a flat cap in his hands, over and over, eyes fixed on the countryside.

Jackman tilted his head to catch his attention and introduced himself. 'Could you tell me exactly what happened?'

Mr Edwards turned to him. His eyes were slightly glazed. 'I'd finished fencing in the willow field at the bottom.' He pointed down in the same direction as Barby. 'I'd just climbed into the Land Rover and revved the engine when she appeared through a tiny gap in the hedge, right in front of me.' He gulped. 'I only just hit the brakes in time.' He shook his head, as if he still couldn't believe what he'd seen. 'She was dirty, her clothes ripped and grimy, her hair matted. But as soon as I saw her I knew it was that girl on the television. The one that was missing. She had no shoes on her feet. God knows what she's been through, poor kid.' He paused, continued to twirl the cap in his hands. 'She'd passed out by the time I reached her. Only woke up briefly when the ambulance and police arrived. They said they wanted to comb the area, find out where she'd come from and asked me for any landmarks. I couldn't think at first. I mean there's a derelict house on the bridle way further back, the industrial units across the way. I didn't even think of these barns until the last minute. Haven't used them in years. We only come up here to dump our farm rubbish.'

Jackman thanked Mr Edwards, left Davies to take his details, donned his overshoes and gloves and climbed over the tape.

The vista from this point offered excellent views over the patchwork of fields that covered the surrounding countryside and reached down to the A3400. The two adjoining barns were situated behind a mound of soil, broken wooden crates and rusted farm machinery. He walked around the exterior. An elder bush almost covered the nearside, so much so that the barns faded into the background, their view obscured from further down the hill. A small copse was set back into the hill nearby. He glanced down. The main road must be at least a quarter of a mile away. He wondered how long the captor had searched for this location — something isolated enough that pedestrians wouldn't hear any calls, but with a track that led up from the highway to a dead end next to the barns. That was his route to transport his prisoners. And with cloned plates, any camera footage that may be available from the industrial units nearby wouldn't help to locate the van. Clever.

A mixture of rubble and broken roof tiles crunched under his feet as he walked into the barn. The first thing he saw was a battered old wooden ladder that leant against the far wall. He sidestepped a CSI who was photographing the entrance to the pit from various angles and turned to find Davies scrabbling over the tape to join him. 'What were these barns used for?' he asked as she joined him.

'Nobody knows. They were built during WWII. Part of the old airfield, but of course that's all gone now. This land was bought by the Edwards family around forty years ago.'

'Looks like they're about to collapse.' Jackman turned and felt the edge of his shoulder catch the sidewall that made a feeble attempt to join the two barns together, loosening a spray of mortar dust that fell to the floor. 'What about the pit?'

'The farmer thinks that maybe it was used to store some kind of weapon during the war, but he doesn't know for sure. Says it was there when they bought it, complete with grill.'

Jackman bent down and took a closer look at the blisters of rust that littered the rungs of the metal grill. 'There's only a pit on this side?'

'Yes. The farmer fixed up the chain to secure it so that either a dog-walker or kids didn't wander in and fall down, although I don't think you get many dog-walkers up here. There aren't any supported paths through this part. The road we took up is privately owned by the farm. There's an entrance further up the A3400 into a bridle way, but it veers off to the other side of the wood and leads in the opposite direction. I'm guessing the kidnapper replaced the lock. It wouldn't have been too difficult to cut the old one off with bolt-cutters.'

Jackman looked up to see daylight streaming in through wide gaps in the roof. It cast distorted shadows over the CSI inside the pit who was now knelt down examining a blanket in the corner. He was just about to climb down and join him when a voice spoke up behind him.

'Careful, sir.' Jackman turned and followed the voice to another CSI in the corner. 'We've only just started down there.'

Jackman nodded and instead crouched down beside the entrance to the pit. Immediately he reeled at the thick stench of urine. The smell was powerful in the confined area and he raised his hand to his nose. The blanket in the corner was so ingrained with dirt that he could only just make out the original tartan effect. He pointed, shouted back to Davies, 'We need to get those bagged up, see if we can locate the seller.'

He scanned the four-metre-square area. At the moment it appeared that Min had been trapped in there for five nights. Lonny for two. The debris in the far corner of the pit indicated their captor had provided blankets, food and water. Why go to so much trouble to keep them alive when the ransom was paid? And why keep them together?

Something in the concrete caught his eye. 'Excuse me?'

The CSI examining the blanket looked up.

'What's that?'

Jackman watched him lean in to take a closer look.

'It looks like she's carved her name into the brickwork and a date. 19.5.14.'

'The date she went missing. Thanks. Get a

photograph of that, will you?'

The CSI nodded and continued with his work. Jackman stared at the powdery floor. Reilly would be strutting around the station as if he'd won the lottery. The discovery of the pit would enable him to gain another twenty-four hours on the custody of Whittaker while forensics meticulously examined the area and a team searched the wider vicinity to see if he had a provable link to the crime scene.

As he wandered out of the barn, Jackman remembered Graeme Ward's claims of seeing a white van matching the description of the one they suspected was used in the kidnapping on the main road. In view of his son's involvement in the Readman murder they'd speculated that he'd possibly got it confused with Carl's van. But his statement said that he walked the fields all around Clifford Chambers. Maybe he had seen the van with the rust mark around the petrol cap along the A3400 after all.

Jackman turned back and looked at the old wooden ladder that leant against the side of the barn that he assumed the kidnapper would have used to transport his victims into the pit., He pictured Whittaker carrying Min down. It would be a struggle. He was a small man, but she was slight so it was feasible. Maybe he drugged her to make it easier. But Lonny? His picture indicated that he was tall and heavier-built. He must have had a weapon. Either that or some help.

Jackman reached for his phone and dialled the incident room. Keane answered on the third ring.

Jackman didn't waste time with pleasantries. 'Check with the officers at the hospital and make sure that both victims have a police presence with them at all times, please.'

# 52

Jackman and Davies nodded to the officer standing outside the hospital room and slowly entered. Min was fast asleep. Her skin was pallid and drawn. Dark circles hung beneath her eyes; a crusted graze ran the length of her chin.

They turned as another figure entered behind them, dressed in a dark suit. An ID tag hung loosely from her neck. 'Can I help you?'

Jackman and Davies flashed their cards. A messy ponytail bounced as she introduced herself as Doctor Carpenter and shook their hands. 'She's in no fit state for questions right now,' the doctor said, picking up the charts at the end of the bed and perusing them.

'How is she doing?' Jackman asked.

The doctor scribbled something on the chart and replaced it in the metal partition at the end of the bed. 'There are no signs of any long-term physical damage. She was very distressed when they brought her in, so we've given her a gentle sedative. We'll keep her in overnight for observations.'

'What about the baby?' Davies asked.

'All seems fine.' Doctor Carpenter moved towards the door and gestured for them to exit. 'But I don't think you guys will get much out of her today. She needs to rest.'

They approached the door. Just as the doctor opened it, Jackman asked, 'Did you treat the other victim, Lonny Cheung?'

The doctor nodded. 'He's in a better condition, but then he wasn't kept for so long. He's on the next floor. I'll take you to him.'

They followed her along the corridor, through a door and up the side stairs to the next floor. The corridor they emerged into was a mirror image of the one below, with different paintings of landscapes lining the walls. Davies' phone buzzed and she hung back to check the message.

'Mr Cheung sprained his ankle?' Jackman asked the doctor.

She took a few more steps, then halted outside a room that was almost directly above Min's. A uniformed officer stood outside, gave them both a single nod. 'Not a sprain as such, more of a nasty twist. He just needs to keep his weight off it for a few hours. It'll be fine with some rest.'

She tipped her head to indicate her task was done, smiled at the uniformed officer and continued down the corridor.

Davies' feet squeaked on the linoleum as she rushed up the corridor to join Jackman. She grabbed his arm. 'Just had a text from Keane. The search team has found a holdall buried deep in the undergrowth of the old copse behind the pit. They almost missed it. Contains some rolls of duct tape and a memory stick.'

Jackman raised his brows.

'The stick is full of photos of Min Li, almost fifty of them, in various different locations around Stratford. Keane said it looks like they were taken without her knowledge before she was kidnapped.'

'What about Lonny Cheung?'

She shook her head. 'Only Min at the moment, but they're still searching.'

'Anything to indicate who it belonged to?'

'Not at this stage. They're sending it all off to be examined.'

Jackman pushed open the door. Lonny was sat up in bed, staring out of the window. He looked up as they entered the room.

Jackman introduced them both. 'You've had quite an ordeal,' he said.

Lonny stared at him and gave a sombre nod.

His body looked odd in the single bed, almost as if it didn't quite fit. 'Feel up to answering some questions?'

'Have you seen Min?' Lonny looked from one detective to the other, his face full of apprehension. 'Is she okay?'

'Yes,' Davies said. Her tone was soft and reassuring. 'She's asleep at the moment but she's going to be fine. Don't worry.'

'They wouldn't tell me.' His face relaxed slightly, but he looked tired, drawn.

'What can you remember?' Jackman asked.

'Not much.' He swallowed, bowed his head.

'Anything will help,' Davies said, but he didn't look up. 'Let's start from the day you disappeared.'

He gave a loud sigh, nodded. 'I was heading down to class on Thursday when I felt a bump on the back of my head.'

Jackman edged forward. 'Where were you?'

297

Lonny looked up at him. 'What?'

'Where were you when you were attacked?'

Lonny thought for a moment. 'Oh the Alcester Road, walking towards town. Almost opposite the college.'

'What time?'

'Around nine. I was late for class.'

'Did you see anyone?'

He shook his head. 'Next thing I knew I was in a van. When it stopped I was taken across some wasteland, a knife to my back, and led into the pit.' He explained how he was bound up and eventually managed to break himself and Min free.

'What did they look like?'

'He wore a mask, never saw his face.'

'Any accent?'

He shook his head. 'Didn't speak.'

Jackman narrowed his eyes. 'He?'

Lonny met his gaze. 'Sorry?'

'You said, 'He'.'

'Must have been a man. He was tall, broad.' He raised his hand above his head. 'Taller than me.'

Jackman tried a few more questions, to seek a description, but it became obvious that Lonny was exhausted and they were getting nowhere. They excused themselves and said that an officer would be sent in later to take a statement after he'd had time to rest.

Jackman replayed the account in his mind as they wandered down the corridor. It was broken, sketchy. Maybe he was drugged? Something else bothered him — there was a vague look of

298

familiarity when Lonny met his gaze, although he couldn't work out why. He didn't recall them ever meeting before. His phone interrupted his thoughts. He glanced down and saw a message from DS Gray. *We've found Qiang Li. Dead.*

# 53

An hour later, Jackman and Gray nodded at the lone officer guarding the entrance and climbed over the police tape that stretched diagonally across the doorway. Qiang Li's flat, in a dingy side street not far from Birmingham's centre, was barely the size of the living area at Min's student apartment. A sink, small piece of work surface and hob filled one corner, a sack of rice another. A folding door sat slightly ajar at the far end revealing a tiny shower room and toilet. The grey sofa that leant against the wall opposite the window still bore the bloodstains of Qiang Li's body, now removed for examination. A roll of duvet wedged down the side indicated that it doubled up as a bed. The room shared the aroma of dirty bedclothes, stale air and chips with the acrid smell of death.

Jackman's eyes rested on a beige blouson jacket that still hung from a hook on the back of the door. He wondered if Qiang wore that jacket to Kitzy's Casino. The place he'd frequented so regularly. The place where he'd indulged his gambling habit. An insatiable habit that had nibbled at his pockets until there was nothing left, then cast him aside for a new victim.

'The house is owned by a Mrs Boston,' Gray said. 'She converted this area into a granny flat for her mother, then rented it out after she died. Qiang Li has been living here for around six months, although she's been trying to get him out for a while. Says he's dirty, doesn't pay the rent. Anyway, she's been away all week. First thing she noticed when she returned today were the flies on the inside of the windows and the smell. When she couldn't get any answer from his door, she called us.'

'Do we know how long he's been dead?'

'The pathologist estimates around forty-eight hours — so sometime on Thursday.'

Thursday, Jackman thought. The day of the second drop. That could explain why it was never collected. It was also the day Davies and he were camped out in Birmingham, waiting for him. 'Anyone see or hear anything?' he asked.

'We're questioning everyone in the local community.' Gray's face fell and he shook his head as he continued, 'But they're all on shutdown. This has all the hallmarks of an organised crime killing, possibly even Triad. Cameras on the main road did pick up three motorbikes with pillions, round the corner at 8.30 p.m. on Thursday. Five minutes later they left and raced off in different directions.'

'Anything on the bikes or owners?'

Gray shook his head. 'False plates. All wore crash helmets with tinted visors. We're awaiting the complete pathologist report, but you don't need a doctorate in medicine to work out that a very large, sharp knife caused the wounds. And meat cleavers are the favoured weapons of the Triad community,' Gray said. 'That combined with the fact that Kitzy's was a regular haunt of our Mr Li just about sums it all up. He lives in a tiny bedsit, works as a waiter yet flashes copious amounts of cash on the gaming tables. He's either into something very dodgy, or he owed someone big time.'

Something caught Jackman's eye, just poking out from beneath the duvet. He bent down and pushed the wadding back. It felt strange through his rubber gloves.

'What is it?' Gray asked.

Jackman ignored him a moment and pushed the fabric back further to expose a black leather jacket. He tugged at it, felt the zip scrape against something set back deeper inside and reached in further, dragging out a dark motorcycle helmet. The yellow forty-six on the back was scored through the centre of the six just like the one in the photo on the wall in their incident room, worn by the motorcyclist who collected the first ransom drop.

Jackman stood and played out a scenario in his mind. He'd read about the work of ethnic gangs like the Triads. They were ruthless in their enforcement of debts. They rarely worked alone. The number of motorbikes with pillions suggested that three of them entered the flat, leaving their riders to keep the engines running. The main house entrance door was undamaged suggesting that Qiang had let them in. Maybe he meant to plead with them. He glanced back at the door to the flat. It was bowed where they'd kicked it in with such force that the lock had broken. Maybe Qiang saw the weapon, panicked and ran to his own flat, locked himself in.

He imagined them blasting in. Qiang Li's fear

at the sight of the knife. He'd look about for a way out. But the room was small. The entrance doubled up as an exit, blocked by them. There would be no escape.

Maybe two of the men grabbed his arms, held him back as another demanded the cash that was owed, meat cleaver in hand. He could almost see the beads of sweat on Qiang Li's forehead as he pleaded for more time — only a matter of hours and the second drop would be made and he would be £40,000 richer. But they were expecting this. They'd heard it all before. No more excuses.

Surely someone would have seen something? Heard something?

Shutdown. Everyone was fearful for themselves, their family. Jackman glanced at the splatters of blood that still covered the walls. If gambling debts motivated Min's uncle to kidnap two students and hold them for ransom, what was Whittaker's role in all of this?

\* \* \*

The ceiling light cast a band of iridescent colours through its crystal shade that blinded Jackman as he opened his eyes. He blinked several times and glanced across at the clock. It was 3.30 a.m. It had been after midnight when he'd returned from Birmingham and fallen onto the bed into a fully clothed exhausted sleep. He hauled himself up, got undressed, turned off the light and climbed into bed.

Jackman shifted position several times and

303

eventually lay on his back. Wide eyes stared into a screen of darkness. He scratched his chest and sighed. The email from the casino entered his head. Maybe he could just take a look.

He pulled back the covers, donned a robe from the back of the door and padded down the stairs, leaving Erik fast asleep on the bed. By the time he'd switched on the lamp, made himself a coffee and turned on his laptop, Erik emerged through the door. He cast a sleepy eye towards Jackman and climbed up on the sofa, curling up next to him.

Jackman stroked the dog's head as he waited for his emails to show. As soon as his inbox filled the screen, he scrolled down, opened the email and waited for it to download.

Chapman had sent three days of footage dating from last Friday through to Sunday. Seventy-two hours of film. He clicked open and waited. A large image filled the screen. He recognised it as the foyer of the casino. Several smaller thumbnails sat across the bottom. He clicked a button in the corner and they enlarged themselves to form a patchwork of views from different areas of the casino: the gaming room, the bar, the lounge, the foyer. He pressed play, sat back and watched. It was a while before anything happened. He could see the girl he'd met on his visit behind the bar serving a drink. The back of what looked like the manager. Then nothing.

Several minutes passed before a thought nudged him. The chef at The Oriental Garden had described Qiang Li as nocturnal. He rarely showed himself in the daytime. He ran the bar across and picked up the footage again just after nine.

The casino was busier at this time. Several bodies milled about. Two couples dressed for a Saturday night out were playing roulette. The black jack table was heaving and several people were in the bar area. Jackman took a gulp of coffee and stared at the different views. Nobody resembled Qiang Li. He pressed fast forward so that he could watch it at twice the speed.

Minutes and hours passed. People moved through the casino, dabbling at the tables, enjoying themselves at the bar. Nothing jumped out at him. Erik's body had heated like an oven and was pressed against his side. Eventually his eyes became heavy and gently closed.

# 54

The ground beneath me felt soft and was moving, like water.

There was a strange smell. A mixture of bleach and toothpaste. Covers that felt heavy pinned me to the bed.

I shifted forward and moved to sit up but my head felt like a dead weight.

The baby. The grazes on the backs of my fingers caught on the sheets and stung as I wrestled my hand to my stomach.

So thirsty.

A rustling in the background. I prised my eyes to tiny slits, opened my mouth, but only a squeak emerged.

A female voice answered. Too faint to make out, but gently soothing.

Was I dreaming? I thought back. The pit. The fields above. The roaring noise in the background.

Lonny. I needed to help Lonny. I opened my mouth, croaked out his name.

A hand rested on my shoulder. I flinched.

More soothing notes. I concentrated on the voice. 'Get some rest.'

I closed my eyes but all I could see was a bright light. Warm and inviting.

# 55

Erik slumped off the sofa with a thump. The sound caused Jackman to wake abruptly. He wrestled with the laptop and caught it just in time before it slipped off his lap. As Erik sat back and scratched his ear, Jackman rolled his shoulders and stared at the screen. The footage was still playing on fast speed. He checked the time. It had automatically scrolled through onto Saturday. He ran it through to the evening and rubbed the heels of his hands into his dry eyes.

He wasn't sure how long he sat there watching the movements on the screen. At one point he moved to make a fresh coffee, then resumed his seated position on the sofa. Just as he was deciding it was about time to get in the shower, an image moved across the screen. It looked vaguely familiar, although he couldn't place it. It moved out of camera range and then back in again. Jackman leant in closer. It looked like Richard Whittaker, although he looked very different to the Richard Whittaker that sat in the police cell back at the station. The thick hair was combed down across the front of his head and he wore an open-necked white shirt and black trousers. He was talking to someone at the bar. Jackman enlarged the photo and zoomed in. He didn't recognise the face of the other person.

Whittaker moved away and a moment later appeared in the gaming room, although he didn't approach the tables. He stood in the corner, a pint of beer in his hand. A man approached him and shook his hand. A Chinese man.

All of a sudden a message flashed up on the screen. Battery low. Jackman jumped up, rushed through to the kitchen, grabbed the charger off the side and plugged it in. The box disappeared.

He zoomed back in. The man was standing in front of Whittaker with his back to the camera.

'Turn around,' Jackman said aloud. The man failed to comply. Another man approached in a smart black suit with a bow tie. Again he stood with his back to the camera.

Jackman shuffled from one foot to another. 'Come on.'

Whittaker was animated, waving his arms in all directions. Jackman slowed the footage down.

When they turned, Jackman leant in closer to the screen. He pressed pause, reached for his jacket and pulled the old photo of Qiang Li out of the pocket. He unfolded the picture, smoothed out the creases and compared it to the image on the screen. The man wore a beige blouson jacket, similar to the one he saw in Qiang's flat, but he couldn't be sure if it was the same person. Jackman couldn't see the left side of his face. He pressed play, hoping to catch him at another angle but the tape moved away.

He rewound and played back the scene. There were three men there, two of them Chinese. He slowed it right down, watched intently at every angle as they moved around. Just as he was about to give up, he caught it — a quick clip of his left profile. He rewound again, pressed play.

His hair was pulled down over the ear, but there was a definite scar running down to his chin line. Qiang Li.

Suddenly, the third man turned slightly and Jackman got a blurred side view. He paused the tape, stood back. Qiang Li's Chinese associate was a figure he'd seen before. In fact it looked very much like a face plastered right across the board in the incident room.

★  ★  ★

As Jackman and Davies trudged through the hospital that morning, Jackman gave her an update on the finding of Qiang Li's body last night.

'Sounds dodgy. You should have called me.'

'No need. Gray has it all under control. There is something else though.'

They'd reached the doors of the lift and she pressed the button. As he relayed what he had found in the casino footage she rounded on him. 'Lonny Cheung? Do you really think so?'

'Pretty much. I've emailed the footage to Keane to double check. He was discharged from this place yesterday. We've got him coming into the station to give us a formal statement this morning, but I think we need to ask him some more questions.'

The lift pinged. The doors rolled open. Two nurses in pale blue jackets stood at the back. They travelled up in silence. As soon as they exited and the doors closed behind them, Davies asked, 'What does this mean?'

'It means there's some kind of connection between Lonny, Qiang and Whittaker.' He lowered his voice as they rounded the corner and reached the entrance to Min Li's room. 'It means that Whittaker lied when he said he didn't recognise them.'

Jackman noticed that the room looked markedly different this morning. Brighter somehow. Much like Min herself who sat on the edge of the bed dressed in a cream shirt and pale jeans. Freshly showered, her hair clumped together on her shoulders where it was still wet. Her eyes were clear and her face held a discernible clarity, in spite of the bruise that clouded her chin.

Jackman put on his kindest smile as he introduced them both. 'I realise you've been through a terrible ordeal,' he said. 'My detectives will need to obtain a formal statement from you later. In the meantime, can you explain to me in as much detail as you can the events of the past week, starting with Monday evening?'

Min Li managed a thin smile, then closed her eyes momentarily. When she spoke her voice was soft and gentle. Her account was surprisingly detailed and articulate. She worked through as much as she could remember: leaving the pub, the boys in the BMW, turning back towards the college. 'I don't remember being taken, but I have hazy thoughts of waking up in the back of a van, blurry images. When I awoke properly he'd already put me in the pit.'

'He?' Davies asked.

'I convinced myself it must have been a man.

310

To carry me, lower me into the pit. And Lonny of course.'

'But you never actually saw him?'

She shook her head. 'His face was always covered.'

'Could you describe him?' Jackman asked gently.

She paused a moment. 'Tall, I think. Well, taller than me.' She shook her head again. 'It all happened so quickly.'

She went on to describe his visit to the pit to deliver provisions. How frightened she had been. How, later, he'd tied her up when Lonny arrived. 'He never came back after that visit. We wondered if you'd caught him?' She looked up at Jackman imploringly.

'When was that?' Jackman asked.

'Thursday. When Lonny arrived.'

Jackman saw Davies make a note. Whittaker wasn't arrested until Saturday, which gave him plenty of time to visit the pit on Friday. Yet he didn't. And the pathologist and police evidence so far estimated that Qiang Li had been killed on Thursday.

Min looked from one detective to another. 'I thought you'd arrested someone?'

'We have,' Jackman said. 'But we still need to iron out a few details. I will be leaving an officer with you for today, just to be on the safe side.'

Min turned her head to the door. 'You still think he's out there?'

'It's just a precaution. Min, have you ever met or contacted your uncle in the UK, Qiang Li?'

She frowned, shook her head.

'Do you know a man named Richard Whittaker?'

'No.'

'What about Lonny? You must have got to know him well over the last few days.'

'What do you mean?'

'What did you two talk about?'

'Home stuff. College. That sort of thing.'

'Did he ever mention those names to you?'

'No, why would Lonny know my uncle?'

At that moment, Jackman's phone trilled. He excused himself and moved out to the corridor. Russell flashed on the screen.

'Hi there,' he said. 'Have you got Lonny Cheung back in?'

'No, sir. We haven't managed to locate him yet. He's not at his flat.'

'Where's the officer guarding him?'

'He sent him away, said he didn't need him.'

Just at that moment, Tom appeared in the corridor carrying two coffees in plastic cups. He stared at Jackman, who stood aside to let him through.

'But you need to come now,' Russell continued. 'We think we've located the van.'

# 56

He sat on the edge of the bed and screwed the covers into his fists. His teeth clenched hard.

Today, he'd seen her. She emerged from the hospital with an officer at her tail, all showered and fresh. Her cream silk shirt fluttered angelically in the late-morning sunshine. She'd looked around, her face pulled into sadness. He was just about to move forward to speak to her when *He* joined her. All tall, gangly and windswept. A flicker of light lit her face as she turned towards him. He'd drawn back into the shadow of the shop awning and watched as they embraced.

It wasn't the fact that she flung her arms around him with such vigour. He could forgive her that. It was the way she buried her head into his shoulder while he stroked her back, how he cupped her chin and raised it to his lips. Afterwards, how she curled her fingers around his, as if never to be parted.

Once again, he was watching her from across the street. She was just like the others. They pulled him in then let him fall, dangling him for a while, before they drew him back in again like a yoyo. Just like his mother.

He could still see his mother now, even though it had been almost twelve years. The sheen of blonde hair that sat in curls on her shoulders, the big blue eyes that fluttered under dark lashes,

313

painted lips that left a mark on his cheek when she kissed him.

There were times when she drew him in and showered him with kindness. Stroked his hair, kissed his forehead at bedtime, let him rest his head on her chest as she sat and read to him.

Then a cloud would descend and her face would change. Dark smudges formed beneath her eyes, her hair grew dull and flat, her gaze fixed. During these periods she pushed him away into his room, turned the key in the lock behind him. Sometimes it was for several days and the only interruptions to his torment were the odd pieces of fruit and bowls of rice shoved into the room before the door to the outside world was shut again.

He remembered trying to call out and bang on the door. But his anguish echoed around the room and disappeared into a well of nothingness. Nobody came to relieve the pain. Not until she was ready.

Then the door would open and she'd be all prettiness and smiles again.

One day he'd pulled the door constantly, listening to the splinters of wood chip and squeak as they broke. Finally, he wrenched it open. He ran down the stairs. He ran like he'd never run before.

As he reached the kitchen a strange metallic smell was followed by a strong feeling of uneasiness. The door was ajar and he pushed it forward. There she sat on the floor, blood spilling like ribbons from her wrists, merging into the pool that surrounded her.

A yoyo. It was always the same outcome. Eventually the string broke and it was game over. Suddenly, a furious rage erupted within him. He couldn't let this happen again.

# 57

Broken glass crunched beneath Jackman's feet as he walked towards the garages. He paused as he reached a uniformed officer standing amongst a group of white-suited CSIs outside number forty-three.

Jackman recognised the wide grin of PS Barby immediately and shook his hand. 'Good to see you again, Bill. What do we have?'

'You guys are certainly keeping us busy. Control room received a call this morning from the owner of number forty-one reporting a break-in and stolen bicycle. When my officers attended they noticed the broken lock on this one and the damage to the door, so they contacted the owner.' He checked his notebook. 'A Mr Blake. Anyway, it appears that Blake has been renting it out. He tried to locate the leaseholder but couldn't, so he came down and checked on the garage. When he opened the door he found the van inside.'

Jackman followed his eyes. The white van with the rust mark around the petrol cap practically filled the small area. He turned back to Barby. 'Is the garage owner still around?'

'Yes, I told him not to leave.'

'Good. I'd like to talk to him.'

Barby nodded and, as he moved away, Jackman stared up at the yellow folding door that was raised at an awkward angle. It looked like it had come off its hinges on one side. He dipped his head and crossed the threshold. The rust mark was more prominent from this angle. He looked down, automatically read the number plate then glanced up the side of the garage. It was empty. He moved across and looked up the other side. Nothing. Even though the van was parked right on centre, there was barely enough room to manoeuvre around the outside. He breathed in and squeezed down to the front. Leant against the wall there were several number plates and a set of screwdrivers.

He turned and called to Davies who stood outside. She walked sideways down the narrow gap.

He pointed to the plates. 'Get these checked, will you? One of them might be the original.'

Davies nodded and reversed out. Jackman followed her back down the side of the van. The sliding door was open. The temporary police lamp cast eerie shadows against the metal inside that was littered with numbered forensic markers. Items that would later be bagged up and examined in the lab. A tartan blanket was folded in the corner. It resembled the blanket that had appeared in the photo on the ransom note. The air smelt musty with diesel and a sickly sweet scent that Jackman couldn't place.

He emerged to find Barby waiting. He led him down to the end of the garages where a man with a bald head and a sleeve of tattoos was standing smoking. 'Sir, this is Mr Blake, owner of the garage,' Barby said.

Jackman nodded at the man, who eyed him

suspiciously. 'Can you tell me who you rent the garage to?' he asked.

Blake scratched the grey bristles that sprouted from his chin. 'My wife organised it. I think his name was Peter Tang. He's used it for about six months.'

'Do you have a written agreement?'

Blake shook his head. 'No. It's an informal thing. I wasn't using the garage so she advertised in the local newspaper. The guy came forward and paid six months' rent up front. No questions asked.'

'What does he look like?'

'What do you mean?'

'Can you describe him?'

'I only met him once. Yeah, tall guy. Chinese, although he speaks very good English.'

'Thanks.' Jackman reached for his phone and dialled Gray's number. He needed a copy of a photo and couldn't waste another moment.

⋆ ⋆ ⋆

Whittaker raised a weary face as Jackman entered the interview room with Davies beside him. He looked as if he hadn't had an ounce of sleep.

As soon as Davies switched on the tape, Jackman made his introductions, pulled a photograph from an envelope and turned it over on the table in front of him.

Whittaker's eyes widened in shock, but he said nothing.

After he'd spoken to the owner of the garage, Jackman left him to work with an artist to give

318

an impression of the man he rented the garage to. He then arranged for DS Gray to email a photo of Qiang Li in the mortuary. This was the photo that now sat on the table in front of them. It was a cleaner image than the one that Jackman had seen the night before, but still dramatic.

Jackman said nothing and pulled another photo out of the envelope. It was the photo he'd showed Whittaker yesterday, the old black and white Qiang Li with the thread of a fold-line running through the middle.

'Do you know this man?' Jackman eventually said.

Whittaker leant in and worked his eyes from one photo to another. 'No.'

Jackman pulled out the image of Lonny. 'What about him?'

'No, I told you yest . . . '

Jackman made a play of pulling out the last of the photos — a still from the casino footage of all three of them together. 'Are you sure?'

Whittaker raised his eyes to meet Jackman's gaze. 'I've done nothing wrong.'

'Then how do you explain this?' Jackman replied.

Whittaker swiped a hand across his forehead and pointed to Qiang Li. 'I know of a man called Peng Wu. Looks a bit like this. He's just an acquaintance from the casino.'

'Why didn't you tell us that yesterday?'

'This one looks so old. I couldn't be sure.'

'His left earlobe is missing!'

Whittaker shrugged.

'Was this the man who asked you to send the email?'

Whittaker nodded. 'They were already written, saved in the drafts folder of a Hotmail account. All I had to do was to log in and send them. I've already told you.'

'They?'

'What?'

'You said 'they'.'

Whittaker suddenly looked sheepish and glanced at his solicitor.

'Are you telling me you sent both emails?'

He cleared his throat. 'I just did as I was asked. I don't know what they said.'

'Did you notice they were sent in different languages? One was Mandarin and one was Cantonese?'

Whittaker shook his head. 'They just looked foreign.'

'Qiang was Chinese. What language did he speak?'

'English, Mandarin. Probably Cantonese too — I know he had a Cantonese girlfriend for a while.'

Jackman pointed to the other man in the casino still. 'What about him?'

'I don't know him. He's a friend of Peng's. His name is Peter Tang.'

★　★　★

Jackman raced out of the interview. The image in the casino was Lonny. That meant Lonny was also Peter Tang. He recalled something Lauren Tate, Min's best friend, had said in her interview. 'Min is everybody's friend. She even helps out

320

the rich kids, lends them her notes to catch up.' Lonny Cheung's sketchy account of his captor and the circumstances of his abduction jabbed at him. Lonny must have been involved in his own kidnapping.

He turned and ran down the corridor, his feet pounding the floor with every step, and climbed the back stairs two at a time. Just as he reached the landing of the incident room his mobile rang out. He cursed and glanced at the screen, just about to turn it off when Dave Benton's name flashed up. He stopped, leant against the wall and pressed to answer.

'Hi Dave, thanks for getting back to me,' he said, trying to calm his quickened breath.

'No problem. It's been interesting to get a sniff of police work again. Made me realise how much I miss it.'

Jackman tried his best not to sound impatient. 'Sure. Did you find anything?'

'I think so. I have a couple of pals that still live out there. Was good to catch up. They know the family. The father's business is pretty big in Hong Kong.' He rambled on for another minute. Jackman was considering ending the call when he said, 'There's something else. Might be something and nothing, but Lonny had a girlfriend over there. A girl by the name of Ting Xú. Was quite besotted by all accounts. Anyway, they had a falling out and she disappeared.'

'What do you mean disappeared?' Jackman almost barked back.

'Police never found her. Went on a shopping trip and never returned. There was speculation that he might be involved, that he finished her off in some way, but nothing was ever proven. Police questioned him but had to release him through lack of evidence. He had an alibi for the afternoon she disappeared. An alibi provided by someone from his father's firm. There's been talk behind the scenes about his father applying pressure. Apparently he wines and dines all the right people there. Two months later, Lonny left to study in the UK.'

'Thanks, Dave. I'll get back to you.' He rang off and raced through to the incident room. All eyes looked up as he entered. 'Where's Lonny Cheung?' he asked.

Keane shook his head. 'Still can't locate him.'

He grasped the edge of the desk, trying to catch his breath. 'What about Min?'

'She left the hospital and went straight home. There's an officer with her.'

Keane took one look at the expression on Jackman's face, drew out his mobile and dialled urgently. Russell did the same. For a moment the room was silent. Until Keane lifted his phone out at an awkward angle. 'Voicemail.'

Russell shook her head. 'Min's not answering either.'

At that moment, Davies rushed in holding an A4 sheet in her hand. 'The artist's impression of the van owner,' she said.

Jackman drew it close. The man staring back at him was cleaner-cut than he'd seen him, the hair shorter, the skin slightly darker, but there was no doubt that it was Lonny Cheung.

# 58

I took my time in the shower. Despite an earlier one at the hospital, I still felt grubby. And there was nobody yelling at me today to cut it short. Even though all the rooms were ensuite, I'd soon learnt that hot water in the building was limited at any given time. But today, with many of the students gone home or visiting friends for the half-term holidays, I could waste as much as I wanted.

I indulged in the jets as they sprayed my back, my chest, spiked into my scalp. I lathered up again. No amount of soap could wash away the filth of the last few days, but the heat was warm and comforting and suddenly this simple pleasure felt like one of life's secret luxuries. I even ignored the plumbing as it knocked and cranked in the background. It never ceased to amaze me how often it broke down in these purpose-built apartments.

When I'd woken up in hospital, I'd been surrounded by a chasm of white. I thought I'd died, the baby had died. People moved in and out of the room and it all felt like a dream, like I was drifting across the ocean on a calm day in a rudderless boat.

But later I woke up properly. My mind felt sharper than it had in days and my stomach screamed for food. I ate three bowls of cereal before a doctor came to see me to explain that I had passed out back in the field from a mixture of shock and dehydration. They'd kept me in overnight for observations. I was going to be fine. And the baby would be fine too.

I opened my closet and pulled out some jeans and a jumper. New jeans that I'd been saving for the end of term party, jeans that had sliced another huge chunk out of my student budget. But none of that mattered now. I tugged at my bedside drawer, was just about to reach for the scissors when I stopped myself. Labels were my nemesis. From a young age they felt like newly manicured nails picking and scraping away at the skin and I begged my mother to remove them. It had become a habit. But six days trapped in a pit had the ability to cure every mild irritation. I pulled them on, embracing the feeling of the label next to my skin; it made me feel warm, safe, alive.

The heat of the shower had a calming effect on my frayed nerves and, after wrapping a towel around my hair, I swiped my hand across the condensation on the mirror and gazed at my reflection. My eyes had brightened, the bruising on my chin from when I was climbing out of the pit had faded. Finally, the fabric of my old self was starting to show through.

I thought about Lonny. He came to see me in hospital this morning and told me about the police rescue. He was able to walk around, his ankle already stronger. He sat next to my bed and we discussed the euphoric relief at being free.

After the police interview, I'd phoned my parents. Listening to their voices, hearing that they were alive and well, was almost too much to bear. They were coming over, due to arrive tomorrow.

It felt strange leaving the hospital with a policeman. Even now, he was situated outside my apartment. They had arrested a man, but were yet to charge, so the police weren't taking any chances.

I could barely believe that I was alive, in my own apartment, with Tom in the front room. Suddenly I realised that for the first time in almost a week I actually felt safe.

The first sound I heard when I stepped out of the bathroom was the television. The volume was cranked up: blasts, bangs and desperate voices filled the background. A rush of happiness oozed through me. Tom was watching a movie. I could never see the appeal with the action movies, but Tom loved to watch them at high volume so that he felt the true extent of the special effects. At one time this might have irritated me, but it didn't matter anymore.

When I entered the lounge I was greeted with another blast and an exploding building on the flat screen in the corner. Tom had his back to me, his body hidden by the armchair he'd pulled in front of the television, one leg hanging over the side. The laces hung loose on his maroon Converse, like snakes hanging from the branch of a tree. I smiled, opened my mouth to speak, then froze. Tom didn't wear maroon Converse. Neither did my other roommates.

The chair whizzed around and I came face to face with Lonny.

'Oh!' I gasped. 'You startled me.' My shoulders relaxed. I scanned the room. 'Where's Tom?'

Lonny didn't answer. As I looked back at him, I realised there was something odd about him. There was a fire in his eyes.

I swallowed. 'Lonny, what is it? What's wrong?'

He stood slowly, his eyes still blazing, mouth shut.

A muffled call came from the kitchenette. I moved towards it, but Lonny was quicker. He pounced across, blocked my pathway. But he wasn't quick enough to obscure Tom and the policeman laid out on the floor, their hands bound together behind their backs, their mouths gagged. The policeman stared at me, the whites of his eyes showing, but Tom . . . he was out cold, his head drooping awkwardly on his chest.

I looked back at Lonny. The blaze behind his eyes darkened menacingly. When he spoke, he sounded different. 'I wouldn't go in there if I were you.'

'Tom.' I mouthed the word but no sound came out. 'What are you doing? We have to help him.'

He met my gaze. 'You don't want him.'

I glanced at Tom, willing him to move, to show some sign of life. 'I don't understand.'

A weird cackle emitted from Lonny's mouth. A sound I'd never heard before.

'Lonny?'

'You've really no idea, have you?'

'What?'

He edged forward, forcing me back. 'You

really didn't guess!' His face was incredulous, as if he was pleased with himself.

I shook my head. 'This isn't funny, Lonny.'

'It was me. The person who kidnapped you, who fooled the police, then set up my own kidnap to join you in the hole. It was all me.'

It was my turn to be incredulous. Lonny? The man I'd helped in the pit, the man I'd shared my food with, the man I'd let cuddle up to me when he was trembling with cold? My mouth suddenly felt bone-dry.

His eyes turned soft. 'I did it because I love you, Min.'

He stepped forward again. I could feel his breath on my face.

'I couldn't get anywhere near you. A popular girl like you would never mix with me. But after you had the chance to get to know me, got close to me . . .'

'But . . . We tried to escape.' I stumbled over the words.

'No, I tried. Just not that hard. The grill was unlocked the whole time. How do you think we managed to get out in the end?'

'We almost ran out of food. You were so angry.'

A malicious grin curled one side of Lonny's mouth. 'I nearly had you, didn't I? Go on, admit it. You really started to like me. Until you came out of that hole and met him!' As he spat out those final words, the fire in his eyes was back.

# 59

The moments before death were not as I expected. My life didn't flash before me. Even as I fought against the binds he tied around my wrists and ankles, all I felt was an overwhelming wave of fear and sadness. It was almost as if the events of the last week had already sucked the life out of my fight.

I was too young to die. Before I'd finished college and showed the world what I was made of. Before I made my parents proud.

I watched him lift the knife and run his finger along the blade, his eyes almost mesmerised. He looked up at me.

My limbs started to tremble. Please, make it quick. No hoods this time, no masks. We don't need those anymore.

He crossed the room towards me, stood right in front and angled his head. Suddenly his eyes turned soft, sad even.

I froze as he reached down and swept his hand down the side of my cheek. He cupped my chin and lifted my face slightly. I wasn't sure how long we stayed there. There was no sound but the soft ticks of the clock on the wall and the rattle of the bed beneath my juddering limbs.

His gaze was soft, as if he recalled some distant warm memory. Until something inside him broke his abstraction and his face instantly turned to stone.

# 60

Lonny moved back, closed the bedroom door and glanced at Min Li, trussed up like a Roman slave. He felt a pang, pulled away. Part of him couldn't bear to see her like that. But she deserved this. She had brought it on herself.

'I remember the first moment you spoke to me,' he said. 'We were visiting London. You stood in front of me in the queue for the London Eye and said, 'The view is supposed to be brilliant from the top.' His eyes turned soft as he recalled the memory.

'Back at the college you sat beside me in English.' He drew in a long breath. 'I loved the scent of your perfume, I could smell it on the books you lent me. And those little smiles of acknowledgement when we passed in the corridor and across campus.'

Min struggled in her ties, but he ignored her, lost in his reverie.

'I tried so hard to find a way to get close to you, spent weeks tracing your uncle, working my way into his sordid life: the little man with the yellow teeth, bad breath and naff beige jacket. Only to later discover that he was estranged from his family. Then I thought up the kidnap. It seemed like a dream at first, almost like a comic-strip story.'

He snorted. 'I remember your uncle's face when I first shared the idea with him. He

329

couldn't wait to get his grubby little hands on the cash. He was even more excited about the second drop.' Lonny's face turned grim. 'But I was too clever for him. I sold him out to his creditors. He'd be dead before he could rat on me.'

He averted his gaze. 'It was the perfect plan until you flew back into the arms of him.' Lonny glanced briefly back at the door, then turned on Min. 'You let me down. Just like the others.'

He cut off as he cast his mind back. His first attempt had almost worked. The plan had been several months in the making, yet thwarted at the last moment. Ting only wanted to be friends. The sting of unrequited love had poisoned his heart. He couldn't let her do that — draw him in and let him drop. He couldn't allow that again.

Killing Ting had been a lot easier than he'd thought. There was none of the wild rage you read about. It had been easy to persuade her to go swimming in the sea together that afternoon, just as friends. She'd struggled initially as he'd pushed her head below the water, but he'd expected that. In fact, he rather enjoyed the warm rush. It made him feel empowered. And as her body went limp, he'd felt a sense of justice.

He shot Min a glance as another spear of rejection penetrated him and crossed the room to her bedside, knife in hand. She squirmed around on the bed, every tendon in her body quivering.

His chest was knotted with a mixture of anger and nauseating guilt at the wretched being that he'd become.

Slowly he lifted the knife and struck hard, sliding it through the flesh. The pain was excruciating. He was aware of a muffled shriek in the background, but he didn't look up. He couldn't. As the blood started to spurt in ripples from his wrist he changed hands and struck the other side, deeper this time.

A line of blood spurted out and splattered across the bed. He fell to his knees. Min continued to squirm in front of him, more and more urgently. He stared at her for a split second through the mist that was covering his eyes. She was so beautiful. Just like his mother. The images faded, the pain seared, then darkness descended.

# 61

As I pressed my hand to my stomach, I felt the grief and sadness rest on my shoulders. It was hard to believe that it was gone: the baby that hadn't been planned, that had been the cause of so much consternation, so much upset. It had gone through so much in its early life. Too much, it seems, for a young life to take.

The crisp hospital sheets scratched at my skin as I wriggled around in the bed. As much as I tried I couldn't get comfortable. It seemed ironic that forty-eight hours ago I was stuck in the pit, filthy and hungry, with only a concrete floor and a couple of blankets. Now I was showered and clean, I'd eaten healthy food and had the luxury of a real bed with pillows and blankets to enjoy, yet I felt no comfort from it. The doctor said it was the shock and trauma that brought it on.

When the inspector came to see me this morning he said that they'd found a whole folder of photos and footage of me on a memory stick in a bag with some duct tape, hidden in the wood near the pit. Fingerprints on the memory stick matched Lonny's. He must have been watching, filming me for weeks without my knowledge, just waiting for the right moment.

I could still see the blade slicing through his forearms as if they were slabs of butter, all the time his pupils bearing into mine. Perhaps there is a limit to shock, it all mounts up and when you exceed that limit something inside of you bursts. Or something bad happens. Like you lose your child.

Thick hot tears snaked down my cheeks. Maybe it would have been better if I had died back there. At least then I could put all those terrible memories behind me. My life wouldn't be haunted by the darkness that now sat permanently within.

Tom had been beaten, struck hard on the head and taped up, but thankfully survived. Like the policeman with him, he'd suffered cuts and bruises and a mild concussion, but would be released today. Tom had been allowed to sit beside me this morning, enveloping my hand in his. He'd tried to comfort me, to be brave, but really underneath the creases on his forehead I knew that he was secretly relieved. A baby was the last thing he needed right now. It was the last thing I needed too, although I couldn't seem to stave off the overwhelming sense of loneliness.

Later today, my parents would arrive. I wasn't sure if they knew about the baby. I'd spoken to my mother and father briefly after my escape. That was when I was initially released from hospital. Before the final stretch of my nightmare began.

I'd decided to go back to China with them, at least for a while. I needed time, to go home, back to what I know, to feel safe and secure, be swaddled in love by my parents. I needed to sit with my father and eat rice noodles, cook with my mother. Only then would the thoughts that swirled furiously around my head start to settle.

# 62

Jackman sat next to Alice and took a sip of water. The rim of the plastic cup was split and he flinched as it caught his lip. He'd spent half an hour explaining where he'd been for the last few days, the surprising end to the case. The week felt like a whirlwind and he started to relax as the details flooded out.

Lonny had taken his twisted obsession with Min to its furthest degree. Qiang Li was just a pawn in his game, the instrument he used to get close to her. The much larger second ransom, Jackman suspected, was intended as Lonny's payment to Qiang's killers — they failed to collect it because the area was too open, the move too risky. An almost flawless plan, apart from Qiang bringing Whittaker in to send those emails, a man that could identify Lonny and confirm his association with Min's uncle. He didn't bank on hurting his ankle in the pit either, an injury that prevented him from escaping with Min and later retrieving the holdall that contained the memory stick and duct tape covered in his fingerprints. He cast his gaze to the side. 'No plan is ever foolproof,' he said gravely.

Alice was sat upright in her bed. He reached across for the hairbrush and pulled it gently through her hair. It felt soft and silky and shone under the gentle sunlight that filled the room.

When he'd finished he laid the brush down and rested her head back. 'There, that's better.' He smiled at her.

'Janus was all sunshine and smiles this morning when she returned to the office to find we'd closed the case.' He snorted. 'But you should've seen Reilly's face. You'd think he'd be happy that we had a charge on the Readman case and a possible link to the Northampton murder. Problem is, Lonny died following police contact. Reilly was furious at the prospect of the case being reviewed by the Independent Police Complaints Commission. Something tells me we'll be stuck with him in homicide for a while. He won't want that to be his epitaph.'

His face fell as his tone grew graver. 'There's talk of another chief inspector's board at Christmas.' He stared at the floor as he spoke the words, almost to himself. 'Not sure if Janus'll support me, but I've gotta go for it, Alice. It might mean working in another area for a while, but I'd make sure I wasn't too far away.' He rubbed his forehead in thought. 'What do you think?'

Alice stared back at him.

For the first time in almost a year a tiny thread of hope wrapped itself around him. As he moved away, his elbow caught the corner of the exercise book Celia had placed beside the bed. It made a gentle splash as it hit the floor. He leant down and read the words she had written on the front: *For Mum. Never give up hope.*

# Acknowledgements

A novel is never fully the work of one person and so many people have kindly helped and supported this one along the way.

I am grateful to Glyn Timmins and Ian Robinson for their input and guidance on not only police procedure, but also the working life of a detective. Thanks also to them and my dear friends Rebecca Bradley and Susi Holliday for reading early drafts and giving excellent feedback.

I owe a debt of gratitude to the wonderful people of Stratford-upon-Avon for their endless assistance in sending maps and helping with the finer details of locations, most notably Joyce Dooley. Thank you for sharing your special town with me.

Special thanks go to Wei Zhao, without whose wonderful insight into Chinese culture this book would never have been written. Any errors or omissions are purely my own.

Appreciation goes to Lauren Parsons, Tom Chalmers, Lucy Chamberlain, Lottie Chase and all the team at Legend Press and also my agent, Kate Nash, for believing in the book in its infancy and supporting me throughout the publication process.

So many friends and family helped with research and provided much-needed moral support including Jimi and Jude Ogston, Greg Hemmington,

Emma Thompson and Peter Arnold, Jill Haine, David and Lynne Anderson, and Derek Archer.

Finally, David and Ella make my writing possible. Heartfelt thanks for their relentless patience, love and encouragement.

We do hope that you have enjoyed reading this large print book.

Did you know that all of our titles are available for purchase?

We publish a wide range of high quality large print books including:
**Romances, Mysteries, Classics**
**General Fiction**
**Non Fiction and Westerns**

Special interest titles available in large print are:
**The Little Oxford Dictionary**
**Music Book**
**Song Book**
**Hymn Book**
**Service Book**

Also available from us courtesy of Oxford University Press:
**Young Readers' Dictionary**
**(large print edition)**
**Young Readers' Thesaurus**
**(large print edition)**

For further information or a free brochure, please contact us at:
**Ulverscroft Large Print Books Ltd.,**
**The Green, Bradgate Road, Anstey,**
**Leicester, LE7 7FU, England.**
**Tel:** (00 44) **0116 236 4325**
**Fax:** (00 44) **0116 234 0205**

## THE TRUTH WILL OUT

### Jane Isaac

Eva is skyping her best friend Naomi, when the latter suddenly disappears from the screen and a menacing figure appears in the background — who then proceeds to attack. Horrified, Eva calls an ambulance and flees Hampton, fearing for her own safety. DCI Helen Lavery leads the investigation into the murder, though there are no leads, no further witnesses, and no sign of forced entry. Slowly, the pieces of the puzzle start to come together; but as Helen inches toward solving the case, her past becomes caught up in her present. Someone is after both her and Eva. Someone who will stop at nothing to get what they want. And as the net starts to close around them, can Helen escape her own demons as well as helping Eva to escape hers?

# PERSONAL

## Lee Child

You can leave the army, but the army doesn't leave you, notes Jack Reacher. Sure enough, the retired military cop is soon pulled back into service, this time for the State Department and the CIA. Someone has taken a shot at the president of France in Paris. The bullet was American — and how many snipers can shoot from three-quarters of a mile with total confidence? Very few, but John Kott, an American marksman gone bad, is one of them. If anyone can stop him, it's the man who beat him before: Reacher. Though he'd rather work alone, Reacher is teamed with Casey Nice, a rookie analyst who keeps her cool with Zoloft. They're facing a rough road full of ruthless mobsters, close calls, double-crosses — and no backup if they're caught . . .

# FIRST ONE MISSING

## Tammy Cohen

There are three things no one can prepare you for when your daughter is murdered: you are haunted by her memory day and night; even close friends can't understand what you are going through; only in a group with mothers of other victims can you find real comfort. But as the bereaved parents gather to offer support in the wake of another killing, a crack appears in the group that threatens to rock their lives all over again. Welcome to the club no one wants to join.

# DISCLAIMER

## Renée Knight

This is a work of fiction. Names and characters are the product of the author's imagination and any resemblance to actual persons, living or dead, is purely coincidental.*

*Everything you have just read is a lie.

What if you realised the book you were reading was all about you? When an intriguing novel appears on Catherine's bedside table, she curls up in bed and begins to read. But as she turns the pages, she is sickened to realise the story will reveal her darkest secret. A secret she thought no one else knew . . .